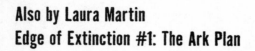

Also by Laura Martin
Edge of Extinction #1: The Ark Plan

CODE NAME FLOOD

LAURA MARTIN

HARPER

An Imprint of HarperCollins*Publishers*

Edge of Extinction #2: Code Name Flood
Copyright © 2017 by Laura Martin
All rights reserved. Printed in the United States of America.
No part of this book may be used or reproduced in any manner
whatsoever without written permission except in the case of brief
quotations embodied in critical articles and reviews. For information
address HarperCollins Children's Books, a division of HarperCollins
Publishers, 195 Broadway, New York, NY 10007.
www.harpercollinschildrens.com

Library of Congress Control Number: 2016960405
ISBN 978-0-06-241625-4

Typography by Ellice M. Lee
17 18 19 20 21   CG/LSCH   10 9 8 7 6 5 4 3 2 1
❖
First Edition

For all the teachers, librarians, and parents working to instill a love of reading in the hearts of the next generation. You are the true heroes of stories.

And to my mom, who first did that for me.

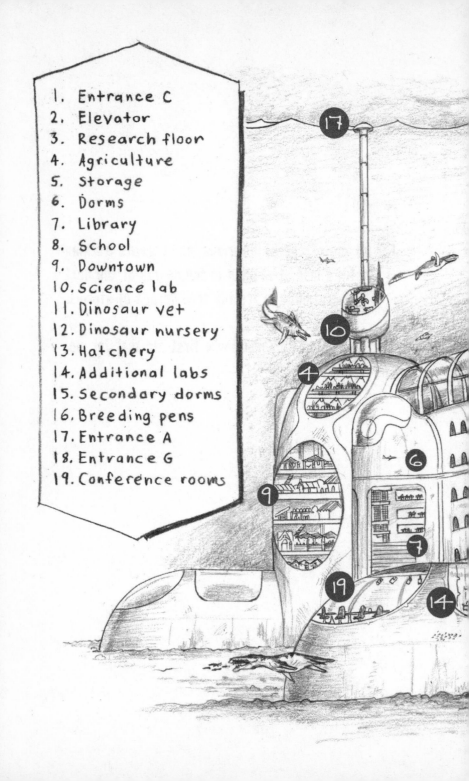

1. Entrance C
2. Elevator
3. Research floor
4. Agriculture
5. Storage
6. Dorms
7. Library
8. School
9. Downtown
10. Science lab
11. Dinosaur vet
12. Dinosaur nursery
13. Hatchery
14. Additional labs
15. Secondary dorms
16. Breeding pens
17. Entrance A
18. Entrance G
19. Conference rooms

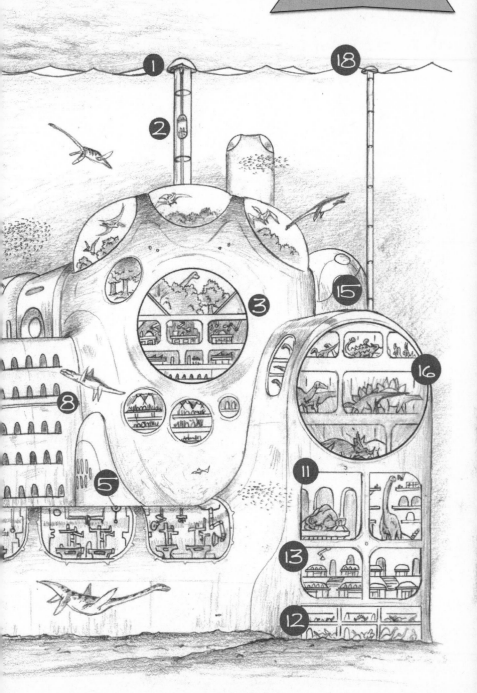

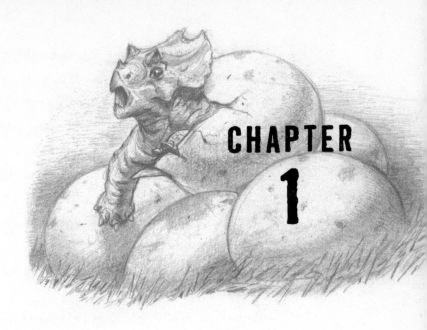

CHAPTER 1

This was a bad idea. Spectacularly bad, actually. It went against everything I'd learned in my short time topside, but all that didn't change what we had to do. I glanced back down at my dad's map, but it showed the same thing it had always shown. The only way to get to Lake Michigan was to leave the shelter of the trees and make a run for it—in the open. My eyes flicked up to take in the sprawling grassland in question, filled, as I knew it would be, with dinosaurs.

A large herd of what I thought had to be *Dracorex hogwartsia* was grazing close enough for me to count the spikes that bristled all over their bony heads, making them resemble the dragons of fairy tales they were named for. But these creatures were not the stuff of fairy tales or history books. At least not anymore. Behind the herd of dracorex was a grassland that used to contain houses, roads, cars, and everything else humans had used to stake their claim on this earth. All that was gone now. Which made sense, I guess, considering the dinosaurs were the ones who ruled things these days.

"I can't believe we're doing this," Shawn muttered, running a hand through his blond hair so it stood up in sweaty spikes. "There is no way we can make it to the lake without getting eaten."

"What's your point?" Todd asked as he swung his arms in lazy circles to stretch out his shoulder muscles.

"My point," Shawn said, grimacing, "is that there has to be a way around this, a way that isn't so exposed. We've always gone around the open areas. Except," he amended, "for that time we almost became a T. rex's lunch." He paused a moment, stifling a shudder. "At least in the trees the only dinosaurs we encountered were little ones. Out there," he said, gesturing in front of us, "there's nowhere to hide, no trees to climb, and nothing to slow down those massive monsters."

"We knew that the closer to Lake Michigan we got, the more open it was going to be," I said flatly. His attitude shouldn't have surprised me. I'd grown up with Shawn in North Compound, and unlike Todd, who'd grown up topside, being aboveground was still an uncomfortable and terrifying experience for both of us. I just hid it better.

"Yeah, but I didn't think it was going to be *this* open," Shawn grumbled, and I tried not to roll my eyes as I turned my attention back to the grassland. I'd read that dinosaurs liked to congregate near a source of water, but this was a little ridiculous. Herds of green-, brown-, and amber-colored dinosaurs were scattered as far as I could see. To our left, a large group of stegosaurs grazed quietly in the knee-high scrub grasses, the sun reflecting off the wide flat plates that sat in single file down their sloping backs.

"Try to relax," I said, even as the knot in my gut twisted a little tighter. "If we read the map correctly, the lake should be just on the other side of those hills."

"Dunes," Todd corrected. "Those things that look like hills are called dunes."

"What's a dune?" Shawn asked.

"Big mounds of sand," Todd explained. "They border the lake."

I glanced back out across the tall wavy grasses, silently wishing Shawn was right and there was another way. While the prospect of finally getting to the lake sent a thrill of excitement through me, Shawn's reminder of our last dash into the open made my already edgy nerves buzz uncomfortably. After a lifetime underground, we hadn't known any better than to run across an open meadow. It had been the first of many near-death experiences. The note and map my dad had left for me, urging me to take his compass and the small memory plug it contained to Lake Michigan, hadn't said anything about how to actually survive topside. That part we'd had to figure out the hard way.

I tugged at my ponytail to free it from the snarled thorns of the bush. A few curly red strands got caught in the branches, and they fluttered gently in the wind. I snatched them and shoved them in my pocket. I wasn't taking any chances. North Compound's marines had found us twice now. We'd eliminated any chance that we were carrying a tracking device, so that left the old-fashioned way of finding us. By foot. Ever since we'd realized this, we'd gone out of our way to hide all traces of our movements. Hopefully it would be enough. I took a deep breath to calm my nerves. The tangy, earthy flavor of this topside world still felt foreign, but unfortunately, it did nothing to slow my hammering heart or shaking hands, so I balled them into fists and mentally commanded myself to get it together.

"Can we just get on with it?" I asked.

"Sure," Todd said as he leaned forward to stretch out his leg muscles.

Shawn scowled at Todd and then turned to me. "How are you so okay with potentially getting eaten alive?"

"Or trampled," Todd added, adjusting his pack. "Don't forget trampled."

"If you were trying to make me feel better, you just failed miserably," Shawn grumbled.

"I wasn't." Todd smirked. A week ago, that smirk would have fooled me. Now I could see the slight tension around his green eyes that gave away his own nerves. Seeing Shawn's glowering face, Todd shrugged. "Look at it this way," he said, gesturing to the massive dinosaurs. "If that many plant eaters are comfortable enough to feed, they don't think there are any large predators around."

"Yeah," Shawn muttered. "But they could be wrong."

"Just keep running no matter what happens," Todd said. "Both of you are still too bad of a shot to turn and fight if something comes after us."

"Hey," I protested. "You said this morning that we were getting better."

Todd wrinkled his nose apologetically. "I was being nice."

"You aren't nice." Shawn scowled again.

Todd laughed. "You *are* improving. Especially since you had that lesson with Ivan. You might actually be a step above horrendous now."

"Well, that's something," Shawn mumbled.

My heart clenched painfully. Ivan should have caught up to us by now. Either he hadn't survived his encounter with the marines two days ago, or something had happened to delay him. I swallowed hard, trying not to imagine all the terrible things that could slow down someone as savvy at surviving topside as my grandfather.

Todd looked at both of us in turn. "Ready?" he asked. I nodded, and Shawn grumbled something unintelligible. Todd must have taken that as confirmation, because he sprang up from the bushes and sprinted into the open.

"Really?" Shawn said, clambering to his feet. "Not even a one, two, three? Or a ready, set, go?" He was still grumbling under his breath as we took off after Todd.

The feeling of being exposed intensified as we left the looming shelter of the trees. Todd flew through the waist-high grasses, his long legs eating up the distance with powerful strides. Shawn and I were not powerful or fast. Short and stocky, Shawn pumped his arms, his face already flushed a bright red as he struggled to keep up. I wasn't sure what I looked like, but I doubted it was much better.

The herd of stegosaurus picked their heads up, bugling a warning to their young, who quickly found shelter under their parents' tree-trunk-like legs. Their wary brown eyes and solemn faces studied us as we passed. If I hadn't been sucking air as fast as I could get it, I would have let out a sigh of relief. Todd had been fairly certain that they wouldn't stampede and squash us, but fairly certain and certain were two very different things.

The wind whipped across the grasses, making them sway and bend like waves, and I looked back to see the trees quickly disappearing behind us. Suddenly my foot caught on a rock and I flew forward. I hit the ground hard, my hands thrown out instinctively in front of me. They landed in something soft and slimy, and an awful smell met my nose. Before I could figure out what I'd just fallen into, I was scrambling to my feet and running to catch up with Shawn and Todd. Glancing back, I saw a gigantic pile of what looked like fist-sized brown balls in a slightly smashed pile. My stomach rolled as I realized that I was liberally coated in what had to be fresh dinosaur poop.

Todd slowed his pace a few minutes later, allowing Shawn and me to catch up enough to run on either side of him.

"See dead ahead?" he asked, pointing. I tried not to be too bitter that he wasn't even breathing hard. Following his finger, I spotted several large circular depressions in the ground, each of them with a pile of white ovals in the center.

"Are those nests?" I asked.

"Yup." Todd frowned. "Not sure of what, though."

"They're everywhere," Shawn huffed as he took in the huge nests that lay in almost every direction.

"It'll take too long to go around. We have to go through," Todd said. "Whatever you do, don't touch the eggs. Somewhere around here are their parents, and the last thing we want is for them to think we're messing with their babies."

"Got it," Shawn said, shaking his sweat-drenched hair out of his eyes.

Todd turned to me, his nose wrinkled. "Did you fall in dinosaur dung?"

I grimaced. "Do you even have to ask?" The smell radiating off me alone should have been clue enough.

Todd shook his head, a smile playing at the corners of his mouth. "Follow me," he called, shooting ahead of us again as we entered the nesting area. The ground underfoot turned to sand, and suddenly running was even harder than it had been before. As we flashed past the nests, I caught a glimpse of the large white eggs, each delicately speckled with brown.

"Jump!" Todd yelled, leaping suddenly into the air. I jumped, glancing down to see a strip of three nests, side by side, impossible to avoid. Shawn was not as quick, and I heard a surprised grunt followed by a shower of sand spraying across my back. I whirled in time to see him sprawl face-first into the middle of a nest. A sharp crack rang out as his head hit one of the eggs. The shell buckled in and started oozing a clear liquid. Shawn sat up quickly, but in his attempt to get to his feet again he bumped the broken egg, sending it clattering into one of its neighbors. It split in two and a slim brown creature flopped out, struggling to free itself from a gooey membrane.

I stared in wonder.

"Not good," Todd said in my ear, and I realized I'd stopped running. He lurched past me and yanked Shawn out of the sandy nest. The little brown dinosaur opened its mouth in a wordless cry, its eyes sealed shut.

"Take your tunic off," Todd barked at Shawn, his face drawn and pale.

"What?" Shawn asked, trying in vain to wipe the goo from the egg out of his hair. Todd didn't wait— ripping Shawn's pack and large bow off his back, he thrust them into my arms and then yanked Shawn's tunic up over his head. Shawn yelped in protest, but Todd was already chucking it away from us. Shawn grabbed his pack from me just as the tiny dinosaur let out a high-pitched cry that made the hairs on the back of my neck stand up.

"Run," Todd commanded. Shawn slung his pack and bow over his bare shoulders, and we took off. The screech of the tiny dinosaur followed us as we wove through nest after endless nest. The sound of an ear-piercing shriek from behind us forced me to turn my head. To our left, still not much more than dots in the distance, was a herd of rust-colored dinosaurs. And they were coming straight for us, fast.

"What are those?" Shawn called.

"The parents," Todd called, putting on a burst of speed. I hadn't thought it was possible to run any faster, but I found a reserve of strength and pushed harder.

The sound of the advancing dinosaurs grew more deafening by the second, their angry shrieks reverberating up my spine and right into my brain. I craned my neck to look back again. They were predators. If their rows of gleaming teeth hadn't made that immediately obvious, the fact that they were running on well-muscled back legs sealed the deal. But it was their eyes that had me doing a double take. Unlike most dinosaurs I'd encountered, whose eyes were along the sides of their heads, these sat in the front under lethal-looking spikes, almost human in their positioning.

Suddenly the sand was deeper than before, and

I looked up to see Todd on all fours scrambling up a mountain. The dunes, I thought as I automatically mimicked his movements. The sand burned under my hands as I fought to keep up. For every step I took, I felt like I slid back down two, and within moments my eyes, nose, and mouth were full of grit. The sound of Shawn's hoarse breathing behind me made it obvious that he wasn't faring much better, and even Todd was gasping for the first time. Despite everything, that fact scared me most of all. If Todd was struggling, did we even have a chance?

Reaching the top of the dune, Todd launched himself off the peak, soaring a good ten feet before landing in the slippery sand of the downhill slope. He immediately jumped again to land with a spray of sand another ten feet down. There was no time to think about it. I jumped. The wind tore at my clothes, and my stomach dropped as the dune rushed up to meet me. When my feet finally touched down, they sank into the soft sand just long enough for me to take off again. But in that second of flying, I felt wildly and amazingly alive.

My elation fizzled when I saw Todd scrambling up another dune even bigger than the first. Blinking the grit out of my eyes, I followed. I hadn't thought it was possible for anything to be harder than that first dune. I'd been wrong. My muscles shook and cramped in protest as I forced them to do battle with yet another endless sand mountain.

When we finally made it to the top, I turned back in time to watch the dinosaurs crest the first dune. The entire herd hadn't pursued us, presumably leaving the majority behind to defend the undisturbed nests. Not that it mattered. Even one of those beasts was more than our match. The handful still following us were much larger than I'd originally thought. At close to twenty feet from muscled tail to blunt snout, they were almost as big as the T. rex.

I looked ahead to see Todd and Shawn already halfway down the second dune, but before I took my own flying leap, I saw something that made me cry in relief. There, spread out as far as I could see, was Lake Michigan. My hand went involuntarily to the compass that hung around my neck. I'd made it. Almost. Three more dunes, smaller than the one I stood on, separated me from the lake and successfully delivering the data plug that, if my dad was right, meant the salvation of the human race. I leapt after Todd and Shawn.

The next two dunes were smaller, but our exhaustion made us clumsy and slow. Even Todd stumbled and slid backward as we made our way up their hot, slippery surfaces. Luckily, the deep sand seemed to slow the smashed-faced dinosaurs down as well, and

I heard their frustrated squeals every time we disappeared from sight over the top of a dune. Finally, we were climbing the last one.

Shawn was struggling more than me. The veins on his neck and forehead bulged, and sand stuck to his sweaty arms and shoulders like a mottled, grainy second skin. He looked to be on the verge of collapsing.

"We got this," I encouraged him, grabbing his pack to keep him from slipping backward again. "We're almost there. The lake is just over the top of this dune."

"Can't. Breathe," he gasped.

A triumphant roar sliced through the air as the dinosaurs crested the dune directly behind us. If we didn't move, they'd be on us in seconds.

"Come on!" Todd shouted, and suddenly he was on the other side of Shawn. Together we hauled him up the dune. Instead of leaping off, we kind of tumbled and slid down the far side, sand spraying up to catch in my hair, tunic, and mouth.

We ran, arms churning, as we battled to make it to the water before the dinosaurs that were already sliding down the last dune. Even though the expanse of blue-gray water got closer and closer by the second, I knew we'd never make it. The dinosaurs were close enough that I could smell them now, a pungent mix of decay and old blood. This was where it was going to end.

CHAPTER 2

When we were still a hundred yards away from the lake, I spotted the brown object floating on top of the water's surface with two men standing inside of it. Sweat stung my eyes, but I didn't notice. Boat, my exhausted brain provided for me, that's a boat. I'd read about boats, of course, but I'd never seen one. Todd must have spotted it too because he immediately veered toward it. It flashed across my mind that those men could be marines, but in that moment I didn't care. The pack of rust-colored scales and flashing white teeth were mere feet behind us now.

The men in the boat were dressed in strange blue jumpsuits and had black guns pressed to their shoulders.

As we approached, a flash of red erupted from each barrel, and I heard an angry shriek as a spray of sand pelted my back. The men fired again as we raced into the icy water. The cold was so shocking after the heat of the sand that it would have taken my breath away if I'd had any left to take. I sloshed through the shallow water, running until it was too deep, and then I instinctively paddled, pulling handfuls of water past me. Moments later my fingernails dug into the rough wood of the boat. One of the men grabbed the back of my tunic and heaved me up over the edge, while the other stood firing shot after shot into our would-be assailants.

Todd and Shawn landed on top of me as they too were hauled in. Managing to untangle myself from the boys, I struggled to my knees and peered out over the edge of the boat. The dinosaurs were slumped across the beach, their legs stuck out at all angles and their mouths hanging open. There had to be at least ten of them, their eyes vacant.

I realized suddenly that the only sound I could hear was the water lapping against the side of the boat, and the silence seemed deafening after the earsplitting roars of moments before. The two men lowered their guns as Todd and Shawn pulled themselves to standing positions.

"Are they dead?" Shawn wheezed, running a trembling hand over his face. "Please tell me they're dead."

"Of course they're not dead," said one of the blue jumpsuited men, as though this should have been obvious, leveling his serious gray eyes on us.

"They sure look dead to me," Todd commented, spitting a gob of sand into the water. He shoved his hands into his hair and tousled it roughly, sending a mist of grainy sand over Shawn and me.

"They're just tranquilized," said the other man with the gun, turning to inspect us. I jumped as I realized that what I'd taken for a slimly built man was actually a girl not much older than me. Her closely cropped black hair stuck out in odd spikes and twists over laughing hazel eyes. Her easy smile was a sharp contrast to the man beside her, whose narrowed eyes held no hint of warmth or kindness. "Those guys won't wake up for at least three hours, and they'll have killer headaches when they do."

"Tranquilized?" Shawn repeated. "Why would you tranquilize them instead of killing them?"

"Wasteful," said the man stiffly. "The carnotaurus numbers aren't stable. Their last breeding season was a bad one. Those right there," he said, pointing to five large dinosaurs slumped near one another, "are probably breeding females. Did you know that their name

16

literally means meat-eating bull? The name came from those impressive horns. Beautiful creatures. Simply amazing. Their eyes face forward instead of off to the side like all the others, one of the reasons they're such efficient hunters. Although," he amended, "it's extremely rare for that many of them to chase prey like that. They prefer to hunt alone. In fact, I've only seen that behavior when they believe their young are threatened." I'd never heard someone talk about dinosaurs with such obvious admiration.

"You mean like if someone fell headfirst into a nest and cracked an egg open with his big head?" Todd grumbled, glaring at Shawn.

"Right," Shawn said. "Because I meant to do that. It was loads of fun on this end. By the way, why did you rip my shirt off?" he asked as he attempted to scrape the layer of sand off his neck and shoulders that the lake water hadn't already rinsed off.

"Because I was trying to avoid that," Todd said, pointing to the beach full of not-dead dinosaurs. He shook his head in disgust. "Obviously it wasn't enough. They were still able to track your scent."

Ignoring the boys' bickering, I studied the girl curiously. "Why do you care about the, what did you call them? The carnotaurus numbers?"

"That is a good question," Todd said, looking from

the man to the girl. "Who are you people?"

"Wait a second," Shawn said. "You don't know them, Todd? Why did you run toward their boat?"

"Did you see a better option?" Todd asked, eyebrow raised.

"Clearly savages," the man sneered, turning to the back of the boat, where a small black motor was perched. "I told you we shouldn't have picked them up, Chaz. Don't get too close, they probably have fleas."

"Fleas?" Todd said in indignant disbelief. "And who are you calling savages?" I put a restraining hand on him; now was not the time to insult the people who had just saved us.

"At least you don't have to report their deaths now. Think of the mound and a half of paperwork you just avoided," the girl said good-naturedly. "Besides, we'll send a team back to attach tags and trackers before the carnotaurs wake up, so it isn't a total loss." The man huffed into his mustache and pulled a handle on the motor. It sputtered to life.

"We will drop you off a mile or so down the shoreline," the man said coolly. "That way other members of the herd won't be able to find your trail. Although I suggest you bathe the one who fell into the nest. The stench of a hatchling can linger for months if you don't."

"Months?" Shawn squeaked, looking pale.

"Actually," the man said, wrinkling his nose, "you would all benefit from bathing. You smell like feces."

"That would be me," I said, raising my hand. I couldn't smell the dinosaur poop I'd landed in anymore, but I'd probably become immune to it. The man had called us savages, and it wasn't hard to guess why. My green tunic and leggings were liberally stained and spotted with dinosaur dung, a film of wet sand still clung to my skin, and my red hair hung in wet tangled ringlets. Shawn and Todd didn't look much better. Shawn was dripping wet sand onto the floor of the boat, shirtless, his hair smashed down on his head in dirty clumps. Todd had somehow ripped a large gash in the shoulder of his tunic so it drooped to the side, his bow and other gear a tangle of straps across his chest. In sharp contrast the girl was immaculate in her crisp blue jumpsuit with its neat red badge on the upper shoulder that depicted the silhouette of a long-necked brachiosaurus.

"Who are you?" I asked.

"Scientists." The girl grinned. "We've been studying dinosaur populations around the lake since before the pandemic." She extended her hand, and I shook it. "I'm Chaz, by the way, Chaz McGuire. This grumpy but brilliant man is Dr. Steve Schwartz." Dr. Schwartz didn't acknowledge his introduction as he fiddled with the puttering motor positioned at the back of the boat. I glanced around, taking in the small craft's flat wooden hull. Narrow benches built into the sides of the boat were the only available seating, leaving the center of the boat open with enough space for the five of us to move around comfortably. Lying open near Dr. Schwartz's feet was a blue duffel bag. Leaning over, I peered inside it to see equipment I was all too familiar with as the daughter of a biologist—small sample bottles, logbooks, and various bits of technology used to measure, catalog, and label scientific findings.

What had that girl, Chaz, said? That they had been studying dinosaurs since before the pandemic? How was that possible? The pandemic, set off by the resurrection of the dinosaurs over one hundred and fifty years ago, had moved swiftly, decimating over 99 percent of the human population within days and forcing the remaining survivors underground. Well, I amended, most of the survivors. Todd's village, the Oaks, was proof that not everyone had found refuge underground. Yet this girl acted as though the pandemic had come and gone and they'd gone right on studying dinosaurs. It made no sense.

"Do you live in a tree village like Todd?" Shawn asked, the confusion in his voice echoing my own

20

thoughts as he shrugged into the damp tunic Todd handed him.

Todd shook his head as he eyed the girl's strange jumpsuit. "There aren't any villages within miles of the lake. Too dangerous. They must be compound moles like you guys."

"Not possible," I countered. "There are only four compounds, and none of them are anywhere close to here." They were in fact located on the northern, southern, eastern, and western corners of what used to be North America. And up until I'd met Todd, I'd believed that they were the last holdouts of the human race, used as safe houses for the survivors of the pandemic. Now I was faced with yet more people who apparently lived outside the Noah's rule.

Chaz grinned as she watched this exchange, as though she was enjoying a private joke. "We aren't affiliated with the compounds or any tree villages. Good guesses, though. Actually—"

"That will be enough, Chaz," Schwartz said sharply, cutting her off midsentence. "You're making me regret promoting you to my assistant. One more word and you'll be back scooping out pens."

Chaz cringed, and I cocked my head to the side as I considered what Schwartz had just said. What pens could Chaz possibly have to scoop? I glanced back at the bag of scientific equipment again. Who were these people? Before I could ask, Schwartz turned a lever on the motor, and the boat suddenly lurched forward. My feet went out from under me, and I yelped, toppling backward into Todd, who hit Shawn. Someone's elbow connected with my head as I landed hard on my back. The boat continued its surge forward, the bottom vibrating underneath me so hard my teeth clattered together.

"Thanks for that," Todd called over the roaring motor as Chaz helped him to his feet.

"Sorry," Chaz said cheerily as she extended her hand to me. "Schwartz isn't really a people person."

"You don't say," Shawn said wryly, shooting Schwartz a dirty look. Grabbing Chaz's hand, I attempted to clamber to my feet, but my pack caught on something, bringing me up short. There was a sharp ripping noise, and I stood up as my pack tore open, and its hastily packed contents spilled out. As if in slow motion, I saw my father's map fall. I'd been consulting it so frequently that I hadn't bothered to tuck it back inside my compass for safekeeping. I lunged for the map but missed as it got picked up by the wind and tumbled across the floor of the boat. Moments before it was about to go airborne and out, a booted foot smashed down on top of it, successfully halting its escape. Sighing in relief, I grabbed for it. The boot didn't move. I looked up into Schwartz's annoyed face.

"What is a savage doing with a map?" he asked, bending down to retrieve it before I could protest. Schwartz's expression went from annoyed to fearful as he surveyed the meandering line that led from North Compound to the center of Lake Michigan. "Chaz, get your weapon out," he snapped. "Don't let them move."

"What?" Chaz asked, looking just as confused as I felt. "You mean the tranquilizer gun?"

"Of course the tranquilizer gun. Don't make me say it again!" Schwartz bellowed. Chaz scrambled to follow orders and whipped her large black gun up to her shoulder.

Dr. Schwartz let the motor sputter out and die as he continued to study my map as though he'd seen a ghost. The boat bobbed up and down in the waves, and my stomach roiled sickeningly. I didn't think I liked being on a boat.

"Tie them up," he finally said, rolling my map up and storing it in the duffel bag at his feet. Shawn opened his mouth to protest, but snapped it shut as Schwartz picked up his own tranquilizer gun. One by one, we put our hands out and allowed ourselves to be tied.

"A tranquilizer probably wouldn't kill you," Chaz

murmured under her breath to us as she tightened the ropes on Todd's wrists.

"Gee, thanks," Todd sniffed.

"Yeah, I'm sure something calibrated to drop a dinosaur would be really great for our health," Shawn muttered with a murderous look at Schwartz. It wasn't until Chaz had double-checked the ropes on our wrists that Schwartz walked up to stand in front of me.

"No one should have a map that leads directly to the lab," Schwartz said, scowling. "Where did you get it?"

I pressed my lips together and looked down. Schwartz grabbed my shoulder roughly and shoved me backward until the hard wood of the boat's edge dug painfully into the backs of my knees. My jaw clenched. If he thought he was going to bully information out of me I wasn't ready to give, he was wrong. I'd come too far, survived too much, to risk failing my dad and the mission he'd given me by trusting the wrong person now. Swallowing hard, I remained silent and met his angry glare with one of my own.

"Maybe I didn't make myself clear," he said, leaning forward so I was forced to lean back farther over the water. "Talk or you go overboard."

I flicked my eyes back toward the shore; it wasn't *that* far away. But with my hands tied together it might as well have been miles.

"Whoa," Chaz said. "Dr. Schwartz, sir, isn't that a bit much? I mean, she's just a kid." I felt the faintest tug of hope. Maybe Chaz wouldn't let this guy do anything too drastic.

"So are you," he sniffed. "Do as you're told."

"Yes, sir," Chaz said, but she sounded uncertain. When I still didn't say anything, Schwartz sighed and backed up a step, giving me some much-needed breathing room. My feeling of relief flitted away when he grabbed Shawn by the front of the tunic and shoved him against the opposite side of the boat. Shawn swayed dangerously backward but his feet stayed firmly planted and Schwartz's grip on him held him upright over the dark waves lapping against the boat. My heart felt like it had jumped into my throat, and I attempted to swallow it as I took in the obvious threat to my best friend's life. It was time to talk.

"It's from my dad," I said. "A family heirloom. No importance." It was a lie. The map was the most important thing I owned. But every instinct I had was screaming at me not to trust this man, and I was not going to tell him anything I didn't absolutely have to.

Schwartz just stood there, his face unreadable as he studied me. I held my breath.

"Liar," he said, but I barely heard him because over his shoulder I'd just seen an all-too-familiar look come

25

over my best friend's face. Before I could tell him not to, Shawn pulled back and clobbered Schwartz on the side of the head with his bound fists. Schwartz yelped, and I saw him lose his grip on the front of Shawn's tunic. Shawn fought to keep his balance for a gut-wrenching heartbeat before toppling backward and off the boat. He disappeared below the surface of the blue-black water, and I screamed, rushing forward even though I knew he was out of reach. A moment later, Shawn came up gasping and thrashing as he fought to keep his head above the waves. With his hands still tied in front of him, he was forced to keep himself afloat with nothing but his legs as his heavy pack and gear dragged him down.

"He's going to drown!" I gasped as Shawn's head went under again. Panic dug its cold fingers into my heart. If I jumped in, all I would do was drown with him. In desperation I attempted to rip at the rope binding my hands with my teeth, but it was no use. The next thing I knew Schwartz had grabbed the back of my tunic and yanked me roughly away from the edge and onto the floor of the boat. He was shouting at me, but I was too lost in my fog of panic to hear him.

"Tell me who gave you that map," he bellowed again, obviously deciding to use Shawn's predicament to his advantage.

"She already did!" Todd yelled. "Can't you see Shawn's drowning?"

I stumbled to my feet in time to see Shawn struggle to the surface, grab a lungful of air, and go down again.

"He'll get eaten before he can drown," Chaz said, her lips pressed in a grim line. "Look." Something in her voice cut through my panic, and Todd and I snapped our heads to follow her pointing finger.

"What is that thing?" Todd breathed. My heart stuttered to a terrified stop as I took in the creature swimming toward us. Its enormous head alone was almost as long as our boat and reminded me of an alligator with long yellow teeth jutting out from jaws that looked capable of crushing a human in one bite. Its massive body was serpentine and fluid as it cut through the water like a snake. A dark blue-black in color, it blended almost seamlessly with the waves, and if Chaz hadn't pointed it out, I might not have noticed it until it was upon us. But now that I had seen it, I knew it was going to haunt my nightmares. I had no clue what kind of plesiosaur it was, but it was one of the scariest things I'd ever seen. Which, considering everything I'd seen since coming topside, was really saying something.

"Get him out," I begged as angry, helpless tears slid down my face. "Please."

"Talk," Schwartz said coldly.

"Sir!" Chaz said, dropping her gun to the floor of the boat as she lunged forward to make a grab for Shawn.

Schwartz shot a hand out to restrain her, his face pinched. "The safety of the lab is in jeopardy. Follow your orders."

Words began pouring out of me, as though if I just said the right combination, I could save Shawn. Whether I trusted Schwartz didn't matter now. Nothing mattered but getting Shawn out of the water. Fast.

"My dad gave it to me. He told me to come here." I choked, frantic. "He didn't say why. Just get him out. Please!"

"Dr. Schwartz?" Chaz said as Shawn spluttered back to the surface. "That's Pretty Boy. It could capsize us." Tearing my eyes away from Shawn, I saw the beast sink down into the murky water. Somehow not seeing it was scarier than seeing it had been.

Schwartz sighed. "Fine, we'll finish this at the lab." Leaning over, he grabbed Shawn's tunic, and with Chaz's help he hauled him back into the boat, where he flopped in an exhausted heap, gasping for air. Schwartz was just turning back to the motor when the boat lurched suddenly, almost toppling Todd into the water. Chaz grabbed him and threw him to the floor of the boat next to Shawn.

"Dr. Schwartz!" she yelled. "It's testing us. Get this thing moving, or we're all dead." Schwartz's face went white, and he grabbed the cord of the motor, giving it a firm yank. The engine snarled and died. He pulled at it again, and it gave another hopeful rumble before sputtering out. The plesiosaur emerged beside us, and if I'd had the inclination to reach out a hand, I could have pricked a finger on one of the teeth that was roughly the length of my forearm. What had Chaz called it? Pretty Boy? What a stupid name for one of the ugliest creatures I'd ever seen. It sized us up before bumping its head into the boat again, making it tilt violently. Its message was clear. It was going to toy with us first, terrify us, before swallowing us whole.

"Dr. Schwartz!" Chaz yelled, going for her tranquilizer gun.

"Saying my name isn't helping," Schwartz snapped. "And don't shoot it. It'll drown if we tranquilize it."

"Good! Drown it!" Todd shouted, but Schwartz ignored him as he gave the cord another yank. This time the engine spluttered to life. He cranked the handle, and we shot off across the water, the shoreline shrinking behind us as we headed toward the middle of the lake. Pretty Boy submerged again, and I waited for it to reemerge and chase us. It didn't.

I sank down beside my soaked and shivering friend. "I'm sorry," I whispered. The words sounded pitiful. Shawn had almost just been shot, drowned, and fed to a monster. *Sorry* didn't really cut it.

"What was that thing?" Shawn gasped, his eyes not leaving the spot where Pretty Boy had disappeared, and I realized that in the struggle to stay afloat Shawn hadn't seen the monster approaching.

"I have no idea," Todd said. "But I'm pretty sure it's the reason my mom said to never swim in Lake Michigan." Shawn's face went green, but before I could ask him if he was okay, he'd crawled awkwardly to the edge of the boat and puked. Not wanting to lose him overboard again, I grabbed the back of his drenched tunic with my still-bound hands and held on until he finally flopped back onto the floor of the boat, his eyes shut.

I bent over him, worried. "Shawn?" I asked, not sure if I should ask if he was okay. Clearly he wasn't. Not that I blamed him.

"He'll be fine," Todd said. "Just give him a minute." I nodded, unconvinced. Just then my canteen rolled against my foot and I looked down to see the contents of my pack scattered across the floor of the boat. Every now and then the wind would catch a packet of dinosaur jerky or a pair of socks and send them flying into the lake. My journal lay in the corner by Schwartz's foot, its pages damp and flayed open in the wind. Eyeing Schwartz to make sure he wasn't looking, I grabbed it and slid it into Todd's still-intact pack. Todd saw what I was doing, and when Schwartz's back was turned, we collected what little supplies were left and tucked them all into Todd's pack. Shawn continued to sprawl on the bottom of the boat, showing no intention of moving despite the bumping and jarring he was getting as the boat skipped across the choppy waves.

"We'll interrogate them back at the lab," Schwartz called to Chaz, shouting to be heard over the slap of the boat's hull on the water.

Todd leaned in so only Shawn and I could hear him. "What lab is that Schwartz guy talking about?" he asked. "Lake Michigan is huge. I doubt this thing has enough gas to make it across the entire lake."

"The lab is in the middle of the lake," Chaz said, making us jump as she crouched down in front of us, her giant black tranquilizer gun slung casually over her shoulder.

I unconsciously clutched my compass. Maybe the lab was what my dad had wanted me to find? After all, he had marked the center of the lake as the location of a member of the Colombe, and how many things could be in the middle of a lake? The Colombe was the secret organization my dad and mom had founded in an attempt to bring people aboveground again. My grandfather, Ivan, had explained that after the Noah had discovered the organization, a few had escaped. Was one of them hiding in this mysterious lab? Five years' worth of questions burned hot inside my chest, but after what had just happened to Shawn, I was worried that I wasn't going to like the answers I got.

CHAPTER 3

"**H**ome sweet home," Chaz crowed later when Schwartz cut the motor down to a crawl. She stood up and stretched, a wide grin on her face. I glanced around in confusion. Surrounding us on all sides was a seemingly never-ending expanse of rolling waves with no land in sight. What was she talking about?

"Are you sure you should stop here?" Shawn asked, sitting up for the first time to peer nervously at the surrounding water. He hadn't spoken since he'd thrown up, and his voice still sounded shaky. Not that I could blame him. The image of Pretty Boy swimming toward my best friend was one I wouldn't be forgetting anytime soon. It had been too loud to do any talking on the trip, and we'd spent what felt like an eternity huddled together on the floor of the boat trying to stay warm as the wind sliced right through our wet clothes.

"Of course I'm sure," Chaz said. "Get ready to duck."

"Duck?" Todd asked, glancing up at the sky. "I thought those went extinct years ago."

Chaz snorted. "They did. Sorry, I meant duck your head. I forgot how hard it is for people to spot the boat dock the first time. Look dead ahead. See where those waves are crashing sort of funny?" I followed her pointing finger and blinked in surprise. About ten feet in front of us the waves *were* behaving oddly, seeming to hit an invisible object before careening back in the opposite direction. I squinted and then jerked back in surprise when my eyes finally made sense of what they were seeing. Rising from the water was a gigantic mirrored bubble, ingeniously camouflaged with reflective glass so that it melded with the shifting waves of the lake. If I hadn't known exactly where to look, I could have passed within a foot of it and missed it. Before I could marvel anymore, our boat slid into a small circular hole in the side of the bubble, and into a network of floating wooden docks that spiraled out from a circular center deck like the spokes on a wheel. Tied to the docks were other small boats like our own, as well as a few larger ones, but the most prominent feature of the entire space was the large glass box on the center deck. The sound of the water lapping against the walls of the bubble echoed around us as Chaz tied up the boat, and we all got out.

"What is this place?" Todd asked.

"Entrance C," Schwartz said briskly, leading us toward the glass box, where he pushed a few buttons on a side panel. Moments later a glass elevator emerged, dripping. It seemed so out of place surrounded by the water and waves.

"So this lab?" Shawn said as the doors slid open. "It's . . . ?"

"At the bottom of the lake," Chaz grinned. "The place was built as a top-secret testing facility pre-Jurassic domination."

"Jurassic domi-what?" Todd asked.

"Jurassic domination is the term we use for when the power shift occurred after the pandemic that deci-mated the human race," Schwartz said stiffly as he grabbed my upper arm and maneuvered me roughly into the elevator. Todd and Shawn followed with Chaz right behind. The elevator was cramped, and I found myself pressed against the cool glass wall, my bound hands smashed awkwardly in front of me. My wrists ached, and I twisted them in an attempt to ease the pressure without much success. Still being tied up seemed redundant at this point. We had nowhere to run, and after what had happened to Shawn, none of us was going to attempt to escape by swimming. Although I wasn't so sure I'd make a run for it even if I had the opportunity. Schwartz and Chaz were my only shot at getting some answers, and after coming this far, I wasn't going to leave without them. The elevator doors slid shut, and with a soft hum we were sinking. The docking area disappeared and the dark blue of Lake Michigan enveloped the elevator shaft.

Schools of silver-and-blue fish swam in dizzying swirls around the elevator as we sank. Larger, darker shapes were also visible, but they were too far away to see distinctly.

"Are those what I think they are?" Shawn asked, pointing to the hazy blobs.

Chaz turned to squint where he was pointing. "Yup, those are Pretty Boy's buddies."

"You seriously named that thing that almost ate Shawn?" I asked. "Why?"

Chaz shrugged. "We've named the big ones. Pretty Boy is a kronosaurus; they are particularly nasty. They can eat you in one bite. But I think I'd actually prefer to be eaten by one of them. It would be better than having an elasmosaurus nibble on you a while." She didn't seem to notice the look of absolute gob-smacked astonishment on our faces because she went on as though this were all completely normal. "We have regular old plesiosaurs and pliosaurs too." She began ticking them off on her fingers. "Let's see, we have the nothosaurs, simolestes, and mosasaurs here. Oh, and a few dunkleosteus. Those suckers have jaws on them like you wouldn't believe! Dr. Schwartz gets the credit for all of them," she said proudly. "If he hadn't tweaked their genes, they couldn't live in fresh water, or our climate for that matter. Most of them lived in the oceans originally."

"I'm sorry," I said, sure I hadn't heard her right. "Do you mean you are still bringing dinosaurs back to life?"

"Well, yes. Sort of," Chaz said with a worried look at Schwartz. "It's a little more complicated than that." All I could manage was to shake my head at Chaz. Were people really still resurrecting the creatures responsible for almost wiping out the human race? I swallowed the tidal wave of hot anger that bubbled inside me as I imagined them bringing back the very monster that had almost eaten my best friend just moments before.

"You made all those plesiosaurs? That's just sick," Shawn said, my own disgust reflected in his face.

"Swimming dinosaurs," Todd sniffed. "I don't care what fancy name you call them."

"They aren't technically dinosaurs. They're swim-ming marine reptiles," Chaz corrected.

"To savages, dinosaurs and plesiosaurs are nothing but something to eat. You are wasting your time with explanations, Chaz. So, yes, Todd was it? They are just swimming dinosaurs," Schwartz sneered. Todd bristled.

"They protect this lab," Chaz said with an apolo-getic shrug at Todd behind Schwartz's back. "No one comes poking around plesiosaur-infested waters."

We continued our steady descent in silence, and soon the sun no longer penetrated the water far enough for us to see the fish or the plesiosaurs. I shivered as the temperature in the elevator became markedly cooler.

Todd was starting to tremble too, but not from the cold. I noticed that his face was white and sweat was running down it. If I hadn't known any better, I would have thought he was the one who'd been thrown in the lake with Pretty Boy.

"Are you okay?" I asked, pulled momentarily from my thoughts about this mysterious lab and the mon-sters they'd created to protect it. "You look horrible."

"I don't like small spaces," he said tersely, clenching and unclenching his fists.

"Wonderful," Schwartz drawled drily, "a claustro-phobic savage." He'd pulled a small port screen out of the duffel bag at his feet and studiously ignored us as he began typing something into it. I gave Todd's shoulder an awkward pat with my bound hands. I wasn't especially fond of the tiny space either. My ears were starting to ache and throb. Noticing my wince of pain, Chaz quickly explained how to clear our ears to relieve the pressure from our descent by holding our noses while simultaneously exhaling through them. It felt a little stupid, but it worked. A minute and one satisfying pop later and the stabbing pain in my head was gone. I made a mental note not to let that happen again. The elevator passed into the insides of a building, and I looked away from Todd to stare. The first floor we slid past was full of lab equipment.

"Whoa," Todd said, letting out a low whistle of appreciation, and I nodded in mute agreement. This place was massive. Unlike North Compound's confining walls of stone and concrete, these walls were made of glass, so you could see through all the rooms from one end to the other, making it hard to tell where one room stopped and another room started.

"Pretty impressive, isn't it," Chaz said proudly. "This is just the research floor; wait until you see the rest of it." The next floor the elevator descended through was covered in wall-to-wall troughs of plants under grow lights, reminding me of the underground chambers in

North Compound where we'd grown turnips, potatoes, and other vegetables. Like the floor above, this one too seemed ten times bigger than even the large meeting auditorium back at North.

"Are you seeing this?" I whispered to Shawn.

"I am," Shawn murmured.

The elevator didn't give us long to gawk before dropping down into the biggest room I'd ever seen. All comparisons to North Compound disappeared as I pressed my hands to the glass and stared in wonder at hundreds of dinosaurs, all housed in enormous glass cages. Arching above the dinosaur pens was a tangled network of glass walkways, bustling with blue jump-suited people.

"No way." Todd breathed. Shawn made a disbelieving choking noise, and I pounded him on the back with my bound hands.

"You keep dinosaurs down here?" I gasped.

"Of course," Schwartz replied. "We run one of the top breeding programs in the world."

"We run the only breeding program in the world," Chaz muttered. Schwartz glared at her before turning his attention back to us.

"We have also tamed and trained some of the brighter species. We've gathered invaluable data from living in such close proximity. They act as message

40

carriers, test subjects, and pets. You may not kill any of them," he said, giving us a hard look. "Everyone who lives down here does so because they believe in the beauty and continuation of the dinosaur. Remember that."

"But why?" I asked.

"What do you mean *why*?" Schwartz sniffed.

I shook my head in amazement as I took in the hundreds of cages. "Why would you breed them? After what happened with the pandemic?"

"The ecosystem," Chaz said. "When people brought the dinosaurs out of extinction one hundred and fifty years ago, no one thought about the impact these guys would have on the ecosystem if they ran wild." She jerked her head at one of the cages. "They were supposed to just stay in zoos, farms, and wildlife preserves, right? Well, obviously, they didn't. After the pandemic, these guys took over and a lot of other animals went extinct. It threw everything out of whack. Our lab has been trying to correct that with selective breeding and repopulation."

Her explanation sounded like a more scientific version of Ivan's table demonstration when we had been back at his house the night before the marines found us again. He'd been trying to explain to Shawn that if you removed all the dinosaurs, the carefully balanced world of predator and prey that we lived in would collapse. And while Chaz wasn't talking about removing the dinosaurs entirely, she seemed to be making the same general point. Had things changed so much in the last one hundred and fifty years that we now *needed* dinosaurs to keep the topside world functional? And if that was true, then what Chaz was saying about balancing out the dinosaur population made a lot of sense. I shook my head as I tried to process this bizarre concept. I had grown up in a compound where everyone talked about the time before the dinosaurs like it was this ideal utopia that could be reclaimed. But what if Ivan and Chaz were right and the dinosaurs were here to stay?

Before I could respond, the elevator continued its steady descent, and I craned my head back to get one last look at the cage of what had to be *Parasaurolophus* before it disappeared from sight. We passed through a floor that looked like a school, glass desks lined up neatly in glass rooms. The place seemed to go on forever, and I tried to wrap my mind around the fact that it was all underwater. If I hadn't been standing in the middle of it, I never would have believed it.

"So much glass," Shawn marveled next to me, and I realized he was right. Glass had been something we'd had to scavenge and reuse over and over again in North Compound, as we were unable to manufacture it.

Chaz leaned forward. "I'm not sure if you noticed while running from that pack of carnotaurs, but we have a lot of sand around here." When neither of us said anything, she cocked her head to the side. "That's how you make glass. You heat sand to really high temperatures. Didn't you know that?" All I could do was shake my head in wonder as we passed through another floor, this one made up of small apartments.

Our elevator finally bumped to a stop, and we spilled out into a gigantic lab lit with harsh fluorescents. Floor-to-ceiling windows looked out into the murk of Lake Michigan. A few scientists glanced up from their large stationary port screens as we entered, eyeing us with interest before turning back to their work. Schwartz gave Chaz a meaningful look before striding away to meet three lab-coated men huddled around a port screen. A small yellow dinosaur that only came up to my knee scurried past us and clambered nimbly up Chaz's leg and onto her shoulder. Chaz dug a large dead beetle out of her pocket and handed it up to the little creature. It cooed happily.

"This is Pip." She grinned as she passed up another treat. "She's kind of the mascot for this floor of the lab. She was supposed to get released back into the wild, but she was so darn cute they decided to let her stay."

"What is she exactly?" Todd asked, slightly less

green now that we weren't in the tiny elevator.

"Compsognathus," Chaz said. "It's Greek for *dainty jaw*. Dr. Schwartz's team was able to extract her DNA from a bone found in Germany. He's one of the most brilliant paleontologists we have here at the lab." The little creature was more bird than dinosaur, and I had to admit that Chaz had a point; she was sort of cute. Vibrant yellow with blue eyes that took up most of her pointed face; she lashed her long, thin tail delicately from side to side for balance as she surveyed us from her perch on Chaz's shoulder.

"Ecosystem or no ecosystem, I can't believe you're still actively bringing new species back to life," Shawn said, his fists clenched. Oblivious to Shawn's anger in her preoccupation with Pip, Chaz nodded happily.

"Ten new species just last year. We have an above-ground facility where we release them. It's really amazing."

"Amazing is not the word I would use," Todd said sarcastically.

"Spoken like a true savage," Schwartz said drily as he rejoined our group. He turned to Chaz. "Dr. Robinson is sending a team out to tag the carnotaurs we stunned. Please accompany him. I'll escort these three to see Boznic."

Chaz nodded and was turning to go when one of

the men in lab coats trotted up, a worried look on his face. He whispered something quietly in Schwartz's ear, and Schwartz scowled and nodded. With a resigned sigh he turned to Chaz, who had stopped to watch this interaction. "Change of plans. Escort them to conference room B. I'll alert Boznic and meet you there after I deal with this." With a curt nod to the man in the lab coat, Schwartz turned and followed him at a jog.

"Looks like you're with me," Chaz said as Pip hopped from her shoulder and scampered away. "Which," she said confidentially, "is kind of shocking. I'm not sure if you noticed, but Schwartz isn't my biggest fan. He only tolerates me because he owes my dad a favor." She stared after Schwartz's retreating form, her forehead scrunched in thought. With a shrug, she motioned for us to climb back into the elevator. Todd's face still had a sickly green color to it, and I saw him give the tranquilizer gun hanging by Chaz's side an assessing look. Not wanting him to pull anything stupid, I gave his shoulder a shove with my own, and he stumbled forward into the elevator. Shawn followed us inside, a preoccupied scowl on his face. Despite the disturbing revelation that these people were breeding dinosaurs, I couldn't help but feel a tingle of excitement. This had to be what my dad had put on his map. It just had to be. As soon as the doors slid shut behind us, Chaz pushed a few buttons and took the tranquilizer gun off her shoulder with a grin.

"I'll make you a deal. If you promise not to deck me, I'll put this thing away. Makes me twitchy pointing it at people anyway." She shuddered and slung the large black weapon onto her back. "Besides, it's about out of battery anyways, and running away is impossible now that you're down here."

"What do you mean impossible?" Todd asked, eyeing the panel on the side of the elevator speculatively.

"Well, you saw how touchy Schwartz was about you guys finding out about this place. It's because no one knows about us—not the Noah, not the compounds, not anybody," Chaz explained. "We're top secret."

"I thought the Oaks was top secret too," Todd muttered darkly, and I winced. His village had been captured when the Noah's marines somehow tracked me and Shawn all the way from North Compound.

When I'd left the compound with nothing but my dad's compass and a poorly drawn map, I'd never expected that the Noah would send General Kennedy and his marines after me. Why would the Noah, the man who controlled all four of the compounds, waste his time on a twelve-year-old girl? The whole idea was mind-boggling, but it was one I'd had to come to terms with.

In fact, there were a lot of things about the world that I'd had to adjust to after coming topside. For one, that people like Todd existed: people who lived outside the Noah's control and the compound's protection. For my entire life, I'd thought survival topside was impossible due to the dinosaurs. Now I was face-to-face with yet another example of that lie. Chaz and the rest of the people in the lab were obviously not descendants of the people the original Noah had shepherded underground over one hundred and fifty years ago. Which meant that, like Todd, they'd never believed the Noah was the great savior of the human race like Shawn and I had. It was simultaneously unnerving and exhilarating.

"What?" Todd cried, and I focused back in on the conversation. Chaz had continued talking while I'd been lost in my own thoughts, and from the look of horror on Todd's face, I'd missed something big.

"Like I said"—Chaz shrugged—"once you're brought to the lab, you have to stay. It prevents information leaks. But don't worry. You'll love it here."

"If you think I'm staying down here, you're insane," Todd snapped.

I bit my lip as I glanced around the glass elevator that was sliding upward past level after enormous level of the lab. "Insane might be an understatement," I muttered. I wasn't sure what I'd thought I was going to find

47

once I got to the lake, but monsters like Pretty Boy and Dr. Schwartz hadn't been it. I forced myself to smile at Chaz. "We promise not to run. My name's Sky, Shawn is the one who almost got eaten, and Todd is the one who looks like he might puke."

"I highly recommend puking," Shawn said with a wry smile. "You'll feel loads better."

"Thanks, but I'll pass," Todd sniffed.

"Nice to meet you." Chaz grinned. "Welcome to the Lincoln Lab."

"And what is it that you do here exactly?" Shawn asked.

Chaz's eyes lit up. "Me? I'm just Schwartz's assistant."

"They let assistants carry tranquilizer guns?" Shawn asked dubiously.

Chaz nodded. "We're always short-handed, and lab kids start working early. It's not that great of a job really. Don't get me wrong, it's a step up from mucking out stalls, but Dr. Schwartz isn't the most personable guy."

"We noticed." Shawn scowled. "About the time he tried to feed me to a sea monster."

"Well, in his defense, you did hit him," Chaz said. "I don't think he *really* would have thrown you overboard." Shawn shuddered and Chaz smiled apologetically. "Yeah, Pretty Boy's a mean one all right. But pliosaurs and plesiosaurs are the only vicious creatures we help proliferate, and that's only to protect the lab."

"Proliferate?" Shawn asked.

"Help multiply," Chaz supplied. "Our main focus is herbivores."

"Okay," I said, trying to wrap my mind around this new information. "Then why didn't you kill that carnotaurus herd on the beach? They were definitely not herbivores."

"It's a lab rule," Chaz said. "It all goes back to the ecosystem balance I mentioned before. No one likes spiders either, but if we killed them all, the bug population would take over. If we kill off all the carnivores, we throw the entire ecosystem off balance."

"Wait a minute," Shawn said, his brow wrinkled in confusion. "Didn't you say this lab had been here since before the pandemic?"

"It has." Chaz nodded. "Originally it was a top-secret testing center for the dinosaurs. Scientists back then were interested in discovering what else the dinosaurs might be useful for besides entertainment and meat. This lab has discovered thousands of uses for everything from the oils in their skin to their dung. Medicines, tools, food, you name it, dinosaurs provide it way better than cows or chickens ever could. Which is good, considering all those domestic animals are extinct now. Plus dinosaurs are exceptionally trainable if you start them as hatchlings, and they make pretty fabulous pets."

"But what about the pandemic?" I asked. The pandemic was one of the main reasons the human race had been struggling to make a comeback for the last one hundred and fifty years. The small portion of the population that had survived it had done so because they'd been blessed with immunity to a disease that should have been extinct for millions of years. And while that immunity did seem to be passed down from generation to generation, it wasn't foolproof.

"Oh, that," Chaz said, waving her hand dismissively. "All the dinosaurs we breed are genetically modified so they help eliminate the bacterial strain that caused the pandemic. I'm not sure how well you know your history, but all attempts at a vaccine have failed. But if the genetic modifications work like Boz thinks they will, we might be able to eradicate it completely in the next thirty years. Pretty awesome, right?" When we didn't say anything, she went on, unperturbed. "Anyways, after the pandemic, the scientists that survived realized that if they didn't step in, the fragile balance of life topside might implode completely. Without us, there might not be a viable ecosystem topside."

"The dinosaurs make it impossible for the human

race to survive topside, so who cares about the viable eco-whatever?" Shawn asked

"It's not impossible," Todd said. "It's just not real easy."

"The word you're looking for is *deadly*," Shawn muttered.

"That's the thing," Chaz said excitedly. "Boz has a plan for us to live in harmony with the dinosaurs. We already have quite a few scientists living in our above-ground facility. Boz says that evolution has proven it isn't just survival of the fittest, but survival of the adaptable!"

"Wait a second," Todd said, "I think I heard about a place like that. Some of the traders mentioned a settlement of scientists near the lake."

Chaz nodded happily. "That was probably us. We trade with some of the tree people from time to time."

"I thought we were all savages," Todd said, his face tight with anger.

Chaz cringed. "Not everyone is as biased at Schwartz," she said apologetically.

"I still think you're all nuts," Shawn said.

"We're not," Chaz countered, sounding slightly insulted. "We do some really amazing stuff here." When we still didn't seem convinced, she huffed and punched a new button on the elevator.

"What are you doing?" Todd asked nervously.

"Proving to you just how awesome this place is," Chaz said. "We have some time to kill before Schwartz gets to the conference room anyways. We'll hit the hatchery first, and then the breeding pens. The dorms and school aren't that exciting."

The elevator dinged, and we stepped out into the gigantic laboratory and my jaw dropped. It was one thing to hear about people breeding dinosaurs; it was a whole other thing to actually see it. Scattered around the room were large metal contraptions with glass domes and heat lamps. I peered inside the closest one. It was filled with five eggs the size of footballs, and the silver plaque on the side let me know that these were apparently ankylosaurus eggs.

"Those are really cool," Chaz said from behind me, making me jump. "They have this fused armor built into their skin. Makes them nearly impossible to tranquilize. Real sweethearts, though, so you almost never have to. We used to have a male named Bubba who would let the little kids climb all over him like he was a jungle gym. He would do just about anything for a cookie."

"I'm not sure if this is impressive or disgusting," Shawn admitted as he turned in a slow circle.

We passed through the enormous hatchery and

walked up a massive set of glass stairs. I looked back and calculated roughly one hundred incubators, each with at least three or four eggs inside.

Chaz punched a code into a large glass door. It buzzed and clicked open, and the smell that wafted through was enough to make me gag. Shawn and Todd immediately covered their noses with their hands. Chaz didn't seem to notice.

We walked into the massive room of dinosaurs we'd caught a glimpse of earlier. With the soaring ceilings and gigantic windows, it was hard to believe we were really underwater. Row after row of oversized glass and iron stalls stretched as far as I could see, each one containing a different breed of dinosaur. We followed Chaz up a ramp that led to a walkway over the top of the cages. We had to maneuver around teenagers in dirty coveralls who were busy wheeling wheelbarrows full of a coarse grain, obviously on their way to fill the enormous feed troughs below. A few of them shot us interested looks, but everyone else seemed much too busy to care about us.

I looked down into the first stall. A small family of triceratops was inside, the female bellowing at three tiny greenish adolescents who head-butted one another and rolled around the floor of the cage. My heart lurched when I saw a small girl in among them, a wheelbarrow and pitchfork in hand as she worked at clearing out a mound of dinosaur poop almost as tall as she was.

Chaz waved down. "Hey, Joyce! How are the three musketeers doing today?" Joyce set down her pitchfork as the three young dinosaurs raced around her in an impromptu game of tag.

"Driving their poor mother crazy. I think we'll move them to their own pen tomorrow."

Suddenly Shawn was gripping my shoulder. "Did you see what was outside those windows?" he whispered.

"What?" I asked, turning to look out the floor-to-ceiling windows that wrapped around the entire enclosure. Outside, swimming in graceful arcs, were plesiosaurs. These had longer necks and smaller heads than Pretty Boy. Their bodies moved smoothly in the water, propelled by four muscular fins. They periodically opened their mouths in soundless calls, giving me a good view of their gleaming rows of teeth. I gulped, and hoped the glass was thicker than it looked.

Chaz turned back to us. "Oh, you spotted our audience. The elasmosaurs like the light the lab gives off. Did you know that some people believe that that particular breed was never actually extinct?" she asked, jerking her head at the long-necked plesiosaurs. "Before the pandemic hit, people claimed that there was a small family of them located in some lake in Scotland. The locals called them Loch Ness monsters or something. Can you believe it? Dr. Schwartz said it's really unlikely, but I would love to travel there someday to see for myself."

Todd craned his head back, taking in the enormity of the space. "What I want to know is how you got all these dinosaurs down here. I know you didn't squeeze them into that tiny glass elevator."

Chaz laughed. She had a low chuckling laugh, and I thought that, under different circumstances, like ones where she wasn't holding us prisoner, I might actually like her.

"We have gigantic freight elevators at entrances A and G," she explained. Before she could go on, the crackle of a loudspeaker reverberated around the room. Everyone froze, looking up as though expecting the voice of God. However, it wasn't the voice of God that came through the speaker. It was Schwartz. And he sounded furious.

"Chastity McGuire! Report to the conference room immediately!" Chaz froze as everyone's eyes turned to stare at us. It looked like our tour was over.

CHAPTER
4

"Your real name is Chastity?" Todd asked, his familiar smirk back in place.

"My name is Chaz," she snipped as she hustled us off the walkway. "If anyone but Dr. Schwartz called me Chastity, they'd get a black eye. Consider yourself warned."

We reached another glass door and Chaz punched some numbers in quickly. It buzzed open and she pushed us inside. This room had lower ceilings and seemed to be some kind of office space. She hurried us down hallway after hallway until we finally reached conference room B. Inside was a fuming Schwartz.

"Did they enjoy your nice little tour of our top-secret

facility, Chaz? You are officially demoted from your position as my assistant. I need someone who can follow a simple order when it's given." Chaz's face flushed red, but she set her mouth in a stubborn line and didn't reply. She had guts. I liked her more for it.

"Relax, Dr. Schwartz," said a large man I hadn't noticed before. His clothes had the pressed appearance of authority. His pale blue eyes were stern, but the wrinkles around his mouth and eyes betrayed that his face was more accustomed to smiling than frowning. "I'm sure Chaz did not mean to be disrespectful. I actually think it might be a good thing to give our guests a glimpse at the importance of our work."

"Sir," Dr. Schwartz said stiffly, "you saw the girl's map. Our safety here might be compromised."

"And if it is?" the man replied with a carefree shrug. "We are not without protection. Before you jump to the grimmest scenario, let's at least hear the girl's story. And for heaven's sake, untie them. They're only children."

Todd snorted. I had to agree. I hadn't felt like a child in a long time. Regardless, Chaz stepped forward to untie us. She looked relieved and gave us an apologetic smile as she deftly unwound the rope.

"Take a seat, please," the man said. "I am Dr. Bartholomew Boznic, head paleontologist here at the

Lincoln Lab, but everyone calls me Boz." He was perched at a long glossy metal table set against another one of those floor-to-ceiling windows that looked out on the lake, complete with frolicking plesiosaurs. Their huge bodies slid past the glass, and some even pushed off it to launch themselves in the opposite direction.

"We didn't tell anyone about your lab," I said as I took a seat across from Boz. "I had no idea what was in the middle of this lake when I got the map."

"That's good to hear." He smiled. "I'd hate to think that the Noah's stealth bombers were winging their way here to destroy my life's work as we speak."

"The Noah doesn't have stealth bombers," Shawn protested, but then he paused, taking in Boz's serious face and raised eyebrows. Deflated, he sank into the seat beside me. "Of course the Noah has stealth bombers," he said flatly, "why am I even surprised?" I rolled my eyes. Even after watching Todd's entire village get captured, and everything that Ivan had told us, it had taken Shawn forever to come around to the idea that the Noah wasn't the savior of humanity we'd always been told he was. I'd been an easier sell. Between my dad's note and the revelation that villages like Todd's existed, I'd very quickly come to terms with the fact that the world wasn't what I'd always been told. Not that I could blame Shawn for taking a little longer. We'd both grown up believing that only one airplane existed, and that airplane's sole purpose was to deliver mail and supplies four times a year between compounds. Then the helicopters had shown up at Todd's village, so Boz's claim of stealth bombers was not all that far-fetched. Unfortunately.

"I can assure you that he does have stealth bombers," Boz said seriously. "And if given the opportunity, he would use them. Our position with the current Noah is tenuous to say the least."

"Tenuous?" I asked.

"He acts like we don't exist, mainly because he can't find us, and we act like he doesn't exist. But I don't want to talk about that now. What I want to know is where this remarkable map came from." He had my dad's map spread out before him, and I could tell he'd been studying it before we came in. I looked at Shawn and Todd, hoping for some guidance about how much to tell. Shawn just shrugged. Todd laced his fingers into the straps of the pack he was still wearing and stared in grim silence at the plesiosaurs outside the window. I decided to proceed cautiously. Boz seemed nice enough, but he and Schwartz worked together. And there was something about Schwartz that made my skin crawl.

"My dad sent it. Just like I told Schwartz before he tried to feed Shawn to that monster Pretty Boy."

"It was an accident," Schwartz sniffed. "The boy attacked me, and he lost his balance." Boz shot Schwartz a disapproving look, clearly skeptical of this explanation, and Schwartz seemed to shrink a bit.

"Our Dr. Schwartz can be a bit overenthusiastic. I'm sorry you had to experience any unpleasantness, Miss, Miss—what's your name, my dear?"

"Sky Mundy."

Boz sat up as though his chair had electrocuted him, leaning forward to look at me over the top of his thin wire-framed glasses. "Are you any relation to Jack Mundy? The biologist in North Compound?"

I sat up too, nodding as my heart lurched with excitement and goose bumps broke out along my arms. This was it. "I'm his daughter."

Schwartz's lip curled in a barely detectable sneer, but Boz looked as though Christmas had just come early.

"I know your father." He smiled, clasping his hands in delight. "He's an old friend of mine from when we trained at the university back at East Compound." I waited for Boz to mention the Colombe, but he did not. He had to be the member of the Colombe my dad was talking about, but I needed to be positive. Pulling my compass out of the neck of my still-damp tunic, I held it up for Boz to see.

"Does this mean anything to you?" I asked. Todd and Shawn leaned forward as one, identical expressions of anxious anticipation on their faces. I wondered what my own face looked like. Hopeful? Terrified? Anxious? All of those feelings were racing through me as I held my breath, waiting to see if this was when I'd finally get the answers I so desperately needed.

Boz's face broke out into a wide grin, and he pulled a nearly identical compass out of the collar of his shirt. "It does," he said. I let out a huge sigh of relief as something loosened inside me, and I felt as though I could really breathe for the first time since I opened that note from my dad a lifetime ago. I grinned at Todd and Shawn. See, I wanted to say, I told you that there was something in the middle of the lake, that everything we went through to get here was worth it, but my smile faded as my eyes flicked over to where Schwartz still sat, glowering at me.

Boz followed my gaze and waved a dismissive hand. "Don't worry about Dr. Schwartz. He was also a member of the Colombe, but he and your father never really got along. He joined me when I escaped East Compound. The same escape," he said sadly, "that killed your mother." I nodded, pushing aside the empty feeling that hearing about my mom always seemed to trigger.

"Then I can tell you everything," I said. "You *are* the person my dad sent me to find."

"Really?" Boz said. "Why did your father send you after all these years?"

"I'm not sure where to even begin," I said, overwhelmed by everything that had happened in the last few days. Boz just folded his hands and smiled encouragingly.

"Five years ago, my dad disappeared from North Compound, leaving me behind," I began, quickly describing how I'd found my dad's note and map, escaped North Compound, met Todd, and survived the takeover at the Oaks. I explained about meeting Ivan and the chaos when the marines tracked us to his house, separating us, and I wrapped up with meeting Chaz and Schwartz on the beach. Shawn chimed in to say that it was a good idea he'd decided to come along because I never would have made it without him, and Todd interjected to tell the story of me taking an impromptu dip in a spinosaur's pond. Both comments earned them well-placed elbows in the ribs. Boz was an excellent listener, nodding and exclaiming, although he seemed saddened when I described the two dinosaurs that we had killed, and he scowled when we mentioned Ivan. Apparently paleontologists and dinosaur hunters didn't quite see eye to eye.

"Well," he exclaimed when I finished. "I'm sorry to hear that Jack went missing. I hope he's alive somewhere out there, but he certainly never made it here." Even though I'd known from the way Boz had reacted to my dad's name that he wasn't here, it still hurt to hear it said out loud.

"May I see the plug?" Boz asked.

I nodded, slipping off the compass and unhinging the hidden compartment. I handed it to Boz. He studied it before flipping it over, as though it might tell its secrets if he just looked at it long enough.

"Well?" Shawn asked. "Do you know what's on it?"

"I don't," he admitted. "I haven't talked to Jack Mundy in years. Why he would disappear and then send his daughter to see me is beyond my understanding."

Todd huffed impatiently. "Well, can't you plug that whatchama dinger into one of those techy devices so we can find out?" He jiggled his foot nervously as he watched the giant sea monsters cavorting behind Boz's head.

"I think that sounds like a very good idea." Boz smiled. "Dr. Schwartz, grab me one of those techy devices. The XI 4000 should fit this." Schwartz nodded stiffly and walked out.

"Now that he's gone," Boz said, setting down the

plug in front of him, "are you absolutely sure that you weren't followed here? This General Kennedy and his marines seem to have had no problem tracking you to Todd's village." His change of subject startled me, and I glanced over at Todd.

"I don't know," I admitted. "Like I said, we ditched everything from the compound that could have potentially held a tracker. Todd thinks they were tracking us the old-fashioned way, by following our trail. But—" I paused—"If they did, our tracks will just lead them to Lake Michigan and then disappear." Boz nodded, seeming satisfied.

Schwartz returned with a large port and propped it up on a stand. Boz pressed his entire hand to the screen, and it hummed for a second, then turned on. Handprint entry, I thought, impressive. With practiced fingers, Boz slid the tiny plug into the port. A black screen appeared, followed by the revolving gold symbol of the ark. The screen blinked and there was my dad.

I leaned forward hungrily, taking in the tiny image on Boz's screen. My dad was wearing a stained and disheveled lab coat, his brown hair sweaty and his face tight and anxious.

"This message is for Dr. Bartholomew Boznic or Ivan Ironarm. You need to enter the ten-digit code we used to pass secret messages within the Colombe. If it is not entered in the next thirty seconds, this memory plug will lock down, corrupt itself, and destroy the hard drive of every piece of technology within two hundred feet."

Boz looked startled at this and frowned.

"Do you know it?" I asked, my throat tight. If Boz didn't know the code my dad was talking about, the plug would destroy the secrets it contained. If that happened, everything I'd been through, everything I'd dragged my friends through, would be for nothing. But even as my heart raced in terrified anticipation, I couldn't help but stare at my dad. It had been over five years since I'd seen him, and in that time my memories of him had faded and blurred. Now everything came rushing back: the way his hair waved across his forehead, the crease between his eyebrows that showed he was worried, the way he used his hands when he talked.

"I think so." Boz nodded. He quickly typed in a ten-digit number, and I held my breath. I wasn't the only one. When the screen beeped, the room let out a collective sigh of relief. This time my dad sat at his desk, sweat shining on his forehead, and from the way the camera struggled to focus, I could tell that his hand was shaking.

"I found something," he said, his words rushed and panicked. "It's what I was worried about all those years ago when I first started the Colombe. I warned everyone that someday the Noah was going to do something drastic. I was right. He's going to wipe out the dinosaurs, but it's worse than I ever imagined. If I don't make it to tell either of you this in person, then hopefully this plug will. We have to stop this." My dad jumped as a loud banging came from behind him. His face went from frightened to terrified. The screen flickered, and a video icon appeared.

I didn't realize I had tears running down my cheeks until Shawn used his sleeve to wipe them away. Boz reached up and clicked the icon.

The port buzzed and then a grainy video began, revealing a windowless room with six men sitting around a table. At the head of the table was our current Noah. He had the same gray-tinged hair and serious expression as his counterparts, and his eyes were dark and hooded behind thick-rimmed glasses. I was struck by how old he looked.

"What is this?" Todd asked.

"It's some kind of meeting," Schwartz snapped.

The Noah cleared his throat. "Today we have reached a monumental decision that will change our world forever." He looked up from his papers to his audience. "Today, by a five-to-one vote, we made the decision to reclaim our world, eradicate the dinosaur pestilence that plagues us, and sacrifice the few for the many. After over a hundred and fifty years of fear, we will triumph."

The Noah wasn't wearing his customary smile, the one that said, trust me, everything will be okay. The one I'd seen him wear countless times in North Compound assemblies, the one designed to help the people of the compounds rest easy that supplies would be delivered and life would go on. Instead, his solemn face was all business and his eyes held a cool resignation. They were the eyes of a man who had set a course and was going to stick to it. Those eyes scared me.

Shawn's hand was on my shoulder; squeezing it uncomfortably, and I wondered if his own stomach was tied in the same painful knot mine was. I bit my lip as the Noah went on. "The fortifications to our nation's four underground compounds are progressing well," the Noah said, "as we prepare to set the second phase of the Ark Plan, code name Flood, into place. We know that future generations will look back on this day and thank us for the decision we have made. Our temporary refuge underground has gone on long enough, and it is time for us to regain what is rightfully ours. Our efforts to eradicate the dinosaurs in the past have failed. But we have found the solution."

The Noah looked straight at the camera. "We know that the dinosaurs of millions of years ago were destroyed by a meteor strike that made the Earth's surface uninhabitable. Modern technology has given us the tools to re-create this phenomenon. We have located enough nuclear weaponry to eradicate the dinosaur population completely." The two serious men sitting next to him nodded solemnly.

Todd was on his feet, gesturing wildly at the screen, his voice quivering. "What is he talking about? Is that who I think it is? Can they do that?" I grabbed his arm and yanked him into the seat next to me.

"Our weapon specialists have developed strategic drop sites that will spare our compounds from structural damage, allowing the human race to survive underground, away from dangerous radiation. Our top scientists are taking samples and DNA from a large number of species and plants, and we feel confident that, when the dust settles, we will be able to rebuild our great nation from a clean slate. Today marks the beginning of a war. One we will win."

The port clicked off, and the silence in the room was deafening. I couldn't wrap my mind around what he had just said. Phase two of the Ark Plan? Code name Flood? Nuclear war? How could it be a war when only one side had weapons?

Boz's face was white as a sheet as he stared at the blank screen in horror. Then he looked at us, his eyes wide and panicked. "They are going to kill us all."

"What?!" Todd yelped, jumping to his feet again.

"They are going to blast our continent with bombs. Wipe the world clean, and start all over again," Boz gasped.

"Why is no one else freaking out right now?" Todd's voice echoed the disbelief I felt.

"There is no way anyone could be that stupid," I said, hoping I could make it true.

"We always knew the current Noah was an extremist, but I never thought . . ." Boz shook his head sadly. "Does he not realize the catastrophic effects of wiping out millions and millions of years of evolution? Every animal will have to be re-created, every plant germinated in a lab, every bacterium grown on a petri dish. It's impossible. The human race would continue to survive underground for a while, but what would be left of the world when they finally did venture aboveground?"

"These bombs would kill everyone who lives aboveground?" Todd asked in horror. "I know of at least three other villages within a month's travel from the Oaks. All of those people are just going to be left to die? So the privileged compound moles can survive? That isn't fair!"

"That might be the understatement of the century,"

I said, feeling sick as I sat frozen in my chair, thinking about everything I'd learned about dinosaurs since coming topside. I kept seeing Ivan's table in a jumbled heap on his floor after he'd demonstrated what would happen to our world without the dinosaurs, the rotten wood crumbled and scattered. Todd seemed convinced that humans could live alongside them. Chaz and these scientists took it one step further, even creating new dinosaurs. Although I wasn't sure yet if I agreed with them, I knew I didn't agree with the Noah, that all dinosaurs should be destroyed.

Todd wasn't done raging yet. "That isn't a solution; that's . . . that's . . ." He stuttered, flailing his arms hopelessly as he searched for a word bad enough to encompass the Noah's plan.

"Genocide," Shawn said quietly. "The word you're looking for, Todd, is genocide."

"You are absolutely correct," Boz agreed. "They are going to kill everything this lab worked so hard to preserve and foster. The years we've spent selectively breeding dinosaurs to even out the population numbers and stabilize the ecosystem. For nothing!"

"I wasn't talking about the dinosaurs!" Todd yelled, slamming his hand down on the table.

"We all just need to relax a moment," Boz said, sinking weak-kneed into his chair. Chaz slumped down into the chair next to me, and I jumped. I'd forgotten she was in the room.

"Why would the Noah have filmed this?" Todd asked as he paced back and forth in front of the long window like a caged animal. "It seems stupid. If this was supposed to be top secret, why document it?"

"My best guess," Shawn said, "was that he was eventually going to show this to us." When everyone gave him a strange look, he jerked his head at me. "To the people in the compounds, I mean. I'm betting that after it was all said and done, after the bombs had been dropped and everything wiped out, he would have sent this to the compounds along with an explanation. It would be considered of historical importance, wouldn't it? The day the decision was made to wipe the world clean and start over again? Of course, he couldn't let it get out before it had all happened or people might freak out."

"So how did my dad get ahold of it?" I asked, thinking out loud. "This had to have been under lock and key."

Boz ran a hand through his thinning hair and looked at us. "Your father was a brilliant man, Sky. If anyone could have hacked the Noah's communication system, it was him." I felt a faint surge of pride for my dad, but it washed away as Boz leaned forward, his

71

face concerned. "How long ago did you say your father disappeared?"

"A little over five years ago," I said. "Why? Do you think maybe the Noah changed his mind since then? That this may be outdated information?"

"No," Shawn said, shaking his head before Boz could respond. He stared at me. "Think about it, Sky. For the last five years, what have we been putting every spare ounce of manpower toward in North Compound?"

I felt the blood drain from my face as realization hit. "Topside fortifications," I whispered. "Of course." I turned to Boz and Todd, feeling numb. "For the last five years, at the Noah's orders, we've been increasing the thickness of the concrete barrier that separated North Compound from the topside world." I inhaled sharply as something else occurred to me, and I turned to Shawn. "The supplies. Remember at the last assembly we went to?"

Shawn nodded. "They talked about how we were going to have to lay up the key supplies we needed from the other compounds in case the mail plane ever couldn't make it. This was why! The Noah wasn't worried about the plane; he was preparing us for this."

I turned to Boz. "We don't have much time. When we escaped North Compound, we were about a month away from being done with topside fortifications. And that was almost a week ago." Everyone fell silent as they took this new information in. The thump thump thump of Todd's booted feet on the glass floor was the only sound in the room as he paced back and forth in front of the long windows, oblivious to the giant plesiosaur that was gliding across their surface. Chaz bit her fingernails, her eyes flicking nervously from Schwartz's angry face to Boz's thoughtful one and back again.

"So what now?" she finally asked, breaking the silence.

"Well," Boz said, hefting himself to his feet. "We can't just let the world end. We have work to do."

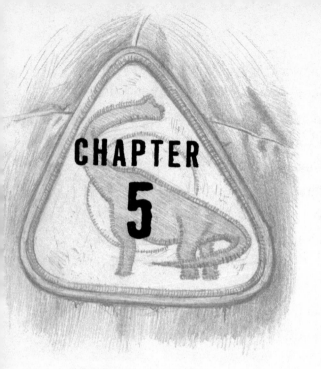

CHAPTER 5

"So, um, this is it," Chaz said as we walked into the small room I'd be sharing with her for the foreseeable future. It was three levels higher than the conference room, but still too far down for any sunlight to penetrate. It contained two twin beds, two small closets, and a lamp. One whole wall was glass and looked out into the lake. Were there any rooms in this place without a monster-infested view? Next door I could hear Shawn and Todd arguing over who would get which bed.

"It's not much," Chaz apologized as she attempted to push a pile of dirty clothes under her bed with a booted foot. "I can get you your own room if you want.

I'm sure Boz could arrange it."

Shaking my head, I walked over to press my hand against the cool glass of the window. "It's great," I said, turning to her with what I hoped was an acceptable smile. "Really."

Chaz nodded, flopping down on her rumpled bed. After the shock had worn off from viewing the video, Boz had gotten himself together and begun giving orders. The first thing he did was swear us all to secrecy. The information would do nothing but cause chaos and panic if it got out, he said.

Todd had been the hardest one to convince. As soon as he heard that the big plan was to do nothing until further notice, he'd pitched a fit. Not that I could blame him. If I hadn't been so overwhelmed by the information overload, I would have joined him.

In the end he'd agreed to a compromise. We would let the lab's head council discuss a course of action before he did anything. Although it wasn't like we had any choice. Boz was incredibly kind about it, but he'd made it clear that leaving wasn't an option.

I jumped as someone knocked loudly on our door.

"Come in!" Chaz called, not bothering to get up from her bed, where she was fiddling with a port screen. Todd stormed through the door, followed by a glum-looking Shawn. I shot him a questioning look, but he just shook his head and plopped down on the foot of my bed.

"How can you stand it?" Todd asked, pacing our small room like a caged animal. "Being underwater. It's horrible. My skin is crawling, the air has no smell, and I feel like my head is going to explode." He looked to Shawn and me for backup, but Shawn just shrugged apologetically.

"I feel at home for the first time in days," he admitted. "This is like North Compound, but bigger and better because of all the windows."

"I don't get how anyone lives like this. It's awful," Todd said. Then he looked over at Chaz. "No offense."

"None taken." Chaz shrugged. Just then a long-necked plesiosaur, what Chaz had called an elasmosaurus, emerged from the darkness, yellow lamp-like eyes glowing, and I jumped instinctively away from the window.

"That is so creepy," Todd breathed.

"You can say that again," Shawn said as we watched the creature disappear back into the murk of the lake.

"Do you realize," Todd said a moment later, breaking the silence, "that your dad might have just saved the entire world by getting that plug into Boz's hands?"

"It hasn't really sunk in," I admitted. "I'm not sure how to wrap my brain around the Noah's plan, let alone that my dad was the one who somehow stumbled upon it." Even though my dad had hinted at the world being at stake in the letter he'd hidden inside his compass, I guess a part of me hadn't really thought he was being literal. Kennedy and his marines coming after me made a lot more sense now.

"What's scary," Shawn said, interrupting my thoughts, "is that I can totally understand why the Noah thinks wiping the planet clean of dinosaurs is going to solve everything." Todd and Chaz shot him identical disbelieving looks, and Shawn held up his hands defensively. "Let me finish," he said. "I understand because if I hadn't seen and experienced the topside world, hadn't heard Ivan and Boz explain things, I probably would have thought his plan was great."

"It's not great," Todd muttered.

Shawn rolled his eyes. "I know that now. I guess we're just lucky Sky's dad found out about all this."

I smiled wryly. "So you really think he's a hero?"

"I'd say he qualifies," Chaz said.

"The thing is," I confessed, "I'm a little disappointed." But even as I said it, I knew *disappointed* wasn't the right word. It didn't encompass the dark emptiness I felt inside, the sense of loss that I wasn't sure I'd ever shake.

"Because you're stuck in an underwater lab, and they won't give you the passcodes to get out?" Todd asked.

"Because the world as we know it might be ending in the not-so-distant future?" Shawn added.

"No." I sighed. "Because part of me still believed that my dad might be here."

"But, Sky," Todd said hesitantly, shooting a worried look at Shawn. "You heard that General Kennedy guy; he said your dad was dead."

I thought back to that moment in the woods where Kennedy had explained without remorse that he had murdered my father within hours of his escape, and shivered.

"I know what he said. But I'm still not sure if I believe it." I saw the look of pity on their faces and flapped a hand at them. "Don't look at me like that. I haven't lost my mind. I just, I don't know, I feel like I'd know in my gut if he was gone."

"Well, my gut says waiting around down here for some council to vote on a plan is suicide," Todd grumbled.

"Just be patient," I said. "My dad sent me here because he thought Boz could fix this. Now we just have to trust that he can."

"If you say so," Shawn muttered.

"I do," I said, wishing I felt as confident as I sounded.

Chaz jumped to her feet, her green eyes twinkling.

"What you need is something to take your mind off everything, and I know just the thing."

"What?" Todd asked dubiously.

"Well"—Chaz drawled suggestively—"since it's kind of your fault I got put back on poop patrol, I thought you might want to help out."

"You thought wrong." Todd frowned.

Chaz snorted and headed out the door, motioning for us to follow. Shawn and Todd shot me pleading looks, but I shoved them toward the door. "It is our fault. We should help," I said.

"You have to be joking," Shawn groaned.

Ten minutes later, outfitted with a pitchfork and a wheelbarrow, I was no longer feeling quite so helpful. We were standing in front of a huge stall door, the thick glass heavily enforced with steel bands. Glancing over at Shawn and Todd, I saw that they were each wearing a pair of blue coveralls that matched the ones Chaz had loaned me. They did not look happy. Chaz, oblivious to our misgivings, was chattering away about the fertilizer and fuel the lab created from the dinosaur poop as she tapped in the code on the stall door. I stood waiting for the giant door to swing open, but instead with a small click, a human-sized door popped open in front of Chaz. She disappeared inside.

We obediently followed her.

"This is Stanley," Chaz said as she rubbed the long narrow head of a strange-looking brown-and-yellow dinosaur two feet taller than her. Stanley cocked his head to the side as he inspected us with wide unblinking brown eyes. He reminded me of the pictures I'd seen of old-world ostriches, with his long neck and legs. I was so preoccupied with looking at Stanley that I jumped when I felt something run swiftly across my foot. Glancing down, I found myself staring into the large, luminous eyes of ten tiny dinosaurs, each of them an exact replica of Stanley, only with muddy green skin instead of Stanley's brown and yellow.

"What are they?" I asked.

"Gallimimus," Chaz said, "a type of ornithomimid."

"You call them all such crazy names," Todd said. "We just call these guys Runners. They are really fast." He bent down to inspect one of the baby dinosaurs. They chattered and swarmed around him, poking their dexterous little front hands into his pockets.

"Do they bite?" Shawn asked cautiously as he took a step back.

"They might nibble at a finger if you offered it," Chaz said. "They don't have teeth, though, so you should be fine. But they are used to getting treats from the handlers, so they can get a little pushy."

"I can see that." Todd laughed as one carefully inspected his ear.

"Okay, Big Stan," Chaz said, offering the dinosaur a handful of small red berries. "We need to get to work. Can you keep your kids under control?" Stanley munched happily on his treat, and then let out a low whistle through his nose, trotting off to the far side of the pen. Immediately the little dinosaurs stopped inspecting us and scampered after their father. All except one who was too busy untying Shawn's shoe-laces.

"I think you better go, buddy," Shawn said, gently untangling his laces from the creature's front paws. Stanley let out a more urgent-sounding whistle, and the little guy snapped his head up and raced guiltily away.

"Think he just got grounded?" Shawn asked as we watched Stanley cuff the miscreant gently as he joined the group.

"Why, Shawn Reilly," I said. "I think you like that little guy. And here I thought you wanted to kill all the dinosaurs."

"Whatever," Shawn grunted.

"Let's get to it," Chaz said, sinking her shovel into a large steaming pile and chucking it into her wheelbar-row. "I'd like to finish this before dinner, and I don't know about you, but I'm starving."

"I'm not sure I'll ever be hungry again," Shawn said as he gingerly poked at the pile in front of him. Two hours later, we were drenched in sweat, and we'd met an ouranosaurus named Cher, two muttaburrasaurs named Bonnie and Clyde, and developed blisters all over our hands.

"You really believe in all this, don't you," I asked Chaz as we washed up that night before dinner.

"In all what?" she asked as she ran a hand through her spiky black hair.

"In humans and dinosaurs living together. One big happy family and all that."

She glanced at me, her trademark smile in place. "Cohabitation? Of course. The lab's whole philosophy is *if you can't beat them, join them*. Although it's worded a lot better than that. The dinosaurs are here to stay, so why not make the best of the situation?"

We ended up getting more practice at making the best of a situation than I would have liked. Over the next two days we were allowed into a grand total of one meeting, more out of politeness than confidence that we would be very helpful. Every passing minute made Todd twitchier and more impatient. He was driving everyone crazy, pacing and trying out different combinations on the lab elevators, hoping to stumble across the code that would take him up and out to freedom. I empathized with his frustration, but if he kept it up, he wouldn't have to wait for the Noah to kill him—I would do it just to get some peace. Luckily for Todd, Chaz kept us too busy and too exhausted for me to do much more than collapse into bed every night.

At least the chores gave me a chance to talk to Chaz. She knew more about dinosaurs than any of the books I'd used to research in the library. Every night I spent hours filling my journal with new sketches and bits of information. As often as I filled a new page, I had to go back to a page I'd written in the compound to fix it, adding in the correct information about what a particular creature ate, their size, what made them dangerous or not dangerous, et cetera. I also made several attempts to sketch out the Lincoln Lab, but the space was just too massive to fit on one page.

I thought I'd feel like an outsider at the lab, but everyone accepted us as though we'd been there for years instead of days. And while I still preferred the freedom I'd experienced at the Oaks, I could see why people liked it down here. The Lincoln Lab had a sense of community to it that had been absent back at North. Every one of the seventy or so residents had carved out a life underwater that they clearly enjoyed. It was refreshing.

I'd just finished scooping out my last pen and

was headed back to my room on our third day in the lab when Boz and Schwartz came around the corner. Schwartz's face was blotchy and red, and even though I couldn't see what he was saying to Boz, it was obvious that he wasn't pleased. Upon seeing me, Schwartz abruptly stopped talking, shouldered past me, and stormed down the tunnel without a backward glance.

"Forgive him." Boz sighed. "Dr. Schwartz has his heart in the right place, but sadly he relates better to dinosaurs than to people."

"Why do you put up with him?" I asked, then winced, realizing how rude that sounded.

"Because he's a genetics genius." Boz shrugged apologetically. "Without him we wouldn't have such fabulous plesiosaurs to guard the lab. But he never really wanted to be down here, and I'm afraid we have differing opinions on how to handle the information found in your dad's message."

"What do you mean he didn't want to be down here?" I asked. "I thought you said he was part of the original Colombe?"

Boz nodded. "He was. But he never wanted to flee East Compound. He did so under duress, and life underwater has soured him a bit, I'm afraid." He watched Schwartz disappear around a corner, his brow furrowed in thought. I shifted uncomfortably, not sure what to say. Remembering me, he gave himself a shake and smiled. "I do have good news, though," Boz said. "We have one last council meeting this evening, and after that we should finally be able to tell you the plan we've developed."

"What meeting?" Todd asked, walking up with Shawn and Chaz. "Where? Can we come?" He was covered head to toe in dinosaur poop and smelled terrible. Boz chuckled and shook his head.

"Patience. We'll brief you on everything tomorrow. Have a good evening." With that he turned and walked away.

I wrinkled my nose in distaste. "Do I even want to know why you're covered in poop?" I asked.

Todd looked down at himself and then grinned sheepishly. "Stanley and the kids were a bit overexcited today."

"He's being modest." Shawn grinned. "He fell head-first into the biggest pile of . . ."

"She gets the picture," Chaz said, cutting him off. "The point is that he needs a shower before dinner."

"We aren't going to dinner," Todd said, looking down the hall in the direction Boz had gone. "We are going to find out what they say in that council meeting."

"But you heard Boz. We aren't allowed," Chaz protested. "We'll get in big trouble."

"And what? They make us shovel more dinosaur poop? Big deal," Todd said, waving a hand dismissively. "You guys can go eat if you want, but I'm finding out what this big plan is we've been waiting so patiently for."

"I wouldn't say you've been exactly patient," Shawn muttered.

"Whatever," Todd said. "Are you all with me?"

I nodded. "Let's go."

CHAPTER

6

"What are they saying?" I asked Todd an hour later. He pulled his ear off the ceiling vent long enough to scowl down at me.

"I can only catch every fourth word or so. Everything is too muffled."

"Then can you get off my shoulders?" Shawn grunted. "You aren't nearly as light as you look." Todd sighed reluctantly and jumped to the floor.

It had taken some convincing, but we eventually talked Chaz into helping us break into the conference room located directly underneath the room where the meeting was being held. Schwartz had never deactivated her authorization code to enter this part of the building, and we made it through the deserted section of the lab with ease.

Chaz frowned at us, shifting nervously from foot to foot. Breaking the rules obviously didn't agree with her. "This is dumb," she said. "I vote we head back and shower. Todd, no offense, but you smell horrendous."

"We all smell horrendous," I agreed, then shot Todd an apologetic look. "But if this was a contest, you'd win by a landslide."

Todd frowned stubbornly but then sighed. "Fine," he grumbled, "but only because I can't hear a thing." We headed back toward the dorms.

"Cheer up," I told Todd. "We will find out everything tomorrow."

"That's too far away," Todd groaned. "I hate it down here."

"I'm going to choose to not be offended by that." Chaz frowned.

Todd didn't say anything, but his face was so downcast and depressed that I felt a pang of sympathy for him.

"What if we just happened to swing by the upstairs conference room where the meeting is?" I suggested. Shawn was already shaking his head in resignation. He'd known me long enough to know exactly where I was going with this. "Don't look at me like that, Shawn

Reilly," I said. "You want to know the plan as much as the rest of us. Besides, Boz never said we couldn't see him *after* the meeting. If we just *happen* to run into him, he might fill us in on the plan."

"Really?" Todd asked, perking up.

"I don't know," Chaz said, biting her lip nervously.

"Why not?" I coaxed. "It doesn't hurt to try."

Shawn groaned. "I've heard those words before. Usually preceding something that earned us an extra week of work detail back at North." I elbowed him in the ribs with a grin.

Five minutes later we were walking down an empty glass hallway toward the conference room where the future of the topside world was being decided. I realized that I barely noticed the plesiosaurs gliding about over and around us anymore. They were just a part of this strange underwater life.

"How long do conferences like this usually take?" Todd asked.

"I have no idea." Chaz shrugged. "I don't think there has ever been a conference quite like this one before. The entire wing is shut down."

"Good point," Todd agreed grudgingly.

We rounded a corner and almost ran headfirst into Boz himself. He yelped, and the box he was carrying flew into the air. Boz made a frantic attempt to catch it, but it slipped through his fingers and hit the hard glass floor with a sharp crack that reverberated up and down the tunnel. The box popped open, scattering dozens of black port plugs the size of my thumbnail across the floor.

"Sorry!" Chaz cried as she dropped to the ground to pick up the plugs.

"What are you kids doing here?" Boz asked, obviously annoyed. I cringed. He'd been nothing but kind to us since our arrival at the lab, and now we'd made him mad. Seeing my reaction, his face softened, and he waved a hand dismissively. "It's all right." He sighed. "Please help me get these picked up, and whatever you do, don't step on one."

"Why?" Shawn asked, crouching to inspect one of the tiny plugs.

"Because those little bits of technology might be what save the world," he said, gingerly plucking the plug from Shawn's fingers.

"So these are part of the plan?" I asked excitedly as I scooped up a handful and put them back in Boz's box.

"They are," he whispered conspiratorially. "We were just briefing the council members on them. Our top scientists have been working night and day to develop these ever since we saw your father's message, Sky. In fact, it was your father's message that inspired them."

"*These* are your plan?" Todd asked before I had a chance to ask what Boz had meant. Todd looked decidedly unimpressed as he held a plug up to the light, turning it this way and that. "They look like a Leather Wing's poop."

"Leather Wing?" Boz repeated in confusion.

I smiled, remembering the huge pterosaurs back at the Oaks that were used for eggs. Not technically dinosaurs, these enormous flying reptiles had leathery wings, long toothy beaks, and smelled terrible. "He means a rhamphorhynchus," I explained to Boz.

Boz burst out laughing, doubling over as tears of mirth rolled down his round cheeks. "Yes," he finally choked a moment later as he fought to get himself under control. "The things that look like rhamphorhynchus poop might just save the topside world, the entire dinosaur population, and millions of species of plants and animals."

"What do they do?" Shawn asked.

Boz sobered again, wiping at his eyes. "It would be incredibly complicated to explain, and I'm not at liberty to discuss it just yet. Besides, I'm needed back at the council meeting. We need at least another hour or two to hash out the details," Boz said, glancing back over his shoulder toward the closed conference room door barely visible at the end of the long glass hallway. "I was just on my way to lock these back up for safekeeping."

"We can take them back to your office for you," Chaz offered.

Boz shook his head, carefully closing the box. "It's quite all right. I will take them." He didn't say it, but it was obvious that he didn't trust us with the technology that could save the world. "What are you four doing here? I thought I made it clear that this was a private council meeting."

"That would be my fault," I said, not wanting Chaz to get assigned any more stall-mucking duties we'd be required to help her with. "I was hoping we could hear something a little sooner? Do we really have to wait until tomorrow?"

"I'm afraid you do," Boz said, not unkindly. "And these"—he patted the box under his arm—"need to go through one last round of tests. There are still a few major glitches in them, and we wouldn't want them to malfunction on us, now would we?" He turned and started walking down the hallway.

"We better go," Chaz said after a minute when I made no move to leave.

"I guess you're right," I sighed, turning to follow her down the hall, but I paused when I saw Todd's face. I'd expected him to look angry at Boz's refusal to share the plan with us, but instead he looked smug.

"Todd?" I asked. Instead of responding, he shot a quick glance over his shoulder to make sure the coast was clear before slipping his hand out of his pocket to reveal one of Boz's tiny plugs.

"Looks like he missed one," he said, and the slightest smirk pulled at the corners of his mouth.

"You hid that one on purpose," Chaz accused.

Todd shrugged. "And if I did? Don't you think we have a right to know what this big plan is that we've been waiting around for?" It was as though he'd read my mind, and I bit my lip, considering. Todd saw my hesitation, and a wide grin of triumph spread across his face. He knew he'd won. Just then we heard Boz's footsteps coming back down the tunnel toward the conference room.

"This way," Chaz whispered, leading us down another tunnel-like hallway. We followed her at a run, finally stopping a few minutes later to catch our breath.

"Where are we?" I asked.

"Just another section of the conference wing." Chaz shrugged. "I figured since the entire section shut down for the meeting, we'd be safe."

"Let me see that plug," Shawn said. Todd handed it over, and Shawn held it up to the light. He turned to

Chaz. "Do you have your port with you?" She nodded, reaching in her pack to pull out the slim black device. Shawn took it, producing his own bulky makeshift port from his bag. He'd cobbled it together from leftover parts back at North Compound and managed to keep it in one piece through all our wild travels. It was a minor miracle. My own journal was looking much the worse for wear these days. Just yesterday one of the baby sauropeltas had gotten ahold of it and chewed up a corner. I noticed that his old port now had a shiny glass shell surrounding it and gave him a questioning look.

"What's that?" I asked, reaching over to poke the case.

"A waterproof case," he said distractedly. "Everyone else's port down here has one, and there were a few extras in the supply room." He gave Chaz a nervous glance, and I got the uneasy feeling that he hadn't exactly asked permission before taking the case. Sometimes my best friend couldn't help himself when it came to new technology, a trait that had earned him almost as many work details as me back at North. "After my little swim with Pretty Boy, I decided water-proofing might be in my best interest." I decided to let it drop. Sensing he'd won, he turned his attention back to inspecting the small holes in the side of each of the ports. A moment later he slid his old port back in his

94

pocket and slipped Boz's plug into Chaz's port. Nothing happened for a second, and then the screen flashed a bright white before going black.

"Uh-oh," Shawn said as he pressed futilely at the power button. Finally, he sat back. "It's dead," he announced in disappointment.

"Dead!" Chaz squawked, yanking the port out of his hands. "What do you mean it's dead? I just got this two months ago!"

"Sorry." Shawn grimaced, looking sheepish. "I didn't know that plug would kill it . . ." He trailed off, a far-off look in his eyes. Chaz looked like she was contemplating decking him when he suddenly jerked upright and stared at us. "It killed it," he repeated, snatching it back out of Chaz's hands.

"Yeah." She scowled. "We caught that the first time."

"No." Shawn shook his head as he held up the blank port excitedly. "Like it's *really* dead."

"As opposed to just kind of dead?" Todd asked, but Shawn flapped an impatient hand at him to be quiet.

"That has to be what the plug does. It kills hard drives. They must be planning on somehow messing with the Noah's technology."

What he was saying finally clicked into place, and I understood what my best friend was getting at. I grinned at him. "It would be pretty hard to launch a nuclear attack if the technology that works the bombs died."

Shawn was nodding excitedly. "Even if they can't destroy the technology that controls the bombs, that many plugs could do enough damage to at least delay the bomb launch. The Noah isn't going to start destroying the topside world when his compound isn't in perfect working condition. Especially if the technology damaged requires replacement parts from other compounds. If nothing else, it buys us some time."

"My dad," I whispered as realization hit me.

"What about him?" Shawn asked.

"Boz said that they got the idea for the plugs from my dad." I grinned. "It all makes sense now. Remember his message? If Boz hadn't entered the correct code, his little plug was going to corrupt all the surrounding ports!"

"Wow," Shawn said, sounding awed. "Do you think your dad put that feature in to try to ruin the Noah's plan? Even if you both failed?"

A smile spread across my face as I stared at the black screen of Chaz's port. Good one, Dad, I thought silently. You really did think of everything, didn't you? But no sooner had this thought crossed my mind than I remembered that he hadn't thought about everything. He hadn't thought about me.

"That tiny thing can do all that?" Todd asked skeptically, interrupting my thoughts as Shawn pulled the plug out of Chaz's dead port.

"I hope it can," I said, taking the tiny plug carefully from Shawn's hand. Chaz reached to take her port back, but before she could, Shawn let out a surprised yelp and dropped it.

"I know it's dead," Chaz said, scowling, "but you don't have to throw it around like that."

"Don't touch it," Shawn cautioned with a grimace as he stuck his fingers in his mouth. "It just got really, really hot." A second later the port sparked, and then with a sharp pop it burst into flames.

"Well," Todd said, stepping forward to stamp the flames out, "that is pretty impressive for a tiny thing that looks like poop." I nodded, glancing from the tiny plug in my hand to the blackened port screen on the floor as I waved away the small cloud of metallic-smelling smoke.

"But how are they going to get them to East Compound? Let alone break in there and get these placed?" Shawn wondered out loud.

Todd raised a questioning eyebrow. "East Compound?"

"It's the largest of the four compounds," Shawn explained. "It was built using the underground subway systems of New York City, and it's gigantic. It's the most logical place for those bombs to be. It's also the Noah's home base, so those plugs would do the most damage there."

Using my thumbnail, I unscrewed the back of my compass. Boz's plug went inside it, nestled into the slot where my dad's plug used to be housed. I didn't want anything to happen to it until I could return it to Boz for that extra testing he'd mentioned.

"Uh, guys?" Todd said. Something in his voice made us all turn to look at him. He was facing the glass wall of the tunnel, looking out into the murky lake. "What's that?"

We scrambled to his side to look out through the glass wall of our tunnel. The Lincoln Lab sprawled out before us, an interconnected web of glass tunnels connecting bubble-shaped buildings. The lights from the lab illuminated the surrounding water in a warm yellow light that seemed to push back against the darkness of the lake. It took me a second to spot what Todd was talking about, but when I did my brow furrowed in confusion. A small silver ball was dropping swiftly through the water toward the top of the conference wing directly opposite our tunnel. A plesiosaur was swimming around the strange object, bumping it with its nose as though testing to see if the ball was eatable. We stood frozen as it sank the last few feet onto the roof of the conference wing. There was a half second of silence, followed by an ear-shattering boom. I screamed as an entire section of the conference wing collapsed in a flash of red roiling bubbles. The ground under our feet shook in the aftershock and tiny hairline cracks zigzagged their way along the tunnel wall we were looking through, making the view blurry and fractured.

"There's more!" Shawn cried. Above our heads five more of the silver balls were floating innocently downward, one directly above our heads. Chaz flew into action, sprinting down the tunnel away from the conference wing toward a panel in the tunnel wall. She hit a red button and yelled into the speaker: "Sector F has been compromised! We are under attack! Institute full lockdown!"

I turned to look back out of the tunnel and saw another of the silver balls illuminated by the lab lights. My breath caught when I noticed the symbol shining on the side of the ball: a golden ark. A second later, thick metal plates slammed shut over the entire tunnel, throwing us into an eerie darkness.

Flashing emergency lights clicked on a moment later, but before I could process what was happening, Chaz had grabbed my arm and was yanking me after her. "We need to get to a lockdown location," she shouted over the blaring alarm.

"What's going on?" Shawn yelled as he and Todd stumbled into action a moment later and followed.

"We're under attack!" Chaz called over her shoulder. "Stay with me!" We were halfway down the hallway when we heard an explosion and the floor rocked violently under our feet. Immediately the pressure in the tunnel changed and a stabbing pain lanced through my head.

"Clear your ears!" Chaz called. "Another one must have hit before the tunnel armor was in place." A deafening roar filled the tunnel, making it impossible to hear anything else. Flashing red emergency sirens illuminated the tunnels in a bloody light as we sprinted down the labyrinth of abandoned hallways. If Chaz wasn't with us, we would have gotten lost within seconds. Rounding a corner, we came face-to-face with a thick metal wall. Chaz shrieked in frustration as we skidded to a stop, and I looked around in confusion. This wall had never been there before.

"We're too late," she yelled. "This part of the lab has been locked down. We're cut off to prevent flooding. We have to get to an emergency elevator." We turned left and sprinted down a corridor I'd never seen before.

Suddenly a panicked Schwartz come flying out of a side tunnel in front of us before ducking into another corridor.

"Follow him!" Chaz yelled. We did, keeping his fleeing form in sight turn after turn. The roaring sound from behind us was getting louder by the second, and a quick glance over my shoulder revealed a terrifying sight. Rushing through the narrow tunnels was a solid, black wall of debris-filled water. And it was gaining on us. Fast. I rounded a curve and saw Schwartz throw himself into a small elevator, the doors already sliding shut.

"Wait!" I cried. Putting on a burst of speed, I dove at the last moment and managed to slip my hand between the elevator doors. They slid back open just as Todd, Shawn, and Chaz hurled themselves inside. Schwartz jabbed frantically at the buttons on the panel, his eyes wide and panicked. A second before the wall of water hit, I realized that we were too late. It careered into us just as the doors began to slide shut. I grabbed on to Chaz and Shawn as the icy water tried to pull us back out of the elevator. The cold was unlike anything I'd ever felt, and my muscles seized painfully in protest.

I felt a sharp thrust upward as the doors closed the last few inches, cutting off the chaos. The elevator began to rise. We stood in chest-deep water, staring at one another in stunned silence. I immediately began to shiver.

"You almost killed me!" Schwartz sputtered as he attempted to hold a small black machine above the water level.

"Yeah, right back at ya," Todd stuttered through chattering teeth. Before he could say anything else, the elevator jerked suddenly, and we all threw our hands out to brace ourselves. The elevator made a strange squealing noise that made my teeth hurt before continuing its shaky ascent toward the surface.

"Too much weight," Schwartz muttered, looking around the small steel elevator nervously. "Much too much weight. We must have at least two hundred gallons of water in here—no, four hundred."

"Why weren't you in the council meeting?" Chaz asked. "Where are the other council members? Where is Boz?"

Schwartz didn't say anything, but there was something in his expression that made me feel sick.

I clapped my hand to my mouth in horror as something else hit me. "Is the whole lab being flooded?" I asked, thinking of the hundreds of people and dinosaurs still inside. People and dinosaurs I'd come to like and care about in the short time I'd been at the Lincoln Lab.

"No," Schwartz said. "Chaz's warning instituted the lockdown and the tunnel armor. I believe the flooding is contained to the conference wing."

Todd narrowed his eyes. "It's awfully convenient you weren't in there."

Before Schwartz had time to respond, a low, ominous beeping began. The emergency lights in the elevator clicked on, throwing us all into a sickly yellow light that reflected dully off the water. Then the elevator stopped.

CHAPTER 7

This elevator was made of steel, not glass, so we could be three or three hundred feet below the surface and we wouldn't know the difference. Schwartz pounded on the elevator buttons in a very un-scientist-like way that did nothing to make me feel better about this situation. I was having a hard time breathing, but I wasn't sure if it was from the icy water surrounding me or from the fear squeezing my insides. My eyes darted around the dim interior of the tiny elevator, and it hit me that it might not be either of those things. I had no idea how much air five people needed to survive, but it was probably more than we currently had trapped inside this elevator with us.

"Oh no, oh no, oh no." Todd panted, his breath coming out in short, frantic little puffs as his fingernails attempted to dig into the steel sides of the elevator.

"Relax," I commanded, amazed at how calm I sounded. I looked into the terrified eyes of my friends. If someone had to have it together, that someone might as well be me. "We don't have much air in here," I told Todd. "Don't hyperventilate it all."

"Not," Todd puffed, "helpful."

"Sky's right: this thing is airtight, and if you keep yelling, we'll all be dead in minutes," Chaz said.

"Why did it stop?" I asked Schwartz.

"Two possibilities," he said grimly. "Either too much weight overheated the engine, or this section of the lab has lost power."

"How close to the surface do you think we are?" Shawn asked, interrupting us.

Chaz shook her head. "No clue. Normally I would have been able to time it, but I think the water slowed us down."

"If we get the elevator doors open, can we swim it?" Todd asked, his eyes wide and wild as he sloshed over to look at the panel of buttons.

Chaz looked doubtful. "Maybe. The pressure might kill us the minute we open the doors. Or a plesiosaur might eat us. Or we'll run out of oxygen before we make it to the surface."

"Oh," Shawn said, groaning. "Is that all?"

"If we stay down here," Todd growled, "we die. Period. At least out there we have a chance."

"Great plan, but do you remember what lives out there?" Shawn shot back. "Because I do. One of them is named Pretty Boy."

"This isn't helping," I said. "We're just using up oxygen. Swimming for it isn't ideal, but we don't have time to come up with anything better. Dr. Schwartz, how much longer do you think the air will hold in here?" His face was a sickly yellow as he turned to me.

"Ten minutes, max, but I'm actually beginning to worry that if we don't get out of here soon, the elevator might start descending. It's a safety measure we installed a few years back in case of a malfunction."

"Why wouldn't you program it to go up?" Todd shouted. Schwartz ignored him, scowling down at the small machine in his hands as he began twisting knobs and turning dials.

"Then we need to get these doors open and swim for it before that happens." Chaz panted as she braced her shoulder in the crease of the door and shoved. Todd, Shawn, and I immediately joined her, our fingers digging into the metal.

Moments later the door gave way and icy water rushed in, slamming me against the back of the elevator. Shawn's panicked face flashed in front of me, and I reached for his hand but missed as we plunged into icy darkness.

I scrambled desperately through the pitch-black water toward where I had last seen the door. Other bodies moved around mine, the water a writhing mass of flailing limbs. My hands met solid metal. Don't panic, don't panic, don't panic, I instructed myself as I pawed blindly along the endless wall of the elevator. The thing wasn't that big, was it? I'd never been forced to hold my breath this long before, and the pressure in my chest seemed to be building by the second. I no longer felt the brush of bodies against mine, and despite the impenetrable darkness, I knew I was alone. What if the door had closed again? My lungs tightened, and the dark water pressed in, making my ears and head throb. As I felt my way up the wall, my hand broke the surface of the water. The elevator had tilted, trapping air in one of the corners.

Desperate, I pushed my face up into the tiny pocket of air, gasping. Panic clawed at me as I hovered there. Everything around me was freezing blackness, and I knew I was going to have to force my head back under the water if I had a prayer of finding my way out. I hesitated, and my muscles cramped with the mind-numbing cold. You can do this, I commanded myself. With one last deep breath, I submerged myself again.

This time my hand curled around the corner of the door within seconds, and I pulled myself through. Terror moved like lightning through my veins as I clawed my way toward the surface, all the while imagining gigantic plesiosaurs circling me. Soon that terror was replaced by the realization that I still couldn't see any light above me. My burning lungs had had enough. They jerked violently inside my chest. I needed air. I inhaled.

Freezing water started to pour into my lungs, but a moment later my head burst through the surface and into glorious fresh air. My body heaved, and I vomited. Water gushed from my nose and mouth as my ears rang. But I was alive. A starry night sky winked above me, and I tried to understand what I was seeing. I'd expected to come up inside the bubble of the dock, and I looked around wildly for my friends. Panic squeezed my still-pounding heart as I took in the empty rolling waves. I was alone.

No, I thought stubbornly. They have to be around here somewhere. I'd fumbled around in that elevator so long that I knew I was the last one to make it out. If they hadn't made it up, then . . . I stopped that train of thought. Thinking about them getting eaten or drowning was too much. To my right, the lake was bubbling as a dark red light shone up through the water. I stared at it in confusion for a minute before I realized that it had to be the remains of Boz's conference rooms.

Suddenly I heard a shout to my left. Turning, I could just make out arms waving in the distance. The relief that washed over me almost made the terror of swimming through plesiosaur-infested water fade away. Almost.

The dark forms were paddling hard away from the bubbling red light. I followed, but my flailing strokes were pathetic in comparison, and I almost lost sight of them twice. I'd never really had to swim before. North Compound had had a small pool, but it was only four feet deep, barely enough to teach us the basics during the survival unit in school. I'd thought learning a skill we'd never actually use was laughable, but it was anything but funny now.

The whine of an engine droned overhead, and I looked up to see four massive black helicopters emerge from the darkness. They each shone a spotlight down on the wreckage of the lab, illuminating water filled with thrashing, snarling plesiosaurs. It was the light, I realized. They were attracted to it just like they had been attracted to the lights of the lab. My heart lodged itself in my throat as I took in the sight of those enormous creatures less than two hundred yards away. I paddled harder, praying that they hadn't noticed me. Over the rushing wind and crashing waves, I slowly became aware of another sound. I stopped swimming, my body bobbing up and down in the waves as I turned, this way and that, trying to spot the new threat. The sound was too low to be another helicopter.

A small arc of light suddenly bounced across the water, catching my attention. I stared at it for a moment, trying to figure out what I was seeing. A second later the light flashed into my eyes, temporarily blinding me. I threw a hand up to block it just as I heard Todd's familiar voice call out. I squinted against the glare and made out a small shape careering across the waves. I felt a flash of relief as I realized that somehow my friends had found a boat. If I could reach it, I could get out of the dark, churning water, and right that second there was nothing I wanted more. I started swimming toward it, the flashlight lighting up the water in front of me. My feeling of relief flitted away a moment later as I realized what Todd had just done.

"Turn off the light," I yelled, my burning lungs and aching muscles forgotten as I put on another burst of speed. "Turn it off!"

"What?" Todd called back.

"The light!" I screamed. "Turn off the light!" He clicked it off, but a quick glance behind me confirmed that he was too late. Two enormous forms were moving swiftly through the black water straight toward me. Even in the near dark, I recognized Pretty Boy's grisly crocodile-like jaw as its head emerged, its eyes flashing and focused. The other plesiosaur wasn't moving quite as fast, but it had a head start on Pretty Boy. Its shape made me think that it had to be an elasmosaurus, but it didn't hoist its long, snakelike neck out of the water like I thought it would. Instead, its small arrow-shaped head darted only a foot or so out of the waves before submerging again. I swam harder, trying to calculate which would reach me first, the boat or the plesiosaurs.

Moments later, I knew the answer to my question. Teeth clamped onto the pack I still wore and jerked me underwater with a violent snap. Black water surrounded me as the long-necked elasmosaurus shook me from side to side. The joints in my neck and shoulders popped as it tried to break my back. A silent scream ripped out of me, but before I could inhale my second lungful of icy water that day, something slammed into the side of my attacker and the elasmosaurus released my backpack. I clawed my way back to the surface, emerging just in time to see Pretty Boy tighten its enormous jaws around the long, muscled neck of the elasmosaurus.

Apparently it didn't appreciate someone trying to steal its dinner. The elasmosaurus let out a high, screeching squeal and craned its head back in a futile attempt to take a chunk out of its attacker. I'd barely processed all of this before a huge paddle-shaped fin came crashing down on top of me, sending me plunging down into Lake Michigan's icy depths again.

The water churned around me, full of thrashing fins and flashing teeth, and I connected with the smooth muscled back of the long-necked elasmosaurus as it struggled violently in Pretty Boy's massive grip. I managed to figure out which way was up despite the chaos and resurfaced midstroke swimming hard, my body one raw nerve of panic. Luck was with me, and when I blinked the water from my eyes, I was only a few feet from the small boat. A hand reached down and pulled me over the side. Someone revved the motor and the boat spun around and away from the fighting monsters. Before I could even register that I was still alive, we were bouncing over the waves, the keening of the dying elasmosaurus filling the air behind us as more plesiosaurs swam over to investigate.

I was shaking so violently my teeth were in danger of biting my tongue off. Todd's face materialized in front of me, and I blinked at him. His mouth was moving, but my ears were still roaring and my heart hammering too loudly to hear anything he was saying. All the adrenaline of moments before suddenly drained out of me, leaving me nothing but a shivering puddle of exhaustion.

"You okay?" Todd shouted again, his face tight with concern. Maybe I'm in shock? I thought fuzzily. How long had he been talking to me? I wasn't sure. My brain felt caught in an impenetrable fog as I relived the last few minutes of horror over and over again. The bombing. The elevator. The plesiosaurs. All those teeth.

"Sky!" Todd said again, grabbing my face between his hands. "You're freaking me out. Say something."

I blinked at him. Why was I still lying on the bottom of this bumping, jarring boat? I felt like a fish out of water, gasping for air and staring up at the night sky as it whizzed by overhead. I should probably respond, I reasoned, but I couldn't remember how to talk.

"Of course she's okay," Chaz yelled. "She's alive, isn't she?"

I glanced around the tiny boat, registering for the first time that it had only two other people in it. The numbness of a moment before evaporated. I sat bolt upright so fast I conked heads with Todd, who yelped and rocked back, rubbing his forehead. This couldn't be right. My hand reached out as if on its own and grasped Todd's shoulder. "Where's Shawn?" I demanded; my voice sounded hoarse and raw in my ears.

Todd swallowed hard, glanced over at Chaz, and then looked down as though he was wishing he could sink through the bottom of the boat and disappear. "He didn't surface," he said, barely audible over the slap, slap, slap of the boat hitting the water and the whooshing of the wind.

"No!" I screeched. "Turn back. We have to go back. He might be in the water somewhere." I would not leave my best friend behind.

Todd shook his head. "We can't."

"We have to," I cried. Didn't he understand? We'd forgotten Shawn! Lunging forward, I attempted to wrench the engine control out of Chaz's hand.

She shoved me back with enough force to knock me on my butt. "Stop it," she snapped. Her face was sad, devastated, and resolved. "He wasn't there. We looked. He never made it up."

"No." I shook my head, refusing to believe it. "He had to make it up. I was the last one out of the elevator." My mind raced frantically back to that terrifying eternity in the pitch black, those last moments underwater. I'd been sure there was no one else in there—I'd never felt so completely and utterly alone in my life.

"I'm sorry, Sky," Todd said slowly, as though he were talking to an upset child. "Schwartz never made it up either. If we go back now, they'll catch us. We can't. He never made it up. I swear." I slumped to the floor of the boat in exhausted defeat. Behind us the scene of the decimated lab played out under the beams of helicopter lights. The water still roiled and frothed red, churned into angry waves by the plesiosaurs that circled and battled one another. Bits and pieces of the destroyed lab had bobbed to the surface, and I recognized the broken remains of a desk moments before one of the plesiosaurs shoved it back under the water. But the scene was quickly swallowed by the darkness, and I shut my eyes as tears were blown off my icy cheeks by the wind that whipped past us. Chaz was steering the boat with a determined precision, but I couldn't make myself care where we were going. The only thing that mattered was that we were going away from the lab, away from Shawn. I shut my eyes again, blocking out the anxious expressions of my friends as I tried not to drown in the pain that was slowly burning through me.

Thirty minutes later, Chaz finally ventured to break the silence. "What took you so long to come up?"

I shivered. "I couldn't find my way out. The water came in too fast, and it was so dark."

"Yeah, I think I just survived my worst nightmare," Todd agreed. I rubbed my hands up and down my arms in a hopeless attempt to warm myself, but the icy cold was just as much on the inside as it was on the outside, and no amount of rubbing was going to fix that.

"Where did you get the boat?" I asked.

"We came up right outside one of the boat dock bubbles. Thankfully someone left the keys in this one, or you'd be a goner." Chaz shook her head, her face sober. "We almost swam right past it. The docks are impossible to see at night. It was a lucky break that my arm brushed against it when we were swimming."

"What now?" I asked, although with Shawn gone I wasn't sure it mattered.

"We get off the water," Todd said. "Take cover and hide until things calm down."

Chaz nodded, her mouth pressed into a grim line.

A long while later, we spotted the shore. We were coming in fast. Too fast. Chaz fumbled frantically with the engine lever, but it didn't seem to be doing much.

"You might want to hold on to something," she warned. "I've never landed one of these before."

"Of course you haven't," Todd said, groaning, as he quickly grabbed the side of the boat, crouching for impact. I had enough time to brace my feet before the boat careered into the beach with a screech of metal and an explosion of sand. When we finally came to a shuddering stop, I had to use my left hand to pry my frozen right hand off the side of the crumpled aluminum boat. The engine sputtered and then died with a hiss of steam. The silence of the forest seemed to press in on us from all sides. We sat there, breathing hard as the sounds of the night slowly started back up.

"That could have gone better," Chaz said, echoing my own thoughts as she slumped in the boat.

"No kidding," Todd said, already pulling himself to his feet.

"If anyone finds out I trashed a boat, I'm so dead," Chaz moaned, taking in the wreckage.

"You really think anyone is going to care about a boat when half the lab just got destroyed?" I snapped.

"I hope it wasn't half the lab," Chaz said, looking worried. "I initiated the lockdown pretty fast."

"Are we supposed to know what lockdown is?" Todd asked.

"You saw it," she said. "Each tunnel is equipped with thick metal plates in case we were ever bombed from above. They are supposed to protect the glass underneath from shattering in a direct hit. There are also those flood walls that drop into place, separating the lab into zones, so if one section does get damaged the entire lab isn't destroyed," Chaz explained. "You don't live underwater without some precautions."

"Well, that's pretty smart," Todd agreed grudgingly.

I waited for Shawn to chime in, knowing this kind of thing was right up his alley, and then it hit me all over again that Shawn would never comment on anything again. That dark cloud of sadness threatened to overtake me once more, but I pushed it away to focus on Chaz.

Chaz shrugged. "We always knew there was a chance the Noah would find us someday, and if he did, he would try to destroy us. I've been practicing emergency flood drills since I could walk. I can only hope that all that practice paid off." She winced and looked away, and I realized that I wasn't the only one who had lost something. We had no way of knowing just how much damage the lab had sustained or what the casualties were. Chaz's whole world lay at the bottom of that lake, and she had no idea how much was left of it. I reached out and squeezed her shoulder. She quickly brushed tears away with the back of her hand and flashed a forced smile.

"We need to get back into the lab," I said. "We can help the survivors, and we need to tell someone what's happened. Schwartz is dead, and all of Boz's council members probably died. Right?" I asked, looking to Chaz for confirmation.

She nodded, looking grim. "The conference rooms were the first hit. Even with the lockdown, the floodgates never would have had a chance to initiate there. We're probably the only ones alive who know about the Noah's plan."

Todd shook his head vehemently. "You can go back to that lab if you want, but count me out. I will never, and I repeat *never*, go into a lab like that again. I spent the last few days listening to everybody rattle on about how safe it was, and then I almost drowned. Nope. Not happening."

"Moot point," Chaz said, shaking her head. "When a lockdown is instituted, it stays locked down until all the systems are stabilized and the threat has been neutralized. That could take weeks. Even if we wanted to get back in, we couldn't."

"Forget about the lockdown," Todd said. "The Noah's guys are swarming around the lab wreckage like flies on poop. If we go bouncing back out onto the lake in this boat, they'll grab us for sure." He gave the crumpled remains of the boat an assessing look and kicked experimentally at the side, where a rock had ripped a large hole. Aluminum buckled and cracked, falling in chunks onto the beach. "Let me rephrase that," he said. "Even if we had a way to go back out on the water, I wouldn't." I stayed quiet as I rolled this new information around, which was why I was the first one to see the trees to our left move.

"Shhh," I hissed as I peered out into the darkness. Hearing the warning in my voice, Chaz and Todd followed my gaze, to where five sets of luminous green eyes were staring at us.

"Here comes the welcoming committee," Todd muttered.

CHAPTER 8

T ime seemed to stretch and slow as we sat staring at the eyes. "Any chance one of you happened to grab a tranquilizer gun?" I whispered.

"No," Todd said, his voice strained and tight. "I sure wish I had my bow, though."

"Bow?" Chaz asked, aghast. "Why? Those can't be more than young adolescents based off of their height. I'm guessing they're either ouranosaurus or iguanodons from the eye shape. Have you two learned nothing these last few days? They are probably just curious."

"Yeah," Todd grumbled. "Curious about how we taste."

"They're herbivores," Chaz said, rolling her eyes in

exasperation. "Just don't turn into a leaf or spook them, and we'll be fine." The words had barely left her mouth before the eyes emerged from the trees to reveal green skin that rippled and gleamed in the moonlight. The dinosaurs' massive heads were wide, tapering down to a square snout. They walked on all fours, their smaller front legs giving them a hunched appearance, but every now and then one of them would hesitate, rearing back to balance on their larger, muscular back legs. At around fifteen feet from head to tail, I had to agree with Chaz: these were young dinosaurs.

"Are you sure they won't attack people?" I asked. I didn't see any teeth, but their billed jaws seemed powerful. Chaz shushed me, her eyes never leaving these strange-looking dinosaurs. They were studying us with the same keen intelligence I'd seen in the dinosaurs at the lab.

"I should tag them," Chaz murmured as the animals approached cautiously. "We haven't seen many young iguanodons around these parts."

"After everything that just happened, how could you possibly still care about the iggi-whatsits," Todd hissed.

The iguanodons came snuffling along the side of the boat, bringing with them a pleasant earthy smell. They dwarfed me by a good four feet, but for the world of dinosaurs that was relatively tiny. We sat in silence as the creatures continued their investigation of our ears and shoulders for a few more minutes. Their hot breath tickled, and I had to fight the urge not to giggle. It wouldn't be funny at all if I scared them and they accidentally smashed us.

When the dinosaurs finally moved away, Todd let out a huge sigh and turned to us. "Time to get under cover."

"I still wish I had the equipment here to tag those," Chaz muttered mulishly as the strange dinosaurs trotted back into the surrounding trees. We followed them, but not before dragging our battered and smoking boat into the lake and sinking it. I could only hope that if a helicopter did decide to look for us, the marines wouldn't notice the huge rut of sand the boat had left behind. With nowhere to go and unwilling to risk a flashlight, we stumbled around in the dark for a while before finding a knobby tree with branches low enough for us to climb. I fell into an exhausted sleep wedged between the elbow of two branches, my heart heavy with thoughts of Shawn.

I woke up hours later stiff and disoriented as the sunlight wove its way through the leaves, casting a murky green glow over the surrounding forest. I tried to sit up to relieve my cramped and aching muscles, but was jerked to an abrupt stop. Glancing down in confusion,

I discovered a long blue strip of fabric looped around my waist and another around my right arm. Following the fabric, I discovered it had been wrapped around the tree branch I was lying on. I carefully undid the tie at my wrist and sat up, the one around my waist pulling tight. Glancing to my right, I saw that Chaz was still asleep, curled up tight with her arms and legs thrown bear-hug style around an enormous branch. She too had thin blue cords of fabric tying her wrist and waist to the tree. When I located Todd, two branches to my left, the mystery of the blue cords was revealed. His tattered blue jumpsuit from the lab was now missing both of its arms. He'd apparently torn them off in order to lash Chaz and me to the tree. However, he hadn't taken the same precaution for himself. Used to sleeping in trees, he sprawled out, his mouth hanging open as he snored softly, one bare arm thrown over his eyes to block out the light. I smiled, appreciating the gesture as I leaned back against my own branch.

The events of the previous day washed over me, and my smile of moments before shriveled and died. The lab had been attacked. We had no food, no weapons, and no way to do anything about the Noah's plan. And worst of all, my best friend was dead. Bending forward, I dropped my head between my knees as the pressure and pain of everything made it hard to breathe. Something slipped loose from the neck of my ripped lab uniform to swing free, glinting in the first rays of morning.

I stared at my dad's compass, selfishly hating it for all it had done. If Shawn had never found that message from my dad, we would both be safe and sound inside North Compound. The topside world would have eventually been destroyed, but I would never have known what I was missing, and I'd never have experienced the gut-wrenching pain of losing Shawn. After all, what was the good of knowing the Noah's plan if we had no way to stop it? Without Boz and the Lincoln Lab, it was all over. I swallowed hard at the lump that seemed to have become a permanent fixture in my throat.

A single fat tear splashed onto the worn bronze surface and slipped off to disappear into the dirt twenty feet below on the forest floor. It was then, feeling more hopeless and lost than I had ever felt in my entire life, that I remembered the plug Todd had swiped from Boz right before the explosion. In all the confusion I'd completely forgotten about it. I carefully unscrewed the back of the compass with trembling fingers and found to my relief that the inside was mercifully dry, the plug seemingly undamaged despite the night before.

Well, that's something, I thought. Maybe all hope wasn't lost, and if it wasn't, I owed it to myself, and to

Shawn, not to curl up in a ball and give up. Even if that was what I wanted to do.

Careful not to disturb the others, I untied myself the rest of the way and climbed gingerly down the tree. I was so lost in my own thoughts that I almost didn't notice the voices. Suddenly General Kennedy's voice sliced through my preoccupation like a knife, and I froze, the hairs on the back of my neck standing at attention.

When his voice came again, it was somewhere ahead and to my left, and even though I couldn't tell what he was saying, I knew from the tone that he was furious. I hesitated. Every fiber of my being wanted to get out of there, but I couldn't. As though acting on their own accord, my feet started moving toward the voices instead of away.

A minute later I found myself back on the beach, peering out from the edge of the woods at a makeshift camp. My stomach flopped sickeningly as I realized that we'd fallen asleep mere steps from our enemy. Black helicopters perched on the sand like giant bugs as the Noah's soldiers milled around, some lounging in front of tents, while others cleaned guns or ate from small tin plates. My eyes found Kennedy immediately, and my heart lurched in surprise when I saw that standing across from him was Schwartz.

I gasped, and then clapped my hand over my mouth, as though I could shove the traitorous noise back inside. Schwartz had survived the elevator, and Kennedy had apparently escaped the pack of saltopus that had attacked him in Ivan's clearing. The cut I'd given him had healed badly, marring his square handsome face, and his hands sported a variety of scratches and half-healed tooth punctures. He may have survived the saltopus attack in that clearing, but it looked like they'd done a number on him.

Schwartz's face was a thundercloud, his sharp eyes narrowed. "I should have known about that insane plan years ago," he said indignantly as he paced back and forth, his hands clasped tightly behind his back.

Barking a laugh, Kennedy removed a knife from his belt. "The Noah's plans do not concern you," he said coldly. He casually began using the end of the knife to scrape gunk out from under his fingernails. It was enough of a threatening gesture that Schwartz took an involuntary step back, his face dark.

"Actually," Schwartz said, holding up a finger in contradiction, "they do involve me. When I contacted the Noah last night I was told that I would be paid handsomely for my services. But all the payment in the world does me no good if the world has been wiped clean by nuclear warfare! Which, did I mention, is absolutely insane. Do you realize how many organisms could be permanently destroyed in this plan? There is no way the topside world could ever recover."

"You've spent too much time in that underwater lab." Kennedy sneered. "Their crazy ideas about balanced ecosystems have brainwashed you. I'm amazed the Noah agreed to use you after all this time."

"He didn't agree to use me," Schwartz spat. "I was working for the Noah when you were still in diapers, marine. Don't forget that. *I* was the one who first told him about Jack Mundy's little club of vigilantes. The Colombe," he scoffed, shaking his head. "What a joke." My hands balled involuntarily into fists, my nails digging into the soft flesh of my palms. Schwartz was a spy and apparently had been ever since my dad started the Colombe.

General Kennedy did not look at all impressed with Schwartz's speech. He sniffed derisively. "You are also the one who disappeared for the last twelve years with that rogue scientist, Boznic."

Schwartz paled. "If I hadn't run with the rest of them I would have blown my cover. What matters is that I got back in contact with the Noah the moment I saw what was on that plug Jack Mundy's brat came dragging into the lab. If it wasn't for me, Boz would have derailed the Noah's entire plan."

"About that," Kennedy said, cocking his head to the side. "Why did you stop Boznic, if you are so dead set against the Noah's plan?"

Schwartz glowered at the surrounding woods. "I was one of the Noah's scientific advisers once, and I believe he will listen to reason. As I'm sure you know, I specialize in DNA. And while I don't share Boz's views on dinosaurs being allowed to run wild, I do see the value in the species. Under the right conditions and with the right containments and safeguards in place, I believe that they could ultimately supply the human race far better than any of the domestic animals of the past. The Noah is a smart man, and I think he will reconsider his plan."

Kennedy snorted. "I highly doubt that."

Schwartz's lip curled into a condescending sneer. "Well, I wouldn't expect a marine to understand the complex workings of science. You aren't paid to think, after all."

Pulling his gun out of his vest, Kennedy pretended to examine it. "It's a real shame that you made it out of that lab alive and Sky Mundy didn't. I would have loved to put an end to her troublemaking life myself." He flipped his gun over, pulling something on it so it gave an ominous click before flicking his cold eyes back up to Schwartz. "You know, if I were to spot a dinosaur over your shoulder, and you accidentally got shot, I'm sure no one would question it."

Schwartz narrowed his eyes. "You wouldn't dare."

"Stop," boomed a voice, and Kennedy's hand froze on his gun. The Noah, dressed in a crisp white shirt and khaki fatigues, strode toward the pair. Behind him, like a well-organized shadow, came ten armed marines that immediately spread out to create a protective guard around their leader. Shell-shocked, I watched the most powerful man on the planet put a restraining hand on Kennedy's shoulder. I'd only ever seen him on the port-casts sent to North Compound and on my dad's info plug, but he exuded the same confidence and authority in person that he did on-screen, making it easy to overlook his small frame and wrinkled face. He carried himself like a man used to being obeyed, and I couldn't take my eyes off him.

"You will not waste your time arguing when your services are needed elsewhere, General," the Noah said in a way that made it clear this wasn't a suggestion. Kennedy snapped to attention, saluted stiffly, and stalked back toward the bustling camp.

The Noah turned to Schwartz, a smile on his lips that didn't quite reach his eyes. "What did I hear you shouting about, Doctor?"

"Sir," Schwartz said tentatively. "Your plan. What I

saw on Jack Mundy's information plug. You can't really be thinking about . . ."

"My plans are of no concern to you," the Noah interrupted with a glance at the marines standing nearby. Clearly he didn't want Schwartz blabbing about his plans in front of such a large audience.

"But," Schwartz protested, "you promised to hear out my ideas in exchange for the location of the lab."

"My dear doctor," the Noah said calmly, "I would have promised you the moon for the opportunity to put an end to Boznic's plotting."

Schwartz's face went white. "You were never going to listen. Were you? I should have known when you lied about invading the lab peacefully."

The Noah turned to his guards. He nodded at the closest one and flicked a hand lazily. "Shoot him."

Schwartz whirled to run, but before he could take even one step, three shots rang out, and he fell. I bit down hard on my tongue, successfully stopping the scream that was already halfway up my throat. The soldiers walked briskly to Schwartz, checked his pulse, and carried his body away.

Unperturbed, the Noah turned his attention to his guard. "Spies bother me," he said. "I never feel as though I can trust them." My eyes were glued to the small patch of bloodstained dirt, the only evidence that Schwartz had been there, and I fought the urge to vomit.

"We will be ready to head out in about two hours, sir," said one of the guards.

"Any progress with the lab?" the Noah asked.

The guard shook his head. "No, sir. We've been unable to find another viable entrance."

The Noah nodded, his brow furrowed. "Very well. Now that we know its location, it will be a simple enough matter to return with more powerful weaponry. Leave a helicopter and a small marine squad here to continue patrolling the area. If anyone surfaces, arrest them and send word to East Compound immediately. From Dr. Schwartz's intelligence, the place has some valuable resources. We may even be able to use it as another compound if we can find a way to remove the dinosaurs." The Noah paused, shaking his head. "The insanity of bringing more of those beasts out of extinction." With a sigh he pulled a port out of his pocket and pressed his hand momentarily to the screen. The guard cleared his throat nervously, and the Noah looked up in annoyance. "Is there something else?" he asked.

"Yes, sir," the guard said, sweat popping out on his forehead. "I just received a report that there have been some issues with the tree villagers we brought to East Compound. They've sabotaged the grow lights in the southern sector. Officer Weston was wondering how you wanted to handle the situation?"

The Noah cast his eyes skyward in exasperation. "Remind me why I am so good-hearted?" he asked. "Next time I'll just eliminate the lot instead of extending my goodwill just to have it thrown back in my face." He sighed. "Tell General Weston to take them off all work crews and leave them in their cell to reconsider their actions. I will decide how to deal with the miscreants upon our return." He looked back down at his port, clearly dismissing the guard.

My heart was thundering so loud that it amazed me the Noah couldn't hear it. I waited for him to leave, but he didn't. I was going to have to be the one who moved. Careful not to make a sound, I began creeping backward, ensuring each foot landed silently, barely daring to breathe. When I was far enough away, I whirled and flew back through the trees, praying I was heading toward Todd and Chaz.

They were still sleeping when I burst from the underbrush panting and sweating and clambered clumsily up the tree. They started awake, but I slapped my trembling hands over their surprised mouths and shook my head furiously. Chaz's eyes went wide with panic when she realized she was tied to the tree, and it took a few frenzied seconds to calm her down and get her untied. That accomplished, they silently climbed down before following me deeper into the woods. When I judged we were out of earshot of the Noah and his marines, I signaled for them to stop and told them everything I'd just heard.

"You mean Schwartz was spying on us this whole time?" Chaz yelped. I shushed her, but she brushed me off, her normally cheerful face flushed with angry red blotches.

"I don't think it was the whole time," I whispered, worried she was going to be overheard by the Noah's marines. "From the way General Kennedy was talking, it sounds like Schwartz went silent for quite a few years while he was in the lab." I shrugged. "Maybe he even began to change his way of thinking?"

Chaz scowled. "Obviously he didn't change it enough. He still gave away our location once he saw your dad's message. Getting shot was too good for him," she spat. "He should have been fed bit by bit to Pretty Boy." I had to agree. Thinking about Schwartz made my insides boil. If it weren't for him, Shawn would still be here now.

Todd grabbed my shoulders and gave me a rough shake. "You're sure he said everyone from the Oaks is at East Compound? You're sure?"

I detached his hands before he rattled my teeth loose. "That's what I heard."

"And they're making trouble," Todd grinned. "That sounds about right."

"What now?" Chaz asked. "Isn't East Compound really far away? And how does knowing where Todd's village is solve the much bigger problem of stopping the Noah?"

"I don't know," I said, sitting down hard on a tree stump to look up at my friends. "Schwartz even tried to tell the Noah that it was a bad idea, and look where that got him."

"But he said that the plan Boz had come up with would have worked?" Chaz asked.

"Lot of good that does us now," Todd said as he gave the closest tree an angry kick with his boot.

"I still have Boz's plug," I said, holding up my compass, "but we have no way to get to East Compound. And if we do get there, we only have one of them. And worse, it's untested."

"So you're saying it's hopeless," Chaz said.

"Now what kind of talk is that?" asked a low voice behind us, and we all jumped, fumbling for weapons we didn't have. My fear turned to relief when Ivan walked out of the bushes as though appearing from nowhere. His grizzled face was just as lined and stern as ever, but his blue eyes were sparkling. I'd never seen such a welcome sight in my life.

"Ivan!" I cried, running forward to throw myself into his arms before I'd really thought it through. He froze a second in surprise, and then patted my back awkwardly with his good arm.

"You're alive." I sniffed, stepping back as I inspected my grandfather. Standing only a little taller than me, Ivan carried himself as though he were seven feet tall. Broad-shouldered with a long hooked nose and a white beard that covered his chest, his most distinguishing feature was the lack of one of his arms. Lost in one of his many encounters with the dinosaurs he hunted, it ended just below his elbow joint.

"Of course I'm alive," Ivan said, sounding insulted. "I told you I'd come after you. But your tracks disappeared into the bloody lake. I've been walking around this beastly bit of water for days now, hoping to catch your trail again. Then the Noah's big buzzing machines showed up, and here you are."

A startled laugh bubbled out of me, and I shot Todd and Chaz a watery smile. "We've been in the middle of the lake," I explained. "Actually, at the bottom of the middle of the lake."

"It was awful," Todd said.

"The middle of the lake?" Ivan asked, his bushy white eyebrows raised. "You found what your father marked on that map of his?"

"We did," I said, my smile and feeling of elation fading as quickly as they'd come. "And we found out what was on his info plug too. And Ivan, it's awful."

"Who's this?" Ivan asked suddenly, gesturing to Chaz. "And where's the blond compound boy?"

I swallowed hard, fighting to keep my emotions in check as Shawn's loss stabbed through me, as fresh and sharp as it had the night before. "This is Chaz," I said with only a slight quaver to my voice. "She's from the Lincoln Lab we were staying at, the one at the bottom of the lake." Chaz stepped forward, her hand out to shake Ivan's until she realized that he was missing the hand she was supposed to shake. Confused and embarrassed about what to do, she stepped back with an awkward half wave and bob of her head.

"Smooth," Todd muttered. Out of the corner of my eye I saw Chaz stomp down on one of his booted feet.

"And Shawn . . ." I took a deep breath to go on, but my words seemed stuck in my throat.

"Shawn didn't make it," Todd finished for me, and I shot him a grateful look that he acknowledged with a nod.

"Hmmm," Ivan said, considering, looking from Chaz to Todd to me and back again. "I think it's high time you told me what's been happening since I saw you last. But first, I think we need a spot of breakfast.

I hate talking on an empty stomach."

"That sounds amazing," Todd agreed, and I realized for the first time that I was starving. We'd missed dinner the night before, and I was on my third near-death experience in twenty-four hours, which, apparently, worked up quite the appetite.

"We can't start a fire here," Ivan said. "The Noah and his muckety-mucks are swarming all over the beach about a quarter mile north."

"I know." I frowned.

"Follow me," Ivan said, turning to march in the opposite direction of the Noah and his camp of helicopters. Ten minutes later, he stopped by a small rock outcropping. He climbed nimbly up the side and disappeared into a cave set in the rocks.

Chaz craned her head back to watch Ivan's progress. "I'm not sure if I should be impressed at how well he climbed that with only one hand or depressed that I can't climb that well with two," she mused.

"Get used to it," Todd muttered. "Ivan does everything better with one hand than we do with two."

"Are you coming?" Ivan called, poking his head over the edge to peer down at us. "Or are you going to just stand down there gabbling? I thought you were hungry."

"We are," Todd said, not wasting any more time as

he grabbed the rock above his head and clambered up almost as nimbly as Ivan.

"He's impressive too." Chaz whistled in appreciation.

I sighed and nodded. "We're topside now. Just expect them to be good at everything."

"I don't know how I feel about that," Chaz said.

I shrugged. "It's frustrating, but we'll get there. You should have seen Shawn and me our first day up here. We could barely stay upright." Chaz laughed as she grabbed a rock and scrabbled up. I waited a second before following her, making sure my face was composed and the tears that had sprung up involuntarily at my mention of Shawn were wiped away. Once I was sure I had it together, or as together as I was going to get it, I climbed up after her. Inside the cave, which turned out to have been Ivan's home base while he tracked us up and down the lake, hung a collection of smoked fish of all different sizes. He used a knife to expertly cut one down and tossed it on an iron skillet. He already had a small fire near the mouth of the cave that he prodded with a stick to revive before putting the pan directly on the red embers.

Todd leaned over the fire and inhaled deeply. "Ah." He sighed, sitting back against the wall of the cave. "I've missed that smell."

"Dead fish smell?" I asked, wrinkling my nose.

He barked a laugh. "No. The smell of a fire. Of fresh air. Of dirt and trees, and yes, maybe even dead fish. The only thing that lab smelled like was glass and dinosaur poop."

"Hey!" Chaz said indignantly.

"Enough," barked Ivan. "Tell me what's been happening. Start with the moment you left me."

Todd quirked a questioning eyebrow at me.

"You tell it," I said, not sure I could get through the whole thing without losing it again.

So Todd began to fill him in. Wordlessly eating the fish Ivan handed me, I listened and thought back over the last few days. The herd of carnotaurs, Pretty Boy, the Lincoln Lab, my dad's message to us, Boz's plug, Dr. Schwartz, the dinosaurs, the elevator, and my near run-in with the Noah. If I hadn't lived it, I wouldn't have believed it.

Ivan just listened, his face stern and serious. When Todd finished, Ivan turned to me. "Let me see this plug that is supposed to save the world."

I dutifully unscrewed the back of my compass and handed it over to him. He held it gingerly between his calloused fingers before offering it back to me with a shake of his head. "It looks like rhamphorhynchus dung if you ask me."

"Thank you!" Todd cried.

Ivan snorted, but then his face got serious again as he turned to me. "You're sure the Noah said he was going back to East Compound."

"Yes," I said, surprised. I'd expected him to ask about the Noah's plan, not his travel itinerary.

"Good, then we can kill two pterodactyls with one stone," he said, nodding decisively.

"Um," Chaz said, shooting me a confused look. "Are we supposed to know what that means? He wouldn't actually shoot a pterodactyl, would he? They're really rare."

"Well," I said evasively. "Let's just say you and Ivan have different views on dinosaurs." Chaz wrinkled her forehead in confusion.

I turned to Ivan. "What *do* you mean?"

"What I mean is we get to East Compound, and we accomplish two things. The first is that we save Todd's village before the Noah has a chance to 'deal' with them." Todd let out a whoop of pure joy that echoed throughout the cave, scaring a few bats from the recesses so we had to duck as they whizzed over our heads and into the sunlight. I glanced nervously out of the cave entrance, even though I knew we were too far away for the Noah's men to hear us.

"The second," Ivan went on as though Todd hadn't

said anything, "is we stop this idiotic plan of the Noah's. If you think Boz's plug will do the trick, then it's worth a try. If it fails, we'll come up with a plan B."

"Both of those sound great," I said. "But how in the world are we going to get to East Compound? It's hundreds of miles away, and we are running out of time." I tried to do the calculations in my head of how long we had before the Noah started dropping his bombs, and failed. It could be days, weeks, or months.

"Well, we certainly can't walk," Ivan said. "That would take us well over a month, and I don't fancy doing that again."

"Again?" Chaz whispered to me. "He isn't serious, is he?"

"He is," I confirmed, thinking back to Ivan telling us about his time spent near East Compound. He'd moved there when my mom, his daughter, had wanted to attend the university. It was where she'd met my dad, and they'd started the Colombe. It was also where she'd died, murdered by the Noah as she tried to flee back to the wild and Ivan.

"But," Todd stuttered, jumping to his feet. "How in the world are we going to get there?"

"We're going to fly," Ivan said, eyes narrowed as he used his foot to scoop dirt over the fire before moving briskly about the cave, packing up various bits of gear.

"Fly?" Todd repeated, looking to me for guidance. All I could do was shrug. I had no clue what my eccentric grandfather had in mind.

"You have a plane?" Chaz asked.

"No," Ivan said. "But I plan on being aboard one of the Noah's before he takes off."

"What!" Todd yelped. "He'll kill us!"

Ivan's blue eyes flashed mischievously. "Only if he sees us." Then he paused, taking in our bedraggled appearance and complete lack of weaponry.

"Hmmm," he said. "Looks like we might need to outfit you a bit first."

"How exactly are we going to do that?" I asked.

"One moment," Ivan said, turning to stride into the dark recesses of the cave. His footsteps echoed through the chamber, and a few more disgruntled bats flew past our heads. Before long he was back, three bows over one arm and three quivers of arrows slung over his shoulder. Todd's jaw dropped as Ivan dug through his pockets, producing knives and small stones I knew to be flint for starting fires.

"How did you know we wouldn't have our bows?" Todd asked.

"Or knives?" I added, inspecting a rather impressive one he'd just handed me.

"I didn't," Ivan said, squinting at me with one eye

as he adjusted the drawstring of a bow a quarter inch before handing it to me. "This is one of my hunting huts. I have about twenty of them in a hundred-mile radius, and the rest are scattered to the east, south, and west. I keep them all well stocked and supplied. Survival depends on weapons. If I don't survive, it won't be because I wasn't prepared."

"Is that a pachycephalosaurus rib bone?" Chaz asked, cringing away from the bow Ivan was trying to pass to her as if it was going to bite.

"It is," Ivan said, shooting me a "what's her deal" look. "They have the most flexibility and workability of the dinosaur bones, although I'll use any dinosaur rib in a pinch." Chaz's face went white.

"Ivan," Todd said, shaking his head as he drew back the string of his own bow. "You're my hero."

"Enough talk," Ivan said gruffly, but I could tell he was pleased. "We need to be on our way if we want to hitch a ride."

I nodded, feeling hopeful for the first time since I'd surfaced from that elevator. Maybe, just maybe, with Ivan's help, we had a shot.

CHAPTER 9

"**E**xplain to me again why this is a good idea?" Chaz hissed in my ear. I brushed a hand at her in irritation. It was bad enough that the clump of bushes we were hiding behind forced us to crouch practically on top of one another; I didn't need her breathing down my neck too.

"She can't, because it's not," Todd grumbled.

I frowned at my two friends. "You heard Ivan. We don't have a lot of time, so we have to work with what we got."

"And what we got is a herd of duck-face dinosaurs," Todd scowled.

"Hadrosaurs," Chaz corrected as she studied the

herd fifty feet away. They stomped their large feet in the cool lake water, occasionally dunking their heads below the surface like the oversized ducks they so resembled.

"What's with the weird bump on their heads?" I asked, inspecting the one closest to us. Although its nose was flat and almost bill-like, the back of its head extended into a bony spike that gave it a bizarre appearance.

"Most hadrosaurs have some sort of crest," Chaz explained. "It acts as an echo chamber, so if a hadrosaur cries out, you can hear it for miles. It's one of the easiest ways to tell them apart. Those, for example, are parasaurolophus. That backward-facing crest makes their heads measure almost a full six feet. And"—she frowned, biting her lip—"they are really flighty."

"Flighty?" I asked.

"They don't tend to stampede in a herd; they scatter," she explained.

Todd swallowed hard. "So you're saying they might just trample us?"

"That is a very real possibility," Chaz admitted.

Wiping my sweaty palms on my shirt, I tried not to imagine what it would be like to be trampled to death.

"How much longer should we give Ivan?" Chaz asked, interrupting my gruesome train of thought.

Todd shrugged. "Five minutes?" Ivan had gone ahead of us to get the lay of the land and to find the best helicopter for us to stow away in. He'd insisted on going alone, muttering something about how we walked through the woods like a herd of water buffalo. I wasn't sure what a water buffalo was, but I was fairly certain he hadn't meant it as a compliment. Instead, we'd been put in charge of the distraction. Ivan had explained that we needed some sort of disturbance if we had any chance of getting on board one of the helicopters undetected. Some distraction, I thought sourly as a dinosaur at the edge of the group lifted its tail and dropped a big steaming glob of yuck right onto the beach.

Todd shook his head, his nose wrinkled in disgust. "This better work."

Chaz nodded. "It should. A herd of dinosaurs charging through a camp causes some havoc. I should know. I was eleven when a herd of stampeding stegoceras almost took out our topside settlement. We were collecting samples from a nearby breeding group . . ."

"Chaz," I interrupted. "Not really the time for stories."

"Right." She sighed. "Well, anyways, even if we can only get half the herd heading in the right direction, it should be enough. Trust me."

Todd sighed. "If you say so."

"I do, but stop poking me, will you," Chaz said, her eyes glued to the beach.

"I'm not poking you," Todd said, shooting me a confused look. I shrugged.

"You are too," she snapped. "Stop it."

That's when I felt the hot breath on the back of my neck. My nerves sprang instantly to attention as adrenaline roared into my veins. A subtle sour smell of rot and decay wafted past me, and I vaguely registered that I'd smelled that particular odor before. I slowly craned my head to look behind me. Two large green eyes peered down at me from the angular face of a troodon, the dinosaur Todd had called a Nightmare when a herd of them tried to eat us back at the Oaks just a few days ago.

"Chaz," I choked. "Todd."

"Shhhh." Chaz shushed me, clearly annoyed. "Hadrosaurs have excellent hearing. Unless you want to spook them early, you *need* to be quieter."

Todd must have caught the terror in my voice, because he turned just as a second troodon nudged Chaz's shoulder, its intelligent eyes sparking with interest. They don't know what we are, I realized. Unlike the pack by Todd's village, these had probably never seen a human before, and they were deciding if we were eatable. I'd read about their superior intelligence, but to see it calculating and studying us in that way was unnerving. The one behind Chaz lifted its nose in the air and opened its mouth as though tasting the air. And for all I knew, maybe it could.

"I told you to knock it off," Chaz snapped. She turned, her arm already swinging to brush us away. Instead, she smacked the troodon right on the nose. It snorted, jerking its head back as Chaz let out a terrified squeak.

Todd grabbed her hand and yanked her out of the woods and toward the beach. As I threw myself after them, a series of excited yips came from behind me, and a moment later sand pelted against the backs of my arms and legs as the troodons launched themselves after us. There was nowhere to run but right through the pack of thirty-foot-tall hadrosaurs.

Their heads jerked up at our approach, and a moment later we were charging into the middle of the startled herd, their earthy, minty smell momentarily overshadowing the rancid one of our pursuers. Catching sight of the troodons, the hadrosaurs bellowed and took off. Chaz had been right: they didn't all stampede together, they scattered, some flying back toward the woods while others headed off down the beach in either direction. I barely avoided being trampled, ducking a whirling tail and dodging a gigantic green hindquarter before my feet hit the icy water of the lake seconds behind Todd and Chaz. Together we plowed into the oncoming waves, water splashing up around our knees and into our faces as we battled to run through ever-deepening water. A huge wave crested in front of me, and I dove beneath its surface. As the freezing water closed over my head, I realized that I had no idea if troodons could swim.

Even with my eyes open, I couldn't see past my fingertips as I swam underneath the surface of the churning waves. It took every ounce of willpower I had not to think about the creatures that lived in this particular lake. Todd stayed beside me stroke for stroke while Chaz pulled ahead. I guess if you grew up at the bottom of a lake, your swimming skills were bound to be good. When my lungs felt like they were about to burst, I gave in and surfaced, whirling to face the beach. To my relief, the troodons weren't chasing us. They'd apparently decided the hadrosaurs were a better bet and were sprinting after a pack of them, right toward the Noah's camp.

"Well, that wasn't exactly the plan," Chaz said, huffing, already swimming back toward the beach. "But it's close enough."

I blinked water out of my eyes, breathing hard as

I paddled after Chaz. "Do you think Ivan had enough time?"

"Only one way to find out," Todd said.

I watched the dinosaurs disappear around a curve. The plan wasn't going to be as simple as Ivan had hoped. We stumbled back onto the beach, and a few seconds later screams and gunshots rang out.

"Come on!" I called, sprinting for the camouflage of the trees. We ran, jumping over fallen logs and tripping over hidden rocks and roots. The screaming and gunshots got louder, and every nerve of my body vibrated in terrified anticipation. We reached the edge of the camp and looked out on utter chaos.

A few of the hadrosaurs had gotten tangled in the ropes of the marines' tents and stood bellowing in fear, while others dragged the tents behind them like makeshift nets, picking up debris and anyone unlucky enough to not get out of their way. The troodons were taking full advantage of the situation, attacking the trapped hadrosaurs in a reckless frenzy. A handful of marines stood their ground, firing shot after shot at troodon and hadrosaur alike, while others ran for the nearest helicopter, swearing and yelling out orders that no one followed. It was dinosaur death and carnage I'd helped orchestrate, and it made me feel ill.

Giving myself a firm shake, I forced myself to focus

on the task at hand. Guilt could come later. Right now, I had a job to do. My eyes combed frantically among the fray, hoping to catch a glimpse of Ivan, but he was nowhere to be seen.

"How are we ever going to find him?" Chaz wailed in my ear. I didn't say it, but the whole plan suddenly seemed hopeless. We hadn't just created a distraction. We'd created a disaster. A disaster Ivan could have gotten caught up and killed in. Not him too, I thought desperately as I scanned the beach again. Shawn's death was already heavy on my conscience, and if Ivan died I might just shatter. The helicopter closest to us suddenly whirred to life, lifting into the air even as marines threw themselves inside.

I was so busy watching it take off that I didn't see what collided with my side, sending me flying into the trees. My breath whooshed out as I landed hard in the underbrush. Out of the corner of my eye I saw Chaz and Todd flying right beside me. If they hadn't shoved me, then who had?

"Cover your head!" Ivan yelled in my ear, pushing my face and Chaz's toward the ground seconds before a wild-eyed hadrosaur thundered past, missing us by inches. A moment later a troodon, yipping in triumph, brought it down ten feet away from us.

"Follow me," Ivan growled in my ear, and I nodded

dumbly, unable to take my eyes off the troodon as it ripped into the still-thrashing hadrosaur's side with terrifying efficiency. Ivan half dragged me to my feet, and I stumbled after him along the edge of the woods, Chaz and Todd right behind us.

Two more helicopters took off, and Ivan quickened his pace, forcing us into a full run to keep up as we skirted the edge of the beach, where our distraction disaster was still going full tilt. He skidded to a stop, feet away from the biggest helicopter of them all. Massive, with five propellers already in motion, it sat next to an official-looking brown tent. Only one marine was standing at the helicopter's door, holding a gun and nervously watching the swirling spectacle of fleeing hadrosaurs and fierce troodons taking place only thirty feet away. The poor man looked like there was nothing he wanted to do more than run, but he kept his feet firmly planted beside the helicopter, sweat pouring down his face to disappear into the black body armor he wore.

"Why didn't you choose one of the smaller unarmed ones?" Todd whispered harshly to Ivan.

"Because there is nowhere to hide in those," Ivan hissed back. "Now hush yourself, and let me handle this."

"This," Chaz muttered under her breath, "is suicide."

Her eyes were wide as she stared at a troodon that had just joined three others to rip into a dead hadrosaur.

"Ivan will figure something out," I said.

"Not that." Chaz frowned. "Those troodons. There has to be thirty of them now. There were only three originally. It's a feeding frenzy. They've alerted every troodon in a fifty-mile radius with the racket they're making."

"What racket?" Todd asked. As if on cue, one of the troodons let out a high-pitched shriek as it flipped a large chunk of hadrosaur thigh in the air and caught it again, shaking it back and forth in enjoyment. "Never mind," Todd said.

"Guys?" I said, suddenly glancing around myself in a panic. "Where's Ivan?"

"What?" Chaz said, prying her eyes away from the dinosaurs. "Wasn't he just by you?"

We looked to the helicopter just in time to see the nervous marine drop like a stone. Ivan stepped from behind him and quickly dragged the unconscious body away from the door. Motioning for us to follow, he disappeared into the belly of the machine.

"Do we just run for it?" Todd asked.

"We need to do something," Chaz said. "As soon as those troodons run out of hadrosaurs, they are going to notice us." She was right. The last of the hadrosaurs had fallen, its body already swarming with the lithe forms of six troodons.

"That's not our only issue," I said, noticing that the brown tent next to the helicopter was beginning to rustle as the occupants inside presumably prepared to make a run for the very same helicopter as us.

"Can't we catch a break?" Todd groaned.

"It's now or never," I said, and gathering all the guts I had, I grabbed Todd's arm with one hand and Chaz's with the other, and dragged them after me as I started a headlong sprint for the helicopter.

There was an excited squeal to our left, and I glanced away from the helicopter to see that four troodons had spotted us, and were heading our way. Luckily, the helicopter was close, and we reached it seconds later. The door was wide enough for all three of us to scramble up and onto the hard metal floor. Ivan was there a moment later, his large black gun out and on his shoulder. He fired four quick shots, and four thumps told me he'd hit his targets. Glancing back, I saw the troodons lying dead, each with a neat bullet hole through the eye. Ivan hurried us to the back of the helicopter to where a pile of boxes was held fast by netting attached to large metal rings in the floor and ceiling.

"In here," he said gruffly, shoving us into a hollowed-out space behind the boxes. "Make yourself as small as possible." Just then, another gunshot rang out, and I jerked my head around to look at Ivan, but his gun wasn't drawn. The gunshot had come from outside the helicopter. "Hurry," Ivan said gruffly, shoving Todd's head down and pushing him in after Chaz. I was next and Ivan squeezed in last, pulling a box over to conceal the gap we'd entered through and deftly refastening the netting. Todd's elbow dug painfully into my ribs, and the boxes had a musty metallic smell to them that made my stomach roll sickeningly. But I didn't dare say anything because through a tiny crack in the boxes, I saw who had fired those gunshots.

The Noah, surrounded by heavily armed marines, had exited the big brown tent and was heading straight for our helicopter.

"This is the Noah's helicopter?!" I gasped.

"Not another word," Ivan breathed. "If we're caught, we're dead."

"What's going on?" Todd whispered. "I can't see anything."

"Shhhhh," Ivan and I both hissed, and I watched as the marines, Kennedy at their head, maneuvered the Noah deftly to the helicopter, gunning down five more troodons and adding them to Ivan's original four. The Noah looked completely unflustered, marching along with the supreme confidence of a man who knew himself to be safe. It was unnerving. The marines reached the helicopter without incident, and one of them helped the Noah inside before the rest of them piled in, the last one slamming the door shut.

"All clear," the one closest to us said into the radio on his shoulder, and another marine pushed his way to the front to slip into the pilot's seat, flipping switches.

"Where's Mathews?" barked General Kennedy.

"Most likely dead, sir," answered another marine. "There were four dinosaurs gunned down by the helicopter entrance."

"Impressive shooting," said the first marine. "Right through the eye. Did we know Mathews was that good of a shot?"

"How many men did we lose?" Kennedy asked the first marine, and I could tell that although he was trying to keep a tough exterior, the stampede and attack had shaken him.

"We don't have a count yet, sir. But first estimates are at around twelve."

Kennedy muttered something under his breath, and stared out the window as the whir of propellers picking up speed made talking nearly impossible. Todd stiffened as the engine roared, and we lifted unsteadily into the air. My own stomach plummeted as we gained altitude, and I squeezed my eyes shut. Vomiting was not an option.

"How long until we reach East Compound?" the Noah asked, and I opened my eyes to see him pulling out his port screen. The helicopter dipped suddenly, tilting in midair, and I had to brace my hands against the cool metal floor to keep myself from sliding sideways into Ivan. The skewed perspective gave me a glimpse out the window, and I saw the distant trees and beach as the pilot turned us east.

"Just under eight hours," the pilot called back.

"Eight hours," Todd squeaked in my ear. I stiffened, but luckily the roaring engines drowned out everything. With no other way of communicating how stupid that had been, I dug my elbow into his ribs. He turned his head to glare at me. I glared back, shifting the tiniest amount in an attempt to relieve already cramping muscles. How would they feel eight hours from now?

The last time I'd been this scrunched I'd been eight and, determined to beat Shawn at hide-and-seek, had wedged myself into a shipping crate. A stabbing pain knifed into my chest as I thought about how much Shawn would have loved riding in a helicopter. He'd have had a million questions about how the massive black machine worked. I let out the tiniest of sighs, drawing a sharp look from Ivan.

As Lake Michigan disappeared behind us, the marines settled into the various seats along the walls of the helicopter, strapping themselves in and getting comfortable for the long trip. Knowing that comfort was out of the question, I shut my eyes. Sleep wasn't going to happen, but with my eyes shut I could focus better on what lay ahead. The most powerful man in the world was just feet away, and I had to figure out a plan to stop him.

1. The Noah's headquarters
2. kids' hideout /
   Old-world maintenance entry point
3. Helicopter landing pad
4. Restroom #5
5. Charging dock
6. Food station

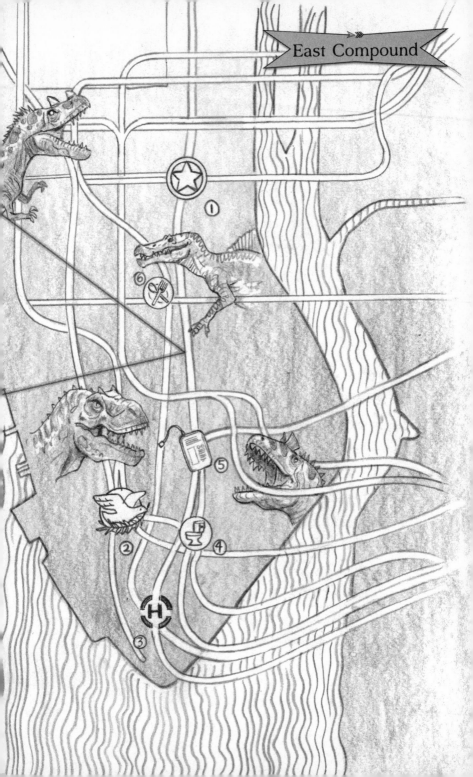

CHAPTER 10

The next eight hours were the longest of my life. My muscles ached, my butt went numb, and the tiny space behind the boxes seemed to get stuffier and smaller as the hours went by. I'd hoped the marines and the Noah would talk, giving us some valuable information about what we were going to find in East Compound, but no luck. The roar of the helicopter was too loud for conversation, and most of the marines sat in silence, dozed, or stared out the window.

But as bad as things were for me, I knew the ride was worse for Todd. I had forgotten about his claustrophobia, and the longer he was confined to the tiny cramped space, the more his shoulders trembled, and the sweatier and sweatier his tunic got. To his credit, he rode out the endless minutes without saying a word. I had no idea how Chaz was doing, but Ivan seemed to be absolutely fine as he sat like an immovable statue beside me. I'd lost track of time and actually felt my eyelids starting to close when I spotted something out the window that woke me up with a start.

Looming on the horizon were the biggest buildings I'd ever seen. Silhouetted against the setting sun, they stood like black monuments of time, immovable and impressive reminders of what the human race used to be. I sucked in an involuntary breath as our helicopter wove its way through at least twenty of them. They all showed the damage and wear of over a century's disuse, but they were still the most amazing things I'd ever seen. I'd thought Ivan's ten-story building was a skyscraper. I'd been oh so wrong. These, with their tops practically disappearing into the clouds, were skyscrapers. Most of them were pockmarked with black holes where windows once sat, while others had lost entire sections, revealing their metal skeletons underneath. We passed more than one that appeared to have cracked off at the middle, toppling into its neighbors to join the deep mounds of overgrown rubble on the ground below.

So this was New York, I thought dazedly as building after building flashed by. The helicopter tilted sharply, turning around one of the buildings, and I saw the ocean for the first time in my life and had to stifle a gasp. Todd looked at me curiously, but I just shook my head as I stared at the never-ending expanse of blue. Unlike Lake Michigan, this blue was vibrant, alive and almost green in intensity. Tears pricked my eyes. I'd never realized, during all those years in North Compound, just how truly big and amazing this world was. I'd confined my dreams to fresh air and the feeling of grass beneath my feet as I wasted my days walking the same few miles of tunnel over and over again in endless repetition. I'd never fathomed that I would get to see an ocean. Or that it would be so heartbreakingly beautiful that it would make the last twelve years of my life feel like they had lacked something vital.

The helicopter dipped again, and this time I saw what I knew to be the Statue of Liberty. We'd learned about it in school, and everything it used to stand for before the dinosaurs and the pandemic changed the structure of our world forever. But like the rest of the topside world created by humans, the once-statuesque lady had fallen into disrepair. She no longer looked like the pictures I'd pulled up on my port screen a lifetime ago. Green moss climbed thickly up her left side, and the arm that was supposed to be holding a torch had cracked off, leaving her looking lopsided. And a little like Ivan, I thought, and had to stifle a giggle. Her crown was missing a few spikes, and perched on one of them was a large pterosaur, its lethal-looking beak tucked under a large webbed wing as it slept. My mouth dropped opened in shock when I saw what lay at the foot of the statue. A spinosaurus, twice the size of the one that I'd killed, was wrapped around the base of the statue, stretched out to catch the last rays of the late afternoon sun. It picked up its gigantic crocodile-like head and watched us pass, twitching its tail lazily. The sight of it made my nerves tingle as I remembered again what it felt like to be inches away from one of those things' open mouths. The helicopter straightened out, and I lost the view of the statue and its strange occupant.

Moments later we started to slowly descend. Floor after floor of broken windows and derelict buildings flashed by the window, and I had to look away as the sight sent my already queasy stomach rolling. A metallic grinding noise filled the air, and I pressed my hands to my ears as the sound vibrated my bones and screeched through the cabin of the helicopter. We must have passed through some kind of door, because the dim glow of sunlight disappeared, and we sank into darkness.

The helicopter thumped to a stop, sending the boxes we'd crouched behind rattling. Ivan placed a heavy hand on my shoulder to steady me. The thrumming engines were turned off, and I felt deaf in the silence. Jumping out of the helicopter with military efficiency, the marines flanked the Noah as he walked away. The pilot remained another few minutes, checking the switches and typing information onto a small port screen. Finally he left, and we were alone.

Ivan still didn't move. The minutes stretched by into what felt like hours. Todd shifted uncomfortably beside me, but Ivan remained a statue. When I'd almost given up hope of ever leaving the helicopter, he reached over to silently unhook the netting that held the boxes in place. A gust of cool recirculated and filtered air wafted past me, and the familiar smell brought memories of North Compound rushing back. East Compound had the same air I'd grown up on, devoid of all the flavor and depth of the topside air.

Ivan silently eased the boxes covering our hiding spot aside and, motioning for us to stay put, slipped out. He was gone only a minute before he was back, waving a hand to show we were supposed to follow him. Moving was painful. Every muscle I had and even some I didn't know I possessed seemed to have frozen in the tiny scrunched position I'd assumed for eight hours. It took everything I had not to yelp in pain, but I followed Ivan as quickly as my howling muscles would allow.

Ivan led us through the abandoned helicopter and out into a massive room. Ten other helicopters sat around us on the cool stone floor, each of them shiny and ready for takeoff. In the far corner was the black plane I'd watched drop off mail and supplies back when I'd believed it was the only transportation the human race had left.

Ivan didn't waste time staring at the helicopters; he was already running on silent feet toward one of the large dark tunnels at the far end of the room. As I scrambled after him, Chaz and Todd at my heels, I couldn't help but compare the tunnel to the narrow ones of my own North Compound. It was at least two or three times their size.

Down the center of the tunnel were two parallel seams of white concrete, marking where the old metal subway tracks had been removed over a hundred years ago. The walls were squared off with thick pillars of concrete embedded every few feet to support the skyscrapers that still towered above. Here and there pipes ran along the walls, poking in and out of the cracked concrete like worms. Some of the pipes were obviously original, but newer pipes had been patched in over the years, snaking along the roofline and twisting into the older pipe network like shiny imposters. The entire thing was incredibly fascinating to me. North Compound's tunnels had been built for the transportation of people, but these tunnels had a history and a life all their own. They spoke of past progress and present decay, and I wished I had time to slow down and really look at them, but it took everything I had to keep up with Ivan as he raced on silent feet through the dark tunnel.

"Where is everyone?" Chaz whispered, her voice swallowed up by the vast emptiness of the tunnel.

"Probably in bed," I said. "If it's anything like North Compound, they probably have some sort of a curfew." Ivan shot us a look over his shoulder that very clearly told us to be quiet, and we obeyed.

Ten minutes later, he stopped, running his hand along the wall of the tunnel. There was a dull click followed by the whine of rusty hinges, and a narrow concrete door opened inward. Made to look like the surrounding concrete, it had blended in seamlessly with the tunnel. Ivan pulled us into it and closed the door. He felt around the side of the wall and flicked on a light to reveal a small circular room. The floor was covered in a hundred and fifty years' worth of dust and bits of crumbled concrete. A rusted ladder was attached to the far wall, leading up to a square metal entrance hatch fifteen feet above us.

"What is this place?" Todd asked, looking around. He was shivering, his sweat-drenched and sleeveless jumpsuit obviously not doing much to keep out the ever-present chill that came with living belowground. It was amazing how quickly I'd forgotten what it felt like to have that damp cold in your bones.

"This is one of the emergency access points," Ivan said. "They were put in for the mechanics to access broken-down subway cars or to evacuate passengers in case of emergency. They are located every few miles along the tunnels."

"Miles?" Todd squeaked. "How big is this place?"

"Gigantic," I answered before Ivan had a chance. "East Compound is by far the largest of all the compounds."

"North, South, and West Compound were all created to house the human race in case of a nuclear war," I explained, trying to remember everything I'd learned in my history lessons. "East was created using the underground subway system already in place in New York City. The pandemic wiped out most of the population, but enough people were left to make the underground portions of the city habitable."

Chaz wrinkled her nose. "Why would they want to stay?"

"Space," Ivan said. "The subway tunnels allowed people to spread out. Although most of the population is fairly concentrated for convenience's sake."

"How many people live here?" Chaz asked.

"Around three hundred," Ivan said, "although I haven't been here in almost twelve years, so that number has probably changed." His eyes darkened and flicked momentarily to me, and I knew he was thinking about the last time he'd been here. It had been the day my mom, his only child, was murdered trying to escape this very compound. Leaving me behind with my dad, who hid all of it from me for twelve years. A fact that still stung.

Taking a deep breath, I pushed those melancholy thoughts aside. We didn't have a lot of time left before the Noah put his horrendous plan into action, and we still needed to locate and free Todd's village, a task that now seemed a lot harder than I'd originally thought. It could take days, weeks even, to search every corner of this compound, and we might not have weeks.

"How well do you know your way around?" I asked Ivan.

"Not well," he admitted. "We're lucky. We landed close to the entrance your mother used to smuggle me in the three times I visited to meet with the Colombe." He motioned to the hatch above our heads. I looked up, my brow knitted.

"But where's the holoscreen?" I asked. "Every entrance at North Compound was required to have one.

How do they scan for threats before going topside?"

"Too many entrances and exits here for that kind of security," Ivan said. "Like I said before, the old subway lines had a lot of utility entrances like this one. Most of them have been bricked over, except," he said, his blue eyes twinkling with obvious pride, "for the ones that your mother uncovered."

Chaz ran a hand down the crumbling brick wall of the room and shrugged. "The lab had way better views with our windows and all, but this isn't horrible."

"Views." Todd snorted. "Yeah. PREviews of what tried to eat us."

Chaz rolled her eyes and turned to me. "What is our plan? Do we have one?"

I nodded, my throat dry. "We need to figure out where we are and where the Noah's headquarters or base or technology hub or whatever is located."

"Wrong," Todd said, shaking his head.

"But, Todd—" I protested.

He crossed his arms over his chest. "No. You don't get to *but, Todd* me anymore. I've helped you without complaining as we almost got eaten more times than I want to count, and you promised that if we made it to Lake Michigan you'd help me save my mom. Well, we made it to Lake Michigan, and now it's your turn to pay up. We are going to find my mom, and we are going to make it a priority."

"Without complaining?" Chaz asked, eyebrow raised. "I find that incredibly hard to believe."

"Plus," Todd went on, ignoring Chaz, "if this place is as big as Ivan says it is, we are going to need all the help we can get to find something big and important enough to stick that plug of Boz's into."

"We need the Noah's headquarters," Ivan said. "My daughter told me once that it was where all of the major technology for the compound is housed."

"Okay," Todd amended. "Well, they can help us bust our way into the headquarters or whatever. The point is that we need their help."

"We aren't going to bust our way in anywhere," I said, shaking my head. "We'll have to sneak in. Even with your entire village, we don't have any weapons."

"Ivan has his gun, and we have these!" Todd said, gesturing to the bow still strapped across his back. I nodded. My own bow had been hard to forget as it jabbed me in the spine the entire ride here.

Ivan raised an eyebrow. "If I recall your story correctly, the members of the Oaks had weapons too." Todd sagged, and Ivan clapped a friendly hand on his shoulder. "While I admire your enthusiasm, Sky's right. Our weapons are not enough. We will have to use stealth. The marines here are heavily armed."

"Really?" I said. "Don't they use the same stun guns as the marines back at North?"

Ivan huffed. "Not exactly. The marines here at East have guns that shoot actual bullets. They need electricity to work, so when the marines are away from the compound, they use small portable generators they carry around in those helicopters. But here at East, they can move freely."

"We have something similar at the lab for our tranquilizer guns," Chaz said. "Only ours run off battery packs."

"Well, that's just great," Todd muttered. "Just what we needed to make this whole thing harder."

"We can worry more about the marines' weapons in the morning," Ivan said, patting Todd's slumped shoulder reassuringly. "Right now, we all need some sleep."

"Sleep?" I yelped. "We don't have time for sleep. The Noah could set off those bombs of his any day now."

"True," Ivan said sternly. "But he left too many of his marines behind at the lake to set off any bombs tonight. Besides, you look dead on your feet."

"I feel dead on my feet," Chaz said, yawning widely. Her yawn triggered one of my own, and I stifled it in irritation.

"But—" I started to protest, but I was cut off by a sharp look from Ivan.

"No buts, granddaughter," he said in a tone that put an immediate stop to any thoughts I'd had about arguing. "We are all going to eat something and sleep here tonight. It's the only safe place I know of in this entire compound. If we venture away from it, we might not find somewhere else for miles. Everything that needs doing can wait until tomorrow."

I looked to Chaz for support, only to find that she was already shrugging off her pack and bow, obviously settling down for the night. Even Todd, who I thought for sure would protest in favor of charging off in search of his mom, just nodded resignedly and unfolded the large, thin blanket he'd gotten from Ivan's cave and laid it across the floor of the small circular room.

With a sigh, I sank down beside him as Ivan produced some hardened strips of dinosaur jerky and passed them out to each of us. Chaz gave her piece a brooding stare, sniffed it, and shoved it in her pocket without taking a bite. I gnawed on mine, hardly tasting the peppery meat as everyone attempted to get comfortable for the night. When Ivan flicked off the light a short while later, I stared into the dark, sure that sleep wasn't a possibility for me. But as the sound of first Todd's, then Ivan's, and finally Chaz's slow, rhythmic breathing filled the room, I discovered I was wrong. I didn't even remember closing my eyes.

CHAPTER 11

I'd woken up somewhere new every day for the last two weeks—the only exception being my time spent in the underwater lab, but even then the view out my window had never been the same twice. So I should have been used to opening my eyes and having that baffling instant where I expected to see the familiar walls of North Compound but instead found myself staring out a tree house window, or through the filmy fabric of my tree pod, or even at the face of a curious plesiosaur as it peered in to watch me sleep. But I wasn't. That first morning in East Compound was especially confusing.

I woke up in darkness so complete, so inky black,

that I wasn't even sure if my eyes were open for a second. After my fingertips assured me that they were in fact open, I sat up gingerly, aware of the heavy sleeping bodies on either side of me. Sometime during the night I'd lost my ponytail holder, and now my hair flopped across my shoulders in a tangled curly mess. A blind search of the surrounding floor didn't turn it up, and I huffed in frustration. I didn't have another one. It was stupid to let something so small and insignificant bother me, but it did. How was I supposed to function without something to get this mess of curls out of my way?

Shawn came immediately to mind. If he were here, he'd come up with some clever way for me to tie my hair back. Probably using something he'd cobbled together out of a bit of this and a spare part of that. He'd always been so good at that stuff. I sniffed, and realized I had tears running down my face.

"What's wrong?" Chaz asked groggily beside me, sitting up. "Is it morning yet?"

"No," Todd groaned from my other side, rolling over. "Go away."

"How do you know it's not morning?" Chaz asked indignantly.

"Because I'm still exhausted," Todd grumbled.

"It's about time you all woke up," Ivan said, and a

176

light flicked on overhead. We all gasped as the sudden brightness accosted our eyes.

"Nice hair," Todd quipped, and I shoved it off my face to glare at him.

"What's wrong?" Chaz asked gently, putting a hand on my shoulder.

I shrugged her off, looked down at the blanket we'd all slept on, hoping to spot my lost hair tie. "Nothing," I muttered. "I just lost my stupid hair tie, that's all."

"What's a hair tie?" Todd asked.

"Here it is!" Chaz said triumphantly, scooping it up and handing it to me.

"Thank you," I sniffed. I let them think I'd been crying over a lost hair tie. It was better than admitting how hopeless I felt. I squared my shoulders and turned to Ivan. "We need a map of the compound. Do you know where we can find one?"

"I might." Ivan nodded. "But a map isn't going to tell us the location of the Noah's headquarters. From what your mother told me, that is kept top secret."

"That's okay," I said, sitting down to slide my boots back on. "We still need a map." I glanced up at Ivan. "Do you know where supplies are kept?"

"I know they are kept in multiple locations," Ivan said, "but I'm not sure where any of them are."

I nodded. "Okay."

"Will you stop saying okay?" Todd asked. "It's too early, and if you say it one more time I can't promise I won't smack you purely on reflex."

"Sorry," I muttered, thinking hard. "We need a way to blend in here. There is no way we can walk around like this," I said, gesturing to our clothes. Chaz, Todd, and I were still wearing the bright blue jumpsuits of the lab, and even in their stained and tattered condition, the red dinosaur badge on the left shoulder stood out like a beacon. Ivan wore a dark brown tunic, a rope slung across one shoulder and wrapped around his waist, his pants a worn and supple black fabric I'd never seen before. None of us was going to be mistaken for a citizen of East Compound.

"That, I might be able to help you with," Ivan said, eyes twinkling. "Sky," he said, "you come with me. The rest of you wait here."

"But!" Todd protested.

"If I wanted to hear about your butt, I would have asked," Ivan said coolly, and with that he opened the door and slipped out. I scrambled to follow him.

"Not what I meant," I heard Todd mutter as I eased the door shut behind myself. I grinned at Ivan in the dim light of the tunnel.

"I didn't know you could be funny," I accused.

"Who's being funny?" Ivan asked, his face completely

straight. I sputtered, but then the corner of his mouth twitched up in the tiniest of smiles.

"Anyway," I said, "where are we going?"

"Do you fancy a shower?" he asked, heading down the tunnel at a brisk jog.

"A shower?" I asked, hurrying to keep up. "Did you really just say shower?"

"I did," Ivan said.

"Yes." I grinned. "But how is taking a shower going to help anything?"

"The locker rooms attached to the bathrooms have places for people to store their clothing while they bathe. We are going to be helping ourselves to some of that clothing. You were right when you said we needed a way to blend. Your mother always used to meet me at the entrance with a compound uniform. She'd insist I shave my beard for those visits too," he said, tugging at the white hair that stretched down past his chest.

"I see," I said, trying to picture Ivan without his beard and failing.

"If I remember correctly, the nearest bathroom isn't far," he went on. "It's early yet, so if we can make it into the showers before any compound residents come in, we should be fine. Find yourself a shower stall and shut the curtain. Get the water running and wait until at least a handful of people have started their own showers.

Then slip out, steal enough for you and Chaz, and meet me back at the utility room. Luckily we are in one of the more heavily populated sections of the compound, so we have a good chance of going unnoticed, but it's still best if we are never seen together. One person that they don't recognize can easily be dismissed, but even this place isn't large enough for a pack of strangers to walk around without being questioned."

"Okay," I said, "I think I can do that."

"Don't think it," Ivan said gruffly, "know it."

I nodded. A moment later we rounded a corner, and I saw two large metal doors embedded in the side of the tunnel. A large plaque above them announced that this was RESTROOM #5. Ivan jogged for the entrance, and I followed, looking left and right down the empty tunnel. One of the doors was marked for women, and the other for men. Without anything but a nod, Ivan disappeared into the men's. I took a deep breath and headed into the women's.

It took everything in me not to gasp at the size of the place, and I realized that I must be standing in the basement of one of the skyscrapers. Thick pillars held up the ceiling that hung low over my head. Dented metal lockers of all shapes and sizes lined one of the walls like mismatched soldiers, while the other wall had been turned into a line of showers. Divided by small curtained stalls, each showerhead hung down from a thick pipe that stretched the length of the room. A stack of dingy gray towels sat on a bench beside the showers, and I turned slowly, taking in the far wall with its sinks and mirrors. I wanted to inspect every nook and cranny, but a sound behind me had me grabbing a towel and scurrying into the closest shower stall seconds before the bathroom door opened and a bunch of talking and laughing women entered. I hurriedly turned on my shower, and icy water shot from the showerhead, soaking me instantly. Trying not to gasp, I ducked out of the worst of the spray, and carefully peeled off my now-drenched blue uniform. Wadding it into a ball, I shoved it on one of the shelves. My leather boots came off next and went up on a second shelf, away from the spray of damaging water. If I'd learned one thing about topside life, it was that good footwear was vital.

Luckily, the water warmed up quickly, and even though my heart was hammering, I allowed myself to revel in the heat and the feeling of being clean. The soap in the dispenser on the wall was an unhealthy green color and smelled oddly minty, but I didn't care. Gobs of it went onto my hair and body as I scrubbed away layers of sweat and dirt. Meanwhile, outside my shower stall, the ladies continued to talk and gossip about husbands and extended work shifts while they undressed and entered their own shower stalls. I listened in on their conversations, trying to judge how many of them were in there. Five? Maybe a few more? When should I make a run for it? Ivan hadn't been very specific. I bit my lip as I scrubbed my hair for the fourth time.

A few minutes later another group of people entered, and I could tell by the giggles and squeals that this crowd was younger. Peeking out of the corner of my curtain, I saw a few girls around my age shoving gray uniforms into lockers. Making a quick mental note of which lockers they used, I ducked back behind my curtain and rinsed the last of the soap out of my hair, and twisted it into a knot on top of my head. The girls entered their own showers, and I turned mine off, wrapping the threadbare towel around myself. I smiled a little at the familiar scratchy feel of it. At least some things about North and East Compound were alike.

I shoved my soggy blue uniform and boots under my arm. There would be questions if they were spotted, but a lifetime of conserving resources wouldn't let me throw them away. The boots especially were the difference between life and death topside, and if I survived this, I was going to want them. A quick glance out of my shower revealed the room to be empty, everyone occupied inside their own curtained shower

182

stall. I went for it. Darting out of the shower, I wove my way through the minty-smelling steam that filled the room and raced on silent feet to the lockers. I pulled the closest one open. Inside was a dirty crumpled uniform as well as a folded and neatly pressed uniform. I was about to snatch the clean one, but grabbed the dirty one at the last second instead, reasoning that it wouldn't be as easily missed. The faint odor of sweat clung to its wrinkled folds as I pulled it on and zipped it up the front. It was a little baggy and the legs were at least an inch too long, but it would have to work. Opening the next locker, I found two more discarded and dirty uniforms and grabbed them too. Maybe one of them would fit a little better than the one I had on, and Chaz could have this one.

I was about to go when I noticed the neatly placed compound-issued shoes on the bench next to the lockers, the same dull gray as the uniforms. How could I have forgotten shoes? One pair went on my feet and I grabbed another two pairs, then beat a hasty retreat out the door, my arms full.

A few moments later I was back in the dim tunnel heading toward our hideout, and I allowed myself a shaky sigh of relief. I'd made it. And to top it all off, I'd gotten a shower out of the deal. One or two people passed me as I walked, but dressed in my new gray compound uniform, I didn't even get a second glance. Minutes ticked by, and I began to worry that I'd missed our hidden door. It was, by its very nature, hidden, and I hadn't paid particular attention to its location when I'd left with Ivan that morning. When I spotted the helicopters and the landing pad in the distance, it confirmed I'd gone too far. Turning around, I headed back down the tunnel. It was getting more crowded now. How was I going to get into our hideout unnoticed? Walking as close to the side of the tunnel as possible, I used my fingertips to brush across the smooth concrete, feeling for the lip of the door, painfully aware of the stolen uniforms under my arm only partially concealing the dripping blue lab uniform and my boots.

Finally, I spotted a familiar-looking scratch in the concrete floor I'd noticed earlier just as my fingers hit the slight edge of the door, and I froze as I heard the sound of running feet coming from behind me. Whirling, I saw five marines charging from the helicopter bay, one of them shouting into a radio. In the distance a faint alarm sounded, and my breath caught in my throat as panic wrapped its icy fingers around my neck and squeezed. It was as though the very air had frozen in my lungs, leaving me rooted to the spot as I watched them race toward me. And for a second, I was back at North Compound again, face-to-face with an electrified gate. I'd been just as trapped then as I was now, staring down a different tunnel with no hope of my best friend saving me this time. He would never rescue me again. In that instant of terror, I missed Shawn with a ferocity that made everything inside me twist painfully. I glanced around at the pipe-riddled walls of the tunnel wildly. Opening the hidden door behind me and condemning Todd and Chaz wasn't an option, so I was going to have to make a run for it. But where? A second later, the marines ran right past me. It took me a moment to realize it. Stunned, I turned to watch them pass. Not one of them even looked at me.

Before I was fully aware of what I was doing, I'd turned and followed them. It made no sense. Every survival instinct ingrained in me was telling me that I should run, not walk, in the opposite direction. But I didn't. An uneasy feeling was tugging at my guts that I knew wasn't just an aftereffect of my panic moments before.

The marines' behavior was odd. I'd lived in North Compound my entire life and had only ever seen the marines act like that once. It had happened three years back when an upper-level tunnel had collapsed. Everyone had panicked, terrified that dinosaurs might finally breach our carefully constructed barriers. None had, but everyone had talked about the incident for months.

You aren't in North anymore, I reminded myself as I hurried to keep the marines in sight. If I was going to navigate East successfully, I was going to have to remember that. A few other spectators in gray compound uniforms stopped what they were doing to run after the marines too, confirming my suspicions that this was in fact an odd occurrence. I rounded the corner by RESTROOM #5 and froze. The marines had entered the men's bathroom and some of them were already coming out, guns held at the ready. The crowd was growing, and I glanced around in surprise. Ivan had been right about this section of the compound being more heavily populated; there had to be at least fifteen people already, and I could see a few more jogging down the adjoining tunnels to investigate. Someone jostled me roughly from behind, and I was suddenly standing at the front of the pack as angry shouts erupted from inside the bathroom, followed by a few strangled screams, gunshots, and a loud thump.

My hand went over my mouth as I swallowed my own scream, because now I knew what was going on. No sooner had everything clicked into place than Ivan was pulled from the bathroom. Two marines flanked him on the right and left, each holding on to an arm as though it was a snake that might bite. Three more marines followed them, guns drawn and trained on my grandfather. Ivan's lip was split, and he had a cut on the side of his head, but the most alarming thing was the small bright-red hole in the shoulder of his newly acquired gray compound uniform. He'd been shot.

"Someone spotted him trying to steal," whispered a voice from behind me. "That's how they knew he didn't belong." I stiffened, unable to take my eyes off Ivan as I became uncomfortably aware of the bulky mound of stolen goods still held under my own arm.

"Where did he come from?" another voice answered back. "Did you see? He's missing an arm!"

"I have no idea. I'm sure his presence will be explained at the next assembly."

"They won't wait for an assembly. This is too big. Keep your port on you. I bet they do an emergency broadcast."

"I don't like the look of him. The marines should have shot to kill."

This last comment had me gritting my teeth to keep from telling those people off. The marines marched Ivan right past the crowd of onlookers. My hands balled into fists around my stolen uniforms, and tears burned behind my eyes. Ivan had his head up, staring defiantly at the crowd, and I knew the exact moment he saw me. His face softened for a fraction of a second, and he gave me the smallest of nods. An instant later his eyes were back on the crowd, blue and angry. It was time for me to get out of there. In the chaos of Ivan's arrest, no one had noticed the other stranger in their midst, but I knew their preoccupation wouldn't last long. Turning, I began slipping back through the crowd, murmuring apologies as I went.

Once I was clear, I headed back toward our hideout, my mind racing. It took everything in me not to sprint for safety. Instead, I forced myself to walk, not too slow, not too fast. Five minutes later I was back and was just reaching for the hidden doorway when I heard voices ahead. Thinking fast, I dropped to one knee, my pile of wrinkled uniforms and soggy boots partially concealed at my side, and made a show of lacing up one of my compound shoes. Glancing up through my eyelashes, I saw two men come around the corner, talking animatedly as they each pushed large metal carts filled to the brim with tangled coils of black hose. Luckily neither of them even glanced at me. As soon as they disappeared around the bend in the tunnel, I slipped inside the pitch-black room and shut the door behind me.

"Freeze or I shoot," said a low voice in my ear. I jumped, dropping my armload of stolen goods.

"Don't shoot," I squeaked.

"I told you it was going to be Sky, you big idiot" came Chaz's voice from the darkness to my right, sounding exasperated. A moment later the light flicked on to reveal Todd, bow drawn, pointing about three feet too far to my right and blinking in the sudden glare.

My heart was hammering, and I put a hand to my chest, bending over in relief. It took me a minute, but I finally straightened again and glared at Todd.

"That voice was you?" I asked. "Why in the world did you do that?!"

"You guys were gone for a really long time," he said defensively. "And then we heard the marines go by and the shouting, and I don't know, I thought you'd been caught and they'd forced our location out of you. I'm not going down without a fight."

"Or," Chaz offered, "you could be a complete buffle brain. I told you all you'd accomplish was scaring Sky or getting creamed by Ivan. Look at her. She's as white as a sheet."

"Ivan was arrested," I interrupted, stooping to scoop up the uniforms I'd dropped.

"That must be what we heard!" Chaz gasped.

I nodded, and the tears I'd been holding back ever since I'd seen Ivan ran down my cheeks. It had been so nice to have him around, to have someone else calling the shots. Now that he'd been captured, the full responsibility of everything was squarely on my shoulders, and the weight of it made anxiety bubble inside me like hot acid. I quickly wiped my tears away with the back of my hand in irritation. I did not have time to cry. "I'm not exactly sure how he got caught," I explained. "We were both supposed to sneak into the bathroom, take a shower, and steal some uniforms on the way out. It worked fine for me. But a citizen must have spotted him stealing the uniforms." I squeezed my eyes shut, trying to push away the image of that awful hole in Ivan's shoulder. Someone gave my shoulder a friendly squeeze, and my eyes popped open to see Chaz's concerned face peering into mine. Giving myself a firm shake, I bent down to pick up the two uniforms I'd stolen, thankful that I'd grabbed an extra one since Ivan obviously wouldn't be getting Todd's.

I quickly sized them up before thrusting one at Chaz. She took it, still looking stunned. Taking Todd by the shoulders, I turned him around roughly so he faced the brick wall.

"What are you doing?" he yelped, twisting his head to look at me. "I said I was sorry. What happened to Ivan?"

"You are going to have to wear the uniform I have on," I explained. "It's way too big on me, and it would be noticed. I think this other one is smaller."

When Todd still looked confused, Chaz groaned.

"She needs to change clothes. So will you turn around already?"

"Oh," Todd said, his face blushing a bright red. "Okay."

When I peered over his shoulder, his eyes were squeezed shut. Reassured, I quickly got out of the baggy uniform and put on the other one I'd stolen. Thankfully this one fit much better, although it smelled marginally worse. It wasn't a perfect fit like compound uniforms were supposed to be, but close enough. Chaz slipped into hers as well, and I nodded in satisfaction. I'd been spot on with her size.

"Your turn," I told Todd. Chaz and I both turned to face the wall as Todd scrambled into his uniform.

"Now what?" he asked a moment later, and I turned to see him wearing the bland gray of the compound. The sight was jarring somehow. I'd only ever seen Todd in the rich hunter green of the Oaks or the vibrant blue of the lab. The gray seemed oppressive on him somehow, much more than it ever had on Shawn and me.

"Putting on the uniforms is as far as I've gotten," I admitted, averting my eyes to stare at the crumbling brick wall in front of me so I wouldn't have to see the look of disappointment on Todd's face. Across from me, partially detached from the bricks, was the rusty iron ladder. I'd noticed it upon first entering the room the night before but promptly forgotten about it. Although with the thick coating of brick dust and rust, it did blend into the wall. Following it up, I saw that it led to a square metal plate in the ceiling.

"We should see what's on the other side of that," I said, pointing up.

Todd cranked his head back to look at the ceiling. "What is it?"

"Hopefully a way out," I said, walking over to the ladder.

"I thought we just flew eight hours and risked our necks to get into the compound," Chaz protested. "Now you want to get back out again?"

"No." I shook my head and rubbed my sweaty palms on the sides of my pants. "But I want to know if that's a way out of here in case this all goes badly."

"It's going to go badly." Todd frowned. "Look at what just happened to Ivan."

"Todd," I said, turning to look him in the eye. "There is a new rule. If it's not helpful, don't say it. Pointing out how hopeless everything is isn't helpful." I tried hard to keep the frustration out of my voice, knowing that most of it had to do with losing Ivan and not Todd's comments, but I wasn't sure I succeeded completely.

"Sorry," Todd muttered.

I sighed. "Think of it this way," I tried again, more kindly this time. "When we were topside, you were the expert, right? You knew what we should and shouldn't do to survive."

"Right," Todd said, and his chin tilted up just enough to show he was more than a little proud of that fact.

"Well," I went on, "down here, I'm the expert." I frowned. "Sort of. Would it have been helpful if I had been reminding you every two seconds topside how dangerous it was? How a dinosaur might get us at any moment?"

"No," Todd admitted grudgingly. "It would have been annoying."

"There it is!" Chaz grinned. "I knew you'd catch on eventually." Todd made a face at her, but I could tell from his expression that my point had sunk in. Satisfied, I turned and gave the ladder a tentative tug to see if it would hold my weight. Two more rungs popped loose from the brick, raining dust down on us. Not an encouraging sign, but not enough to make me abandon the idea.

"That seems safe," Todd said drily from behind me.

"Todd," I warned.

"That was sarcasm," he protested, "totally different. And sarcasm can be incredibly helpful." He shouldered past me to inspect the ladder himself. "I was letting you know it didn't seem safe before you climbed it and broke your neck."

Chaz groaned from behind us, and I had to suppress a smile. Todd was impossible sometimes, but right at that moment, he reminded me of Shawn. A feeling that was both comforting and incredibly lonely all at the same time.

"Do you think it will hold me?" I asked.

"Yes," Chaz said, at the exact same time that Todd said no.

"Only one way to find out," I said as I grabbed a rung and began pulling myself up hand over hand. The iron creaked and groaned, but by some miracle it held. A minute later I'd made it to the top to inspect the metal plate. It was thick, with no apparent lock on it. But that couldn't be right. The engineers who had helped convert the subway tunnels into East Compound never would have left an entrance unlocked. Unless, I thought, as I ran my fingers over the rough metal, they really hadn't known about this entrance like Ivan had said. Something small off to the left of the plate caught my eye, and I leaned in closer, squinting against the dim light. My breath caught in my throat when I realized what I was looking at. There, etched in the stone, was the image of a dove holding an olive branch, and I knew instinctively that I was looking at the symbol for the Colombe. I reached for it with a trembling hand. Someone, maybe even my mother, had carved this into the stone. Tears burned against the backs of my eyes, and for a second, things didn't feel quite so hopeless. Tilting my head, I pressed my ear against the metal plate, listening hard. All I could make out was the softest of rustlings.

Well, I thought, let's hope this isn't a horrible mistake. It took some muscle, but with a creak, the plate lifted a few inches. Immediately a flood of dust, sticks, and rubble cascaded down on my head. I let the plate close, coughing hard as I tried to blink the grit out of my eyes. Below me, I heard Todd and Chaz yelp as the debris that had missed me hit them.

"Are you okay?" I called softly when I could finally breathe again.

"Been better," Todd said, brushing at the sticks and dirt that now liberally covered his uniform. Before I could lose my nerve, I opened the hatch again. This time, less dust came through and I was able to shield my eyes enough that it didn't blind me. When it finally cleared, I looked out at what had to be the inside of a building, although something felt off about that. The walls were too far apart to be a building. Littered around the hatch were piles of overgrown rubble. Weeds, vines, and even a few small trees had sprouted, making their home among the garbage left behind by humans hundreds of years ago. A few beams of light streamed in from an opening at the far end, and I squinted to make out what looked like a particularly large mound of dirt with smooth white ovals perched in its center. My mind barely had a second to register that I was looking at a dinosaur nest before something let out an angry bellow and a gigantic square head with a sharp beak thrust itself into the gap underneath the entrance plate. I yelped, barely pulling my fingers back before the lethal beak took them off. The plate dropped and the dinosaur's thick snout was caught for a second. It squealed in protest before yanking its head backward, allowing the hatch to clang shut. Drops of blood, not mine thankfully, dripped from the plate onto my shoulder as I clutched the ladder, breathing hard.

"What was that?" Todd called.

"The reason we won't be using this as an exit," I said as I began climbing down shakily.

"Are you okay?" Todd asked when I reached the ground again.

I nodded, staring back up at the metal plate. "It's a nesting area," I explained. "I didn't get a good look at the dinosaur, but based on that gigantic head and the beak, I'd say a triceratops?" I glanced at Chaz for confirmation.

"I doubt it was a triceratops. I got a look at the snout when it came through. Triceratops aren't quite that narrow through the nose. Maybe it was a centrosaurus or even a pentaceratops." She sighed, looking wistful. "Now that would really be something."

"Yeah," Todd said drily. "It would be a real honor if Sky had gotten eaten by one of those."

Chaz snapped out of her wistful haze and looked at Todd in surprise. "Oh, ceratopsians aren't carnivores, so they'd never eat Sky. They are extremely territorial about nesting grounds, though, and they can be deadlier than a T. rex. Their heads are some of the most lethally designed in nature."

I shut my eyes, trying to remember the sketch I'd made of a pentaceratops in my journal. Which, unfortunately, was still back at Boz's lab. "I bet it was a pentaceratops," I said.

Todd groaned. "You two are impossible. The only really important things you need to know about dinosaurs are if you can eat them or if they can eat you."

"What matters is that we can't use that as an exit." I sighed.

"Okay," Todd said. "But before we worry about exits, let's worry about finding my mom and stopping the Noah's plan." He smiled broadly and elbowed me in the ribs. "Did you see that?" he asked. "Helpful."

Chaz snorted. "Congrats."

"You're right," I said. "We need to get going."

"Which brings us back to the question I originally asked," Chaz said, crossing her arms. "Where are we going? We need a plan."

I bit my lip. "We need to find a map of the compound. And don't ask me how we do that," I warned Todd before he could interrupt me. His jaw snapped shut with an audible click. I sighed. "I'm still working on that. Once we have a map, we start searching for the Noah's headquarters. Ivan seemed to think that our plug could do the most damage there, and since we only have one shot, we need to make it count." Taking a deep breath, I inspected Todd and Chaz. Stepping forward, I busily brushed off the last bits of dust that had dropped on them when I'd opened the hatch. Before she could protest, I used the last of our water to smooth down Chaz's spiky hair. No one in the compound had hair like that. Satisfied that they'd pass a cursory inspection, I gave myself a once-over. The dinosaur blood on my shoulder was unfortunate, but other than that I was okay. I put my hand up to my hair to smooth it and froze.

"What's wrong?" Todd asked.

I turned to them, wide-eyed. "My hair," I said.

"What about it?" Todd asked. "It doesn't look that

bad. In fact, it's downright tame compared to the usual mess it's in."

Chaz elbowed him hard in the ribs with a groan of exasperation. "What?" Todd said defensively. "It usually looks like a squirrel or something tried to nest in it!"

"It's red," I hissed.

"Right . . . ," Todd said slowly, looking to Chaz for support. "Am I supposed to understand what you're talking about or is this some kind of girl thing?"

I rolled my eyes. "I have to do something to cover my hair," I explained. "It's an unusual color, and it won't take long for people to realize they've never seen me before. I got lucky earlier that it wasn't noticed."

"Want me to cut it off?" Todd offered, pulling out the small knife he'd received from Ivan.

I considered the idea for a moment, then shook my head. "No. A bald girl would stand out just as much as a redheaded one would. Besides," I said, giving the knife a dubious look, "I can't imagine you'd do a real good job using that thing."

"So what you're saying is that you'd like to keep both your ears." Chaz grinned. Todd looked slightly insulted, but she just pushed past him to pick up one of the discarded jumpsuits that lay in a heap on the floor. She grabbed the fabric between her teeth and ripped off a long section from one of the legs. With the ease of years of practice, she deftly wound the fabric around my head, tucking loose red curls inside the makeshift turban. When she was done she stepped back to survey her handiwork.

"There," she said with a satisfied nod. "That should do it."

"It's, um, interesting," Todd said.

Chaz shrugged. "I used to have to do this every time I went in the pterosaurs' cage. They confused a good head of hair with prey a little too often. Eventually I just cut it," she said with a gesture at her head. "It simplified things." I nodded, grateful for her ingenuity. It wasn't perfect, but it would work.

"Time to go," I said. "Everything we brought from topside stays in here." Todd looked about to protest, but must have seen something in my face that made him reconsider. Instead, he grudgingly took his bow off and emptied his pockets. Once Chaz had done the same, we were ready.

"You need to follow my lead out there," I said. "And it might be best if you didn't talk at all," I told Todd. "Our cover will be blown in seconds."

"Thanks for the confidence," he grumbled.

"Remember when you made me carry my bow around for an entire day before you taught me to shoot?" I asked. He nodded. "This is a lot like that," I said. "Compound life is different than topside life."

"Does Chaz get to talk?" he asked.

"She does," I said. "Lab life is close enough to compound life that she'll be okay." Chaz grinned smugly at Todd, who scowled. "Are we ready?" I asked.

"As we'll ever be." Chaz nodded, her grin of moments before nowhere to be seen. I pressed my ear to the door, as I'd seen Ivan do that morning. Hearing nothing, I put my hand on the handle, ignoring the slight tremor of nerves, and pressed down.

"Then here we go," I said as I opened the door and stepped out into East Compound.

CHAPTER
12

I quickly shut the door behind us. Disembodied voices drifted from either end of the immense tunnel, but no one was in sight.

"Look here," I said, quickly pointing down at a distinctive scratch in the concrete floor. "Remember that. I almost couldn't find the door last time." I gave them a second to look and then turned and walked briskly down the tunnel in the direction of the bathroom Ivan and I had visited that morning. Todd and Chaz hurried to follow me.

"Look like you are going somewhere," I whispered, flashing a quick smile at a group of men who had come around the curve of the tunnel. "There is very little downtime in a compound," I went on as soon as they had passed us.

"Got it," Chaz said. Todd just nodded, his eyes flicking nervously from the dim lights above us to the worn concrete below. The tunnel got busier and busier as we walked. People went about their business, chatting to one another about work schedules and the meal menu for the week. I even heard a few people discussing Ivan's arrest, and it took everything in me not to stiffen as they gossiped about how the criminal should be punished for attempting to steal. Thankfully, no one's gazes lingered on us for more than a second. We made it past the bathrooms, and I saw that they still had two marines posted out front, not letting anyone in. A few people grumbled about this, complaining that the next bathroom was over a half mile away. We walked on by. Every nerve in my body buzzed; any second someone could realize that we didn't belong and sound the alarm. But no one did.

"This is so weird," Todd said, looking up and down the tunnel. I looked too, on high alert, but nothing was out of place.

"What's weird?" I asked.

"This!" Todd said, gesturing around himself. "Everyone is walking around unarmed, relaxed."

Chaz wrinkled her forehead in confusion. "It was like this at the lab too."

"Sort of," Todd said. "But not really. For one thing, you had those giant swimming dinosaurs outside the window, and who can relax with those things inches away? Plus, there were still dinosaurs on almost every level. There was a certain degree of awareness, of caution. Everyone down here just seems so . . . so . . ." He shrugged helplessly. "It feels like one of my senses has gone dead or something."

I nodded. He was describing the exact opposite of what I'd experienced going topside for the first time. The world had suddenly contained too many sounds, smells, colors, and tastes. I'd almost forgotten what it was like in the compound: the recirculated scentless air, and the calm feeling of safety.

"It's why people moved underground in the first place," I explained. "So they could live without fear."

"Dumbest idea ever," Todd muttered. "What this place needs is a good dinosaur infestation."

I snorted, but before I could reply we came around a corner, and entered what had to be one of the old subway stops where people had been able to get on and off the trains. To our right were stairs leading up to a long narrow platform. The words "Canal Street" were spelled out in chipped yellow and orange tile up and down the tunnel wall. All along the platform, people sat leaning against the thick metal support beams that held up the ceiling, eating from compound-issued gray trays. The familiar smell of roasted potatoes filled the air, and my stomach rumbled. It was breakfast time, I realized, and this must be where people could come to get their meal allotments.

"Any chance we could get something to eat?" Todd whispered in my ear.

I shook my head. "We don't have the proper meal tickets."

"Well," he said, "how do we get those? I'm starving."

"Just keep walking," I growled.

"Really?" Todd groaned. It was only then that I noticed that Chaz was no longer near us. I whipped my head around in a panic before I saw her standing underneath the platform, where a long narrow shelf had been built into the wall of concrete. A few people were standing around chatting while they waited for their port to charge in one of the many electrical outlets located in a special strip along the wall. And there was Chaz, standing shoulder to shoulder with them as though she did this every day, turning her head this way and that as she studied the charging ports with interest.

"Chaz," I hissed, not wanting to draw too much attention to ourselves. She jumped guiltily, turned quickly away from the shelf, and hurrying back over to us, her hands jammed in the pockets of her uniform. "Stick with me," I admonished. "You're worse than Todd."

"Hey," Todd started to protest, but when he saw the look on my face his jaw snapped shut. The people standing along the charging bar were starting to give us odd looks, so I hurried my friends down the tunnel again. We'd barely made it twenty steps when a high-pitched beeping noise rang out. I froze, glancing around me in terror as I tried to figure out what was happening. Was it some kind of alarm? Had we been spotted?

Up and down the tunnel people were stopping as they each produced a port screen, staring down at it as though waiting for something.

"What is this?" Todd asked. "It's the weirdest thing I've ever seen."

"I think it's a compound-wide announcement," I whispered under my breath.

"Hey," Todd said, interrupting my thoughts. "Where did you get that?"

"Get what?" I asked distractedly as I tried to catch a glimpse of what was on the port screen of a woman a few yards to my right.

"Not you; Chaz," Todd said, pointing to where Chaz stood with, of all things, a port screen in her hands. Peering over her shoulder, I saw the words COMPOUND ANNOUNCEMENT in large bold letters flashing on the screen, along with a small digital timer busily counting down the seconds until the announcement. We had only thirty left to wait.

"It would be really great if you could explain what in the world is going on," Todd hissed in my ear as he craned his head to see the screen.

"It's a way to get information out quickly. North did this sometimes if they needed to tell us something before an assembly." I elbowed Chaz in the ribs. "Where did you get the port?"

"There were a bunch of them charging on that platform we just passed," she murmured without taking her eyes off the screen. "I swiped one. I thought it might come in handy."

"You thought right," I said. Before I could say anything else, the face of the Noah flashed onto the screen and my blood ran cold. We'd had compound-wide announcements at North Compound before, but never directly from the Noah. Nervous murmurs reverberated up and down the tunnel, letting me know that this wasn't the norm here either.

"Good morning, citizens of East," the Noah said, his face serious, pale eyes concerned. "As many of you have heard, an intruder was apprehended and arrested this morning in the southern wing as he attempted to steal from compound residents. I know this alarmed many of you. And while this issue will be more formally addressed in this week's assembly, I want to make you aware of a few things. The first is that this intruder is a criminal who snuck aboard a shipment of grow lights from North Compound."

A picture of Ivan flashed on the screen, and I sucked in a breath. He was barely recognizable as the man I'd followed to the compound bathrooms just that morning. Both eyes showcased large purple bruises, and his nose was dripping blood and obviously broken. His white beard hung in bedraggled clumps, and his shoulder sported a bloody bandage. I wondered for a second why the Noah was claiming Ivan was from North Compound before I remembered that no one in the compounds knew anyone lived topside. Ivan's image disappeared and the Noah's face filled the screen again.

"Because of his dangerous nature and the threat to our people, our marines took swift action. They are to be commended for bringing him in so quickly and efficiently." The Noah cleared his throat and glanced down as though reading something. "While I do not want to alarm you, I do want to make you aware that we have had recent intelligence that this criminal may not have entered our compound alone. There is a strong possibility that three young juveniles accompanied him."

Todd made a strangled choking noise beside me, and I dug my elbow into his ribs, unable to take my eyes off the port screen.

"These children, also criminals escaped from North Compound, are extremely dangerous and are not to be approached. You cannot believe anything they tell you. If you see them, alert the nearest marine using the emergency locator link on your port screen. I repeat, do not approach them. We are searching our security footage, and our technology specialists assure me that if they are here, we will have images of these juveniles for you within the hour. We believe that they are between the ages of ten and fifteen. One of them, a girl, has red hair. Please be on high alert if you see any children who you don't immediately recognize." My breath caught in my throat, and my eyes flashed up to the tunnel, but luckily, the citizens of East Compound were still too engrossed in their port screens to notice that the children in question were standing only a few feet away.

"Our marines are being mobilized as we speak, working to locate these young criminals," the Noah said. "I can assure you that we are doing everything in our power to keep you safe. Thank you, citizens."

"We have to run," Todd whispered, eyes wide as everyone around us looked up from their ports and began muttering worriedly to one another. A man to our left was staring at us suspiciously. A moment later he was walking directly toward us, a wary look on his face.

Before I could stop him, Todd took off, sprinting at full speed back down the tunnel. I cursed under my breath; he'd just blown any chance we had of playing it cool and staying undetected. Chaz and I had no choice but to whirl and follow his retreating form. A few people yelled in surprise, but I didn't glance back. Any second now, they were going to push the alert button on their ports, signaling our exact location. Our only hope was to reach our hiding spot before that happened. The cool tunnel air pumped in and out of my lungs, and before I realized it, my makeshift turban flew off. I skidded to a stop to retrieve it, but not before an elderly lady spotted me and let out a shriek of alarm. I left the turban behind and tore off after Chaz and Todd, who were now a good ten feet in front of me. We were almost there. But the angry shouts echoing down the tunnel behind us were getting louder and louder. It was going to be close.

I came around one last curve of the tunnel, and spotted the scratch in the floor. Chaz and Todd were nowhere in sight. I hurtled toward the hidden doorway, and it opened two seconds before I was about to throw my shoulder into it. I flew headlong into the now-familiar circular room. Todd shut the door behind me, and Chaz appeared with a broken rung of the ladder that she thrust through the door handle, successfully locking us in.

"Did anyone see you come in here?" Todd panted.

I shook my head. "I don't know." Bending over, I propped my hands on wobbly knees as sweat poured off me. A moment later, Todd's question was answered as the sound of heavy boots reverberated in the tunnel outside, followed by loud voices calling out orders. The marines had arrived. We froze, staring at the door. Seconds ticked by, and the sounds outside the door got louder and louder, until, by some miracle, they started to fade. I glanced at Todd and Chaz in disbelief. Was it possible? Were we safe?

Todd flopped down onto the concrete floor. I let my shaky knees give way and sprawled beside him. A soft thump let me know Chaz had taken our lead. We lay there, staring at the ceiling as our breathing slowed from ragged gasps and our thundering heartbeats faded from our ears. We were alive and, for the moment, safe.

CHAPTER 13

The marines searched for us for the rest of the day without success. Our relief over our near miss wore away quickly as we realized we were trapped. Above us was a nest of very temperamental and territorial dinosaurs. And outside our door was a fleet of marines intent on bringing us directly to the Noah.

"If we step outside that door, we're caught," I said as I picked at the crumbling concrete under my feet. We'd been over this same topic dozens of times already, but it was the only topic worth talking about. I sat with my back against the wall farthest from the door, my shoulder propped against the rusted ladder. Todd was pacing back and forth like a caged animal. In sharp contrast to Todd, Chaz lay on her stomach, perusing her stolen port as though she had all the time in the world. And I guess, in some ways, she did. We had nowhere to go. No plan. And, as far as I could tell, no way out of this mess.

"And if we go up, we're dead," Todd pointed out as he made another sharp turn to pace back the other way.

"You're making me dizzy," I said, shutting my eyes and leaning my head back against the hard stone. Some of it crumbled, and bits of dust and gravel rained down into my hair. I didn't even bother to brush them away.

"Going up isn't an option," Chaz said absentmindedly as she stared at the port, sliding her finger across the screen, brow furrowed.

"Well, going out isn't an option either," Todd snapped. "Those marines have nothing better to do than walk up and down this tunnel looking for us."

"Shhhhh," I cautioned. "Keep your voice down."

He stood still, fury rolling off him in waves for another minute before his shoulders slumped in defeat. He sank down against the wall to my right and tipped his head back to join me in staring at the ceiling. Above us the square metal hatch that separated our world from the dinosaurs was surrounded by crumbling concrete. A large crack wound its way across the entire length of the ceiling before breaking off into a spiderweb of finer fractures around the metal plate. It was kind of amazing that it hadn't collapsed after all these years.

"Do you know what this compound's problem is?" Todd asked after a minute of silence.

"Other than the fact that it's being led by a man whose grand plan to free us from the dinosaurs is going to make the topside world uninhabitable?" I asked.

Todd snorted. "Yeah, other than that."

"What?" I asked, deciding to play along.

"Everyone feels too safe," Todd said. "I'm telling you, walking around those tunnels was so weird. I felt like I was on another planet. It's why those marines have nothing better to do than look for us. If they were topside, they'd be too worried about protecting their own skin to worry about a couple of kids." His words were a bolt of lightning straight to my brain. I jerked upright, my thoughts tumbling over one another as I rolled this new idea around in my head. Was it possible? It was crazy. But what if it actually worked?

"Todd," I said, jumping to my feet. "You're brilliant." Craning my head back, I stared up at the metal plate fifteen feet above me, trying to do some fast mental math.

"Thanks," he said, glancing at Chaz in confusion and then back at me. "Um. Why am I brilliant?"

I tore my gaze from the entrance above my head to grin at him. "Remember what you said when we were in the tunnels this morning?" I asked. "What you said this compound needed?"

"I wasn't allowed to talk in the tunnels, remember?" Todd asked.

I flapped a hand at him dismissively. "Right. Like that really stopped you. You mentioned you felt like you'd lost one of your senses being down here? Remember? And then you said that what this compound needed was a good dinosaur infestation?"

"Yeah," Todd said slowly, still not seeing the genius in that simple statement.

"Well," I said. "You were right. That's exactly what this compound needs. Dinosaurs!"

"What are you saying?" Chaz asked, getting to her feet and brushing herself off.

"I'm saying that we need something to distract the marines from us. Right?" They both nodded. "So we give them a distraction. A ten-ton distraction! We let dinosaurs loose in the tunnels. Everyone will be so terrified they'll be hiding out in their apartments, and the marines will be too busy to worry about a couple of kids. We'll be able to search the compound for the Noah's headquarters and everyone from the Oaks!"

I decided to ignore for a moment the fact that

East Compound was absolutely huge and that even if the marines were distracted for a week, we probably couldn't search the whole thing. Somehow that detail seemed trivial now. I felt certain that if we could just get out of this little room, we'd find the Noah's headquarters, or at least something large enough for Boz's plug to do some significant damage. I started pacing the same path Todd had taken earlier, my mind whirling. Of course, I reasoned, we would also have the dinosaurs to contend with, but given the choice between Kennedy and his marines, I think I'd take the dinosaurs.

"So let me get this straight," Todd said slowly. "You want to somehow bring dinosaurs into East Compound?"

"Yes."

"That's insane!" he cried.

I nodded. "Totally. But insane might just work. Do you have a better plan?"

"No," Todd admitted. "But you don't either. What you have is a death wish."

"It's not a bad idea," Chaz said, tilting her head to the side. "What did you have in mind?"

I glanced at Todd, who still looked unconvinced. "Do you remember the herd of carnotaurus that almost caught us at the lake before Chaz and Schwartz tranquilized them?"

"They're hard to forget," he said drily.

"The reason they came after us like that was because Shawn fell into their nest."

"Like I told you before," Chaz said, "a lot of dinosaurs are very territorial about their nesting grounds."

I smiled. "What would have happened if instead of just falling into a nest, Shawn had actually taken one of the eggs?" I asked.

Chaz grimaced. "It wouldn't be pretty."

It was everything I could do not to jump up and down in excitement as the idea took shape. "We have a nesting ground right above us. I saw the eggs and everything before I almost lost my hand. All we need to do is steal one, and those dinosaurs will tear this place apart."

"Right," Todd drawled. "And how do you recommend we do that?"

"Carefully?" I offered.

"Even if we do manage to steal one, which is suicide by the way, and by some miracle we get dinosaurs down here, which won't be easy, and we somehow avoid getting trampled to death, which might be unavoidable, then what?" Todd asked. "We still don't have the faintest clue about where to put Boz's plug or how to find my village."

"Well," Chaz said, "Sky's plan might help with that

too. Any dinosaurs we let in will have to be dealt with before the Noah can put his plan into action. Right? If nothing else, it buys us even more time. Time to find your village. Time to find Ivan. Time to come up with a better plan for stopping the bombs."

"I didn't even think of that," I said, realizing that even one dinosaur let loose in the tunnels could probably do more damage than Boz's plug. But, I amended, without disabling those bombs, we were just delaying the inevitable. And unbidden, thoughts of my best friend surfaced again, sending a fresh wave of pain ripping through my chest. Disabling bombs would have been right up Shawn's alley. He'd know exactly where to put the stupid plug so it would do the most damage. The only thing I could think of was finding where the Noah was hiding the nuclear bombs and hoping someone had conveniently left out a port screen lying around that said *bomb control* on it or something equally obvious.

Todd sighed. "Your plan is stupid. I want to go on the record for that. But I guess it will have to do."

I glanced back up at the ceiling with equal amounts of hope and terror bubbling inside of me. Breaching the barrier that had separated the dinosaurs' world from ours would make me a traitor to the entire human race. My lips twisted upward in a smirk despite myself. That was exactly what everyone at North Compound had called my dad. But my smile faded as I thought about the innocent citizens of East who were about to be thrust into the paths of dinosaurs. At least I wasn't letting loose something really dangerous. Right? They would cause just enough chaos for us to search the compound without getting arrested or shot. Todd was right. It *was* insane. But it was the only chance we had. I tried to imagine what Shawn would say about my plan and grinned. He'd hate it.

Turning back to Chaz and Todd, I nodded. "Let's do this."

My plan was easier said than done. For one thing, we would have to figure out a way for the dinosaurs to get through the tiny opening in the ceiling and then through the almost equally tiny door out to the tunnel. I was hoping that the incredibly strong pentaceratops above us would do most of the heavy lifting once they figured out we'd taken an egg, but I couldn't be sure. So the first order of business was to start chipping away at the concrete around the entrance hatch and the door. I took the lead on the entrance hatch and was pleased to discover that since it was already in the process of crumbling, it took very little effort to gouge out chunks with a knife. The small piece of concrete containing the Colombe's symbol went into my pocket for safekeeping. Unfortunately, since we had to be quiet or risk discovery, I had to transport the biggest pieces to the floor rather than letting them fall. Todd and Chaz devoted themselves to thinning out the concrete around the door that led to the compound. It was tedious, messy, choking work, but no one complained. When we called it quits hours later, my arms felt like jelly and I had so much grit between my teeth and in my eyes I didn't think I'd ever get it out.

"What time do you think it is?" I asked, plopping down on one of the only rubble-free parts of the floor that was left. My legs burned from my countless trips up and down the ladder, and I grimaced as I stretched them out in front of me.

"Late," Todd grumbled, coming over to sit beside me. He flipped his hands palm up to show me the large blisters that had bloomed across the surface.

"It's one a.m.," Chaz said, pulling out the port to consult it. "We've been at this for over eight hours."

"Do you think it will be enough?" I asked as I stared up at the ceiling.

"I hope so." Todd moaned, leaning his head against the wall and closing his eyes.

Chaz tilted her head back to look up. "I just hope the ceiling doesn't come down on our heads tonight."

"Cheerful thought." Todd yawned. "Thanks for that."

I groaned, putting my head between my knees and

shutting my eyes. "If I wasn't so exhausted, I might care."

Chaz laughed.

I sat back up and rolled my neck in a futile effort to ease the permanent kink eight hours of looking up had created. "We should get some sleep. If this is going to work, we need to set it in motion early, before the compound is up and moving."

"Fat chance of falling asleep in this," Todd said, giving a chunk of concrete by his foot a good kick. "We can't even lie down in here now."

"Do your best," I said, settling back against the wall and closing my eyes. Tomorrow, I was going to change the people of East Compound's lives forever. The thought made me feel sick, but not as sick as the thought of what would happen if the Noah carried out his plan. With that in mind, I fell asleep, hoping that Chaz's fear of the ceiling falling in wouldn't come true.

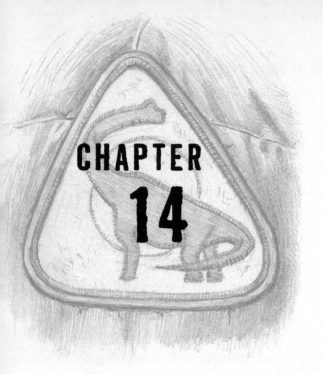

CHAPTER
14

S omeone was shaking my shoulder roughly, and
I opened my eyes to find Todd's panicked green
ones only inches from mine. It didn't take long for me
to figure out why. Loud shouts and banging were coming from the other side of our door. We'd been found.
Chaz lurched to her feet beside me, and I scrambled up
on shaking legs. Together we stared at the door in hor-
rified silence as the concrete around its frame started
to crack and crumble. We'd done too good of a job
weakening the wall that separated us from the outside
tunnel, and any second now it was going to give way
and allow the marines inside. And from the sound of
it, there were a lot of them out there.

I stood frozen for another second as my sleep-befuddled brain tried to catch up with what was happening, and then I moved, lunging for the ladder. A second later my hands were on either side of the metal hatch.

"Get ready," I shouted down to Todd and Chaz, who snapped their heads up to gape at me in surprise. They'd been so involved in what was happening at the door that they hadn't even noticed my climb. After a second's hesitation, Todd darted across the room, slinging his bow over his shoulder, followed by his quiver of arrows. It was then that I realized my own bow and quiver still lay at the foot of the ladder. Oh well, I thought, too late now. I heaved the hatch out of the way. It hit the floor above with a tooth-rattling clang. Before I could think better of it, I was pulling myself up through the hole and into the middle of a dinosaur nesting ground.

My eyes fought to adjust to the dim light as I glanced around frantically. As they did, I finally figured out where I was. This wasn't the inside of a building like I'd originally thought. I was standing on what used to be a street. Shards of broken and cracked blacktop jutted out between the mounds of rubble and tufts of weeds, and here and there a faded yellow line could be seen marking the midpoint of what used to be a road.

Above me, arching high overhead, was the underside of some kind of concrete overpass, probably part of the network of interlocking roads that cars used.

Sensing movement to my right, I whirled and saw the wide, crested head of a dinosaur turn my way, dark eyes flashing in the dim light. Letting out a snort, it lumbered to its feet so it stood silhouetted against the early dawn light coming from behind it. Chaz had been right. It was a pentaceratops. The large frilled crest on its head curved backward, while two lethal-looking horns pointed forward directly above its eyes. A small horn adorned the top of its beaked nose, while two others sprouted from the wide cheeks. Built for battling the biggest and baddest predators ever to walk the earth, the pentaceratops made a terrifying picture.

Out of the corner of my eye I caught sight of the nest I'd spied from the hatch roughly twenty or so feet away. I began backing toward it slowly, unwilling to take my eyes off the watching dinosaur. Now that it was standing, I could see it was at least fifteen feet from nose to tail and stood at least three or four feet taller than me. Its body was wide, like pictures I'd seen of old-world elephants, with a barrel chest and stocky muscled legs that reminded me of tree trunks. It cocked its head to the side, studying me. As I took another step back, I couldn't help but think that the marines down below were suddenly looking like a pretty good option.

I continued my slow progress toward the nest, trying not to alarm the creature. And it seemed to be working. The pentaceratops snorted and snapped but it didn't charge. Risking a glance back to check my progress, I barely stopped myself from stepping on a tiny blue dinosaur. At only around twelve inches or so, it was a miniature version of the giant that was still staring me down. Tiny nubs on its face showed where horns would eventually grow, and its beak, though small, was just as sharp and pronounced as the adult's. It cheeped a challenge toward me and lowered its head as though it was going to ram my ankle. Instead, its tiny legs got tangled and it tumbled over them to land in a heap. It would have been funny if this whole situation weren't gut-wrenchingly terrifying. Raising its head, it let out a plaintive cry.

As though this was a signal, the dinosaur across from me let out an enraged bellow and charged. Up and down the cavernous space came thundering replies, and I knew that, if I survived this, that noise was going to haunt my nightmares for the rest of my life. The ground under my feet began to tremble, and out of the corner of my eye I saw more crested and horned heads descending on me. It was too late to grab an egg from the distant nest. I dove, scooping up the still-bawling baby dinosaur, and ran for the entrance hatch.

I was at least ten feet away, and the dinosaur across from me was eating up the distance faster than I thought its huge frame was capable of. A sharp pain sliced into my hand, and I glanced down to find the tiny blue creature latched firmly on to the fleshy piece of skin between my thumb and fingers, with apparently no intention of letting go. It took more willpower than I knew I possessed not to drop it right there.

A second later I realized that I wasn't going to make it. The charging dinosaur was going to reach the hatch before me. Even though I had nowhere else to go and a herd of angry dinosaurs at my back, my survival instincts took over and I attempted to change direction. The uneven rubble beneath my feet gave way and I slipped and fell just as the giant pentaceratops reached the hatch. One of its huge hind feet disappeared through the entrance hole, and it fell, its chest hitting the ground with a resounding crack. It bellowed its fury, and I screamed, shoving myself backward with my free hand to get clear of its thrashing limbs. The dinosaur under my arm wriggled in alarm, its tiny muscular body thrashing to free itself.

Behind me came answering bellows and shrieks, and I struggled to my feet in time to see even more dinosaurs racing toward us from the opposite entrance.

I was trapped, my only way out plugged by a dinosaur. And then the floor gave way. With a sound like a gunshot, the trapped dinosaur disappeared, leaving a gaping hole in the floor. I blinked for a second in shock. It had actually worked. Even though I'd chipped away at concrete for hours the day before, I hadn't really been able to picture a dinosaur falling through the floor. The ground vibrated under my feet, and I jerked my head up to see that the herd of pentaceratops was getting closer by the second. Not knowing what else to do, I ran for the now-huge hole, skidding to a stop at the edge to peer down. By some miracle, the ladder was still clinging to the side, and I jumped, grabbing it with one hand just as the snap of a massive beak resounded inches above my head.

I cowered, the baby dinosaur clutched tight to my chest, as a chaotic swirl of crumbling concrete, screeching dinosaurs, and dust flew around me. Below, the fallen pentaceratops was on its feet and had its head stuck in a hole where the door used to be that led out to the tunnel. Todd and Chaz were nowhere in sight, but the dust was so thick it was nearly impossible to see. Were they down there somewhere? Hidden underneath the pentaceratops's thrashing body and huge stamping limbs? The thought made my insides clench sickeningly, and I prayed my friends were okay.

I was stuck. If I went any farther down the ladder, the dinosaur below was going to accidentally trample me. Although, considering I was still holding the baby dinosaur, I kind of deserved it. A mere three feet above me, I could see a herd of snorting, furious pentaceratops staring down from the gigantic hole in the ceiling. Huge and bulky by nature, they were thankfully unable to lever themselves down into the hole far enough to reach me. Nevertheless, they were close enough that I could smell the earthy tang of their breath every time one of them bugled a challenge. The baby dinosaur wriggled in protest at being held so tightly, letting out angry little squeals that could barely be heard above the racket.

Then, with a sound like thunder, the dinosaur below me burst through the weakened concrete wall into the tunnels of East Compound. Half climbing, half falling down the remaining feet of rickety ladder, I stared in wonder at the enormous hole it had created in the tunnel wall. It was large enough for five people to walk through side by side and reached almost to the roof of the tunnel outside. Remembering Chaz and Todd, I whirled, frantically scanning the floor of the destroyed room, but thankfully I found no traces of my friends. They hadn't been in here when the dinosaur fell. The relief at this realization was almost painful. But if they weren't here, where were they? A piece of falling rubble the size of my head missed me by inches. As I threw myself against the wall, my foot slipped on something, and I glanced down to see my bow and quiver. By some miracle they'd avoided being trampled, and I quickly yanked them free of the rubble before running for the door.

That's when I heard the screams. They echoed around me and down the tunnel, making my blood run cold. The pentaceratops was already twenty feet away, bugling angrily as it charged after a pack of retreating marines. Five women, dressed in the somber gray of compound citizens, huddled against the tunnel wall ten feet to my left. They must have been on their way home from a nightshift based on their sweat-stained and rumpled uniforms. Now they stood frozen, huddled together in hysterics as they watched the charging pentaceratops disappear around a corner. One of them, a short woman with long blond hair, fumbled to pull out a port screen and jammed her finger against it. A second later an alarm sounded, and I almost dropped the baby dinosaur to clasp my hands over my ears. The wailing siren blasted from speakers up and down the tunnel, echoing and reverberating until the noise was so loud I could feel it pulse in my bones. Which was why I didn't hear the crash behind me.

Instead, I felt the sharp sting of rock and concrete shrapnel hit my back, and I turned just in time to dive out of the way as three more pentaceratops came charging past me. Hitting the ground awkwardly to avoid smashing the baby dinosaur, I rolled out of the way and pressed my back against the tunnel wall. The compound's alarm system was drowning out even the trumpeting calls of the pentaceratops. One of them went charging out to the left, while the other two trotted off to the right. I peered back into our ruined hiding place and saw in a moment what had happened. The hole leading to the nesting ground was now twice as big as before, the edges crumbling and caving under the weight of the angry herd above. Suddenly another three-foot-wide chunk of the ceiling gave way, and two more dinosaurs spilled into the room below. Again, I threw myself backward to avoid getting smashed as they took off into the tunnels. The pack of screaming women had disappeared, and I was alone.

"Todd!" I yelled. "Chaz!" But the alarm was too loud. There was no way they'd ever hear me. I couldn't even hear me. Where had they gone? Had the marines managed to get them while I was topside? Just then another dinosaur fell into the hole, and I pressed myself back against the wall as it charged out. The tiny dinosaur under my arm squirmed angrily, trying to free itself, and I used both arms to hold it close, although I wasn't sure exactly why. It had served its purpose. But I still didn't want to let it go. It was so small. The first compound citizen it came across would kill it, and I didn't want that on my conscience. And even as I thought it, I realized how ridiculous that sounded. I'd just let loose a herd of angry, stampeding, fifteen-foot-long, five-ton dinosaurs into one of the last safe refuges for the human race, and I was worried about the fate of one tiny dinosaur? If Shawn were still alive, he would have made me drop it. But Shawn wasn't here, and now neither were Todd and Chaz.

The blaring alarm made it hard to think straight. Should I wait here and hope Todd and Chaz showed up? Follow the retreating marines? Run in the opposite direction? One thing was for sure: no one in the compound was going to be worrying about me anymore. I quickly tucked the baby dinosaur into my half-empty quiver. It immediately clamped its sharp beak onto an arrow, snapping it cleanly in two to show its displeasure. Not wanting it to do the same to my ear, I tore a strip of fabric from my compound uniform and tied its beak shut. Satisfied it couldn't get out, or take a chunk out of my face, I slung the quiver onto my back next to my bow and took off in the same direction as the retreating marines.

The tunnels were deserted. The alarm had done its job, and everyone had taken cover. I flew past the bathroom where Ivan had been arrested and the subway platform where Chaz had stolen the port. A few tunnel entrances flashed past me, and I wished again that we'd been able to find a map of East Compound. Ahead was a crossroads where five different tunnels intersected. The floor was thick with strips of discolored concrete showing where old subway tracks had merged and crossed over one another. I skidded to a stop, not sure which way to go. The alarms chose that moment to turn off. It was like I'd gone deaf, and my ears rang and throbbed in the unexpected silence. Suddenly a high, screeching roar echoed down the tunnel behind me. It was immediately followed by a chorus of answering shrieks and the rasp of claws on concrete. That wasn't the sound of one of the pentaceratops I'd let loose. For one thing, they didn't have claws. The tiny dinosaur on my back suddenly started squirming and bucking frantically. When I glanced over my shoulder, its eyes were wide and rolling as it fought desperately to escape the confines of my leather quiver. Its terror was contagious, and its message was clear. Whatever was coming wasn't going to be good.

Just as I was whirling to run, I heard a sound that stopped me dead in my tracks. Turning slowly, I stared back down the dim tunnel. I shook myself. My sleep-deprived and stressed brain had played a nasty trick on me. I listened again, but heard only the shrieks and grating of claws on stone. And whatever was making that sound was getting closer while I stood there. Move, you idiot, move, I commanded myself. But I didn't. I stayed right where I was, waiting for a sound I knew I couldn't possibly have heard.

"SKY!"

I jerked as though I'd been shot. This time, I knew I'd heard it. My feet finally started moving, and I sprinted back the way I'd come, back toward a sound I'd been convinced that I'd never hear again.

It couldn't be him.

It had to be him.

A second later Shawn Reilly burst around the corner, Todd and Chaz running hard beside him.

"Shawn!" I screamed, fully aware now that I'd lost it. It was the only explanation for why I was seeing my dead best friend running toward me. It was then that I registered that Shawn was gesturing wildly and shouting something.

"Turn around!" he bellowed. "Run the other way!" A second later, I saw why. The hole I'd created into the compound had apparently let in more than just the pentaceratops. No more than twenty feet behind them came a pack of flashing green scales. I wasn't sure what they were, but they could have been the T. rex's smaller and meaner-looking cousins. Standing roughly six feet tall, with the short, toothy snout that labeled them as a predator, they ran hunched with their front legs held in tight to their chests while their powerful back legs ate up the distance between them and my friends. I skidded to a stop and turned back the way I'd come with Shawn, Chaz, and Todd at my heels.

"Take the next tunnel on the right," Shawn yelled. We did, our feet almost sliding out from under us on the smooth concrete floor before we tore down the new tunnel. A quick glance over my shoulder revealed that two of the dinosaurs had fallen sideways trying to make the turn too quickly. The other three had stayed on their feet, their claws sliding along the floor with an earsplitting screech that made my skin crawl.

"Those are condorraptors," Chaz called, glancing back over her shoulder. "They're incredibly vicious."

"I noticed." Shawn panted, and hearing his voice sent a shock through me all over again. I reached out and touched his shoulder. It was solid. Sweaty. But solid. So this was real. He was alive. But how? I didn't have time to think about it, though, because Shawn was giving directions again.

"There's an old subway platform on the left," he

yelled. "Follow me." A surge of hope shot through me. Maybe Shawn had a plan besides running until one of the condorraptors eventually caught us. Which, up until a few seconds ago, had been mine. I saw the platform he was talking about up ahead. The condorraptors were snapping their jaws only feet behind us now.

We reached the stairs leading up to the platform, and Shawn charged up them two at a time with Todd at his heels, followed by Chaz. I brought up the rear. My right foot had barely landed on the platform when a stabbing pain lanced through my calf. I screamed, falling forward. A sharp ripping tug jerked me backward before I'd even hit the ground, and I shrieked again, scrabbling frantically for something to grab on to. There was nothing but smooth concrete under my nails, and I was yanked back another step. The pain in my leg was unbelievable, but my panic almost drowned it out completely. I didn't need to look to know that one of the dinosaurs had clamped its jaws around the meaty part of my calf and was doing its best to get at the rest of me. The rasp of claws on the narrow stairs drowned out my next scream, and I knew I'd be dead the second it managed to get its footing and some leverage.

The sharp twang of an arrow zipped past my ear and the pressure on my calf disappeared. Shawn suddenly had me under the arms, dragging me onto the platform. Chaz was there a second later, and with their help, I was hauled to my feet. I turned to see Todd fire three more arrows into the herd of snapping and screeching dinosaurs that were attempting, unsuccessfully, to navigate their way up the narrow stairs simultaneously. One of them lay motionless halfway up the stairs, an arrow in its eye, my blood dripping off its teeth. Bile rose in my throat, but before I could pull myself together enough to puke properly, Shawn and Chaz were yanking me across the platform toward a double set of stairs on the far end. They dragged me about halfway up, my calf throbbing with each step, before I remembered Todd.

Twisting out of Shawn's grip, I glanced back. Todd was running in a dead sprint across the platform, his bow clutched in one hand, an empty quiver bouncing on his back, and panic in his eyes. Behind him on the platform steps were two dead condorraptors. Unfortunately, the others had managed to use the fallen bodies as leverage to claw their way up the stairs, and three of them were hot on Todd's heels.

"He's not going to make it," I said, twisting out of Shawn's grip. My leg buckled underneath me and I slid back down the stairs on my butt. The fall jarred my injured leg, but I managed to stop myself after only a few painful steps.

"What are you doing?" Shawn cried, appearing at my side a moment later. I brushed him off. Todd had gone back for me. There was no way I wouldn't do the same for him. I pulled my quiver and bow off my back.

I thrust the baby dinosaur into Chaz's hands. She grabbed it, looking surprised. Bracing the quiver between my trembling knees, I pulled out an arrow, notched it to the string, aimed, and fired. I'd targeted the eyes, like Todd had taught us, but my shot was a little low, and just as the condorraptor opened its mouth to lunge for Todd, my arrow slammed into the back of its throat.

It went down hard. The two dinosaurs behind it tripped, becoming momentarily tangled in the fallen dinosaur's flailing limbs. I'd bought Todd the extra two seconds he needed to make it to the stairs. I turned and hobbled back up after Shawn and Chaz. Chaz was still holding the squirming baby dinosaur, and Shawn's face had turned the color of the concrete wall behind him. My bow and quiver went back over my shoulder, and I grabbed the dinosaur from Chaz as soon as I reached her. Weirdly, it stopped struggling as soon as it was back in my arms, and I was able to easily tuck it back into my quiver as I climbed. To my surprise, the climb wasn't nearly as painful as I'd expected. I wasn't sure how much damage had been done to my calf—there was an awful lot of blood I was doing my best to avoid looking at—but I must not be too damaged if my leg was still functioning. Right?

We reached the top without further incident. Below us, on the platform, the remaining condorraptors had given up attempting to squeeze their bulk between the narrow railings of the steps and were wandering off. One of them stopped to rip into the dinosaur I'd killed, and my already queasy stomach rolled again.

"This way," Shawn called, leading us at a run down one narrow hallway after another. The concrete floor sloped upward, and metal doors flashed past, all of them shut. I hoped that all the citizens of East Compound had managed to get to a secure location. The thought of those condorraptors charging into a school or apartment sector made me feel sick. I hoped that they were the only carnivores that had found their way in.

Shawn peered around a corner cautiously, and then took off again, motioning for us to follow. Dressed in the gray uniform of East Compound, he was making his way through this maze of tunnels and hallways like he'd been doing it his whole life. How was that possible? A minute later, he slid to a stop outside a metal door and quickly typed something into the keypad embedded in the wall. The door clicked, and we tumbled inside. Shawn threw a dead bolt before sagging against the door in relief. I looked around the small room, my hands on my knees as I fought to get air into my burning lungs. There was a small desk in the corner, as well as a cot with a rumpled blanket and pillow.

"We can't stay here long," Shawn said, panting. "Kennedy will send his marines to look for me as soon as they untangle themselves from those gigantic dinosaurs with the horns."

"Pentaceratops," Chaz corrected. "A relative of the more common triceratops."

"Glad to see you haven't changed," Shawn said, smiling wryly.

I finally had enough air to function again, and I stood up, making my way across the room in two steps to pull Shawn into the biggest hug of his life.

"I thought you were dead," I choked out, blinking away tears.

"Right back at you," Shawn said, pulling away and wiping at his own watery eyes.

"Yeah, about that." Todd frowned. "Why aren't you dead?"

"Gee, thanks," Shawn said drily.

"Seriously, though," Todd said, "you never came up from that elevator. We thought you drowned or got eaten."

Shawn's smile slipped away and his face darkened. "It's kind of complicated," he said. "To start with, I thought you guys were the ones who were dead. I almost didn't believe my ears when I saw the Noah's announcement yesterday. I barely let myself hope, but after I found out that they had Ivan in custody, I knew it had to be you."

"Do you know where they're keeping Ivan?" I asked. "Is he alive?"

Shawn shook his head. "The last thing I heard, he was being interrogated for information."

"First things first," Chaz said. "You need to explain how you survived and ended up here. Something smells fishy about all this."

"I agree." Todd scowled, looking around. "It seems a little convenient that you not only survived, but somehow ended up here with your own comfy room."

I glanced at Shawn as their words sank in. They were right. Something did feel off about this. In my elation at seeing him, I hadn't let myself think about it. Now that I was, I didn't like where my mind was going. I took a step back from my friend and winced as pain shot through my leg.

"Sit down," Shawn instructed, guiding me backward until I could sink down onto the bed. "I totally forgot about your leg. I think there is a first aid kit in here. Give me a second." He hurriedly yanked the small desk across the room and propped my injured leg up on it. The adrenaline of moments before was wearing off, and I realized just how badly my leg hurt. My uniform was drenched in dark red blood up to the knee, and torn down the back. Shawn crouched down in front of me, and before I had a chance to shut my eyes, he'd gingerly peeled back the sticky fabric to reveal my leg. Todd whistled in appreciation, and Chaz leaned in to get a closer look. My stomach roiled, and I looked away quickly.

The good news was that the condorraptor had only managed to grab my calf with its front teeth. Ten ragged and torn holes, each the size of my thumbnail, marched down my leg, oozing a sluggish stream of red. A purplish-black bruise stretched from my ankle to wrap around my swollen knee, making my leg look less like a leg and more like a stump of wood. Shawn poured something with a sharp smell over the puncture wounds that bubbled and sizzled. Squeezing my eyes shut, I bit down hard on my lip to keep from screaming. Whatever that stuff was, it felt like fire was racing through my veins.

"Sorry," Shawn said. He shot a quick glance at

Chaz. "Those things weren't poisonous, right?"

She shook her head. "They aren't. But they do have all sorts of bacteria and stuff on their teeth that could cause a major infection."

"That's what I thought," Shawn said, dumping even more of the stuff onto my leg. I yelped as the pain seemed to double in seconds. Moments later the stinging eased, and I hazarded another glance at my leg. Now that the blood was washed away, it didn't look nearly as bad as before, and I felt my queasy stomach ease slightly. As far as dinosaur wounds went, I'd gotten off easy.

Todd was watching Shawn clean and bandage my leg with a skeptical eye.

"Thanks for coming back for me," I told him.

"Right back at you," he said, turning to grin at me. "So has your plan worked the way you thought it would?"

"Not exactly." I winced. Just then the dinosaur on my back squirmed, making its presence known.

"Chaz?" I asked. "Would you get it out for me? So it can walk around a bit?"

Chaz moved around to my back and gingerly took the tiny pentaceratops out. She glanced quickly under the protesting dinosaur's tail before setting it on the floor.

"It's a girl, by the way," she said, smiling as the dinosaur wobbled unsteadily for a second, and then lumbered off on its tiny stout legs to investigate.

"I should be surprised that you got a pet out of this disaster, but somehow I'm not," Shawn said, not looking up from my leg.

"The plan was to steal an egg," I explained, "but things didn't go exactly the way I thought they would." I turned back to Todd and Chaz. "What happened to you guys? You weren't supposed to leave without me."

"And you weren't supposed to send a dinosaur through the roof until we were well out of the way," Todd pointed out. "Besides, the plan never involved being raided by armed marines."

"Both good points," I said. "But what happened? And how did you meet up with Shawn?"

"And Shawn still needs to explain how he survived and ended up here," Todd pointed out with a meaningful glare at Shawn. When he didn't get a response, he sighed and turned back to me. "About the time that dinosaur's leg came plummeting through the ceiling, the marines apparently gave up trying to get in the door and blasted a hole in the wall. We decided that the marines looked like a better option than getting smashed by a two-ton dinosaur."

"Actually," Chaz began, but Todd held up an impatient hand to stop her.

"Don't you dare correct me on that dinosaur's weight. The point is it was heavy enough to squash us." He shook his head in exasperation. "Anyway," he went on. "Chaz and I made a run for the opening the marines had just created, and two of them grabbed us. They only managed to hold us for about five seconds, though, because then that dinosaur fell through the ceiling and they had bigger problems."

"About four tons bigger," Chaz muttered, and Todd rolled his eyes, his jaw tight. He paused, as though daring her to say something else; when she didn't, he went on.

"Everything went nuts after that. They were trying to shoot the dinosaur, which was stupid because their bullets didn't do anything but make it mad. When it became obvious that it was going to make it into the tunnel, they ran. Unfortunately, that guy Kennedy had us at gunpoint, ordering us to retreat right along with them."

"So how do you come into all this?" I asked Shawn just as he was sitting back to survey his handiwork. I looked too, and saw that he'd encased my leg from ankle to knee in a neat white bandage. Dots of blood were already starting to seep through where the puncture wounds were, but on the whole it looked and felt a lot better. "Thanks," I said, flexing my foot experimentally.

"I hacked into the marine network as soon as I got here," Shawn explained. "So I was following their communications. I intercepted the marines with Chaz and Todd at a tunnel crossroads. To be honest, I had no idea how to save you, but then those massive dinosaurs you let in suddenly started panicking."

"That's because they could smell the condorraptors," Chaz explained.

"I never meant to let those in," I protested.

"Well, when you open up a gigantic hole into the compound, you don't exactly get to choose what decides to pay a visit," Todd pointed out.

"Never really thought of that," I admitted sheepishly. I glanced back at Shawn. "Go on," I prompted. "What happened next?"

Shawn nodded. "Well, those, what did you call them? Condorraptors? Came flying around the corner and took down one of the huge dinosaurs." He caught Chaz's look and sighed. "Sorry, sorry. They brought down a pentaceratops. In the confusion, I was able to get Todd's and Chaz's attention, and we took off down the tunnel."

"It's what triggered the condorraptors to come after us," Chaz explained. "They have a very strong chase instinct when it comes to hunting."

"That's when I saw you at the far end of the tunnel." Shawn shrugged. "You know the rest."

"Okay." I nodded; that all made sense. "But how did you end up here? In East Compound?" Shawn's brow furrowed and his mouth went tight as he glanced down. I'd only seen that look on his face one time before, and it was back at North Compound.

It had been less than a month ago, but it felt like a lifetime. Shawn had just shown me the note he found hidden in my dad's compass, the note that told me I had to deliver an information plug to the middle of Lake Michigan. He'd gotten that exact same look of guilt when I found out that he'd failed to tell me that North Compound was in the process of putting locks on all the entrances, locks that would have guaranteed that I never left on my dad's mission. Whatever he was hiding now was bad. Really bad.

"Shawn," I said slowly, pulling my leg off the desk and staring at him. "What's going on?"

He sighed, suddenly looking exhausted. His golden hair was matted with sweat and clung to his head in twisted ropes.

"Do me a favor?" he asked without looking at me. "What?"

"Don't hate me after I tell you this," he said, glancing

up quickly before returning his gaze to the floor.

"I'd never be able to hate you," I said, feeling the truth of that statement in my bones. Shawn and I had grown up together. He was more family than friend, and there was nothing he could say that would change that.

"I hope not." He sighed; then he looked up at us, his face drained of all color. "You know how we haven't been able to figure out how the Noah was tracking us? How the marines managed to follow us to the Oaks and Ivan's?" I nodded, feeling numb. "That was all my fault," he said. "I'm the tracker they were able to follow."

CHAPTER
15

I felt numb. Too shocked by Shawn's words to move or respond. Todd had no such problems.

"What?!" he roared, and without further warning, he'd launched himself across the room at Shawn. Shawn threw up his hands just as Todd tackled him, sending the desk crashing to the floor as they both tumbled across the concrete. The baby dinosaur squawked in fright and came running to cower behind my legs. Within moments, Todd had Shawn pinned and was pounding on him with his fists, yelling about his village, his mom, and Roderick.

"Stop it," I cried, lurching forward to pull them apart. Todd just batted me away and went right on whaling on Shawn, who I realized was doing nothing to fight back. He lay there, arms thrown protectively over his head, taking every blow Todd gave him. "Help me," I yelled at Chaz in desperation.

Together we managed to pry Todd off Shawn. For a second, I was worried that Shawn had been knocked out cold because he didn't make a move to stand up. Todd ripped himself from Chaz's hands and moved to jump on Shawn again. Maybe it came from a lifetime of looking out for Shawn, or maybe it was seeing him lying on the ground like that, but before I even realized I was doing it, I had my bow and an arrow in my hand and pointed at Todd. He froze, shock and betrayal on his face as he stumbled back, arms thrown instinctively in the air.

"How can you possibly stand up for him?" he growled. "Think about it. My village, Roderick, the lab, Ivan's place . . . he's been telling that Kennedy guy exactly where to find you this entire time."

My resolve wavered as I let Todd's words sink in. Turning back to my traitorous best friend, I said quietly, "Shawn, you better start talking."

He sat up, grimacing at the effort as his nose dripped blood onto his torn uniform. His right eye was already beginning to swell as a dark purple bruise spread across his cheekbone. "It was an accident," he said, wiping the back of his hand across his mouth. "But I totally deserved that."

"And we deserve an explanation," I shot back.

"I never meant to hurt anyone," Shawn said.

Todd snorted in disbelief, and I glared at him.

"My aunt asked me to test something out for her," Shawn went on as though he hadn't heard. "Months and months ago, back at North Compound. It was this emergency tracking prototype they were working on developing for the marines. It was tiny, no bigger than my pinkie nail." He held up his finger to demonstrate the size and then shook his head in disgust. "I agreed to help. It sounded cool. It was implanted in my upper arm, and they were able to track my movements throughout the school day. It was going to help the marines locate one another in an emergency, so it was all for the good of the compound. I thought I was doing something really great, you know? I even helped them untangle some of the coding so it functioned better on the marines' ports."

"So when I met you, you knew you had a tracking device!" Todd growled.

"I did," Shawn said, hanging his head. "But I thought the tracker had been disabled months ago, once they were done with the testing. And even if it hadn't been disabled, it was only supposed to work within a mile radius of the compound. It should have been completely useless within minutes of Sky and me making it topside."

"But it wasn't," I breathed.

Shawn shook his head. "No. Although I didn't know it at first. I'd completely forgotten about it until the marines showed up at Todd's village. Then I convinced myself that it was just a fluke. We were only a day's travel from the compound, and it was totally possible that the Noah would have already known about his village. But then when the marines showed up at Ivan's, I knew," he said, shaking his head. "There was no way that could have been a coincidence. Do you remember how I asked you for a knife the night after we escaped Kennedy and his marines?"

I nodded, vaguely remembering. None of us had had one, having lost them in the scuffle with Kennedy and his marines.

Shawn yanked up the sleeve of his shirt, showing a jagged cut on his shoulder, just beginning to heal.

"I wanted to slice the tracker out, but I couldn't figure out how without a knife. Finally I got desperate and used a sharp rock. I destroyed it two days before we got to the lab."

I sank down heavily onto the bed. "Why didn't you tell me about all this?"

"Well, initially, because my aunt told me not to. It was a top-secret government project, and I guess I let that go to my head. And then, to be honest, I completely forgot about it in the chaos of going topside. That is, until Todd's village." He looked at Todd, who was still fuming, arms crossed. "I can't even begin to apologize for that. It is completely, one hundred percent my fault."

"It's not," I said, shaking my head. "It's mine. I'm the reason you were there in the first place."

"It's both your faults," Todd growled.

Chaz tilted her head to inspect Todd. "Tell me, Todd, if they hadn't shown up at your village, what would you be doing right now?"

"I'd be home," he snapped. "My mom would be safe and so would everyone else."

"Right." Chaz nodded. "And in a few days or weeks when the Noah drops his nuclear weapons? What then?"

Todd sagged visibly, and his anger seemed to drain out of him as he sat down heavily on the bed next to me. Chaz turned back to Shawn. "I'm not letting you off the hook. You should have mentioned that tracker long before now. And you still need to explain how you ended up here."

"I'm so sorry," Shawn said, shaking his head.

"Stop apologizing and talk." Chaz frowned. "You said yourself that we didn't have long here. I'm not sure about you, but I have no desire to run into those marines again."

"Right," Shawn said, straightening up. "Do you remember when we were in the elevator?"

"How could I forget," Todd mumbled. "It's literally the stuff my nightmares are made of."

"Well, I'm not sure if you know this. But Schwartz was working for the Noah," Shawn said, his face twisted in anger. "Communicating with him and everything. He's the one who told them that we knew about the Noah's plan. It was just dumb luck that we ended up being in that wing of the lab when the bombs hit." When none of us reacted, he glanced around in surprise.

"We knew that," I said.

"Okay," Shawn said, looking a little unsettled. "So, one of the Noah's guys must have told him about me, the tracker, and who my aunt was, because when those doors opened, he grabbed me. The next thing I knew, I had this hose thing in my mouth, and I could breathe."

"So that's what Schwartz was working on in the elevator," Chaz cried. "It was a Water-Gil. It must have been one of the new prototypes he's been developing for underwater observation." When the rest of us just looked clueless, she sighed in exasperation. "They let you breathe underwater."

I thought back to those terrifying moments in the elevator and vaguely remembered that Schwartz had been messing with a small black box right before the elevator doors had opened.

"Whatever it was, it allowed me to breathe, and I had no choice but to swim next to Schwartz until he surfaced. And when we did, you guys were nowhere in sight. A helicopter picked us up almost immediately, and I was brought back here. The worst part was that Kennedy congratulated me. Said I'd done a great service for the human race by helping them track you." He sniffed, his face bright red with shame. "It was awful. I let him know exactly what I thought about the Noah's awful plan, and about tricking me with that tracker." He shook his head. "I thought you guys were dead, and I had nothing to lose. So they locked me up in here," he said, gesturing around. "And I've been in here ever since."

"But you aren't locked in now," I said, glancing at the door nervously.

He shook his head. "The coding system for the door locks here were super easy to crack. I also had this," he said, holding up his old familiar port screen from North Compound. I gaped at it in surprise. How had it survived the bombing?

Seeing my glance, Shawn shrugged sheepishly. "I had it in my pocket that day, and since it had a waterproof case, it survived. The marine who searched me saw that it was drenched, figured it was busted, and let me keep it. It's how I heard the Noah's announcement about you guys and hacked in to find out about Ivan. Up until then, I was just lying around here feeling pretty awful about myself and trying to figure out how to stop the Noah on my own." He shrugged. "You know, to make your deaths have some meaning."

"And did you come up with anything?" I prompted, thinking of our own feeble plan to use Boz's last lone plug.

"Sort of," he said, perking up. "I think I was able to get a message out to the Lincoln Lab."

"You what?!" Chaz cried. "How? Did anyone respond? Do you know if there were any casualties besides the conference wing?"

Shawn shook his head. "I didn't get any response." Chaz sagged visibly, disappointment etched in her every feature. "But," Shawn said hurriedly, "that doesn't mean no one survived. I had to use the same program Schwartz used to betray the lab to the Noah. They might not trust anything coming from that signal if they figured out it was Schwartz who betrayed them."

"What did you send in your message?" I asked.

"The basics of the Noah's insane plan." Shawn shrugged. "I realized that there was a good chance that none of the survivors would know about it; Boz kept things pretty top secret. I also sent them a map of East Compound with the Noah's headquarters circled."

"You know where his headquarters are?" I asked.

"I *think* I know," Shawn corrected. "I'm not positive. If you guys hadn't shown up, I was going to try to break in myself tomorrow."

"What's at his headquarters?" I asked eagerly.

"No idea," Shawn said. "But I figured I'd start smashing stuff and hope I managed to damage something important before I got caught."

"We still have one of Boz's plugs," I said. "It survived the elevator. Maybe there is something there that controls the bombs that we could use it on?"

"It's worth a shot," Chaz said. "Besides, if there isn't, we can always fall back on Shawn's plan and start smashing stuff."

Todd nodded approvingly. "I like that idea."

"The headquarters aren't the only thing I found," Shawn said, shooting Todd a wary look. "I think I know where the people from your village are too."

"Really?" Todd said, jumping up so quickly the bed almost toppled over. "Where?"

"The same place as the Noah's headquarters," Shawn said. "Grand Central Terminal." Before I had a chance to ask what that meant, Shawn's port buzzed. We all stared at it like it was a snake that might bite. Shawn quickly swiped his screen. When he looked up, his face had lost all color.

"We have to go," he said, "now. Kennedy and the marines are heading right for us."

"How do you know?" Todd asked suspiciously.

"Because my port is still intercepting their communications. That's why," Shawn snapped as he moved quickly around the room, shoving things into a bag.

"Where are we going?" Chaz asked.

Shawn threw his bag over his shoulder. "I already told you, Grand Central Terminal. Well, actually, underneath Grand Central Terminal. I'll explain more once we're on the move. We've already stayed here too long." He glanced at me uncertainly. "Can you run?" he asked.

I stood, forcing myself not to wince, and nodded. Convinced, he turned toward the door. Todd followed, but not before snatching a handful of arrows out of my quiver and shoving them in his own. I didn't argue. Of the two of us, he was by far the better shot. Turning toward the door, I was brought up short by an indignant squeak as the tiny dinosaur came rushing out from under the toppled desk to skid headfirst into my injured leg. The pain made black spots bloom in my vision, but I shook them off to pick her up.

"I almost forgot about you," I apologized as she squealed indignantly at me, proving that she'd managed to get the tie off her beak at some point.

"That's odd," Chaz said as she stared at the dinosaur.

"What?" I asked defensively as I slid her back into my now almost empty quiver. To my surprise, she made no move to bite me again.

"Where did you find the baby pentaceratops again?" Chaz asked.

"She found me, actually," I said. "I think she came out of a nest nearby that had a bunch of eggs in it."

"Well, that explains it." Chaz sighed. "She's imprinted on you."

"She's what?" I asked.

Chaz rolled her eyes impatiently. "Imprinted. Birds do it, and so do some dinosaur breeds. They attach to the first thing they see after hatching. She thinks you're her mother."

"Well, that's just great," Shawn groaned from the door. "But did you two not hear what I said about the marines? They are going to be here any minute. Move!"

We followed Shawn out the door and began to weave our way through a maze of hallways. There was a noticeable limp in my step, but the pain had settled into a dull throb. With the amount of adrenaline I had pumping through my system at the moment, I could have probably lost the entire leg and kept going. The tiny dinosaur on my back warbled and chirped as we ran. She needed a name.

"I'm going to call her Sprout," I announced as we reached a set of steep stairs and headed down.

"Really?" Shawn asked, glancing back to eye my tiny passenger.

"Really," I said with a look that dared him to argue with me. Sprout chirped nervously, and I reached a hand back to stroke her head to calm her. Thankfully, she didn't take the opportunity to take off one of my fingers. Was Chaz right? Had she really imprinted on me? And what did it mean if she had? Was I supposed to be her mother now? Shaking my head, I shoved those thoughts aside. I'd worry about it if I survived the next few hours.

"How far away are we from Grand Central Terminal?" Chaz whispered as we paused for a second to catch our breath on the platform in front of the tunnel.

"Two miles through dinosaur-infested tunnels," Shawn answered.

"And you're sure everyone from the Oaks is at this Grand Central Terminal?" Todd asked.

"No," Shawn said. "But it's my best guess. I was able to hack into the system and pull up a map of the place, and nothing showed up about the Noah's head-quarters or a prison. But," he said, holding a hand up before Todd could interrupt him, "I was also able to pull up some of the original plans of the station, blue-prints from over three hundred years ago when it was first built. They show a huge area set aside for the tech-nology that ran the subways. Well, that area no longer shows up on the current compound map."

"And we no longer use subways," I finished for him as I started to understand what he was saying.

"Exactly." He grinned. "My guess is everything in those rooms was salvaged years ago, leaving a huge empty space no one else knows about."

The sudden crack of a gunshot echoing from the tunnel we'd just left made us all jump. The marines had apparently found their way to Shawn's room. With-out saying a word, we charged down the steps into the main tunnel. Shawn took a right, and we followed at a dead sprint. We ran full-out for a good fifteen minutes before any of us felt confident enough to slow down to a brisk jog.

"So tell me about Grand Central Terminal," Todd said, barely breathing hard. "What do we need to know?"

"The original station was built a long time ago," Shawn explained between gasps of air, "like a hundred years before the pandemic."

Todd whistled in appreciation.

"The outside was beautiful," I added, remembering the pictures I'd seen of it. "It looked like something from ancient Greece."

"We don't really have time for a full-blown history lesson," Todd said with a nervous glance over his shoulder.

Shawn flapped a hand at him impatiently. "I'm getting there," he said. "Well, like fifty years or something after the original station was built, they built a skyscraper right behind it. I guess the skyscraper's construction wasn't so great, because during the chaos of the pandemic, it collapsed—right on top of Grand Central Terminal. But here is the really cool thing. The original structure of the station was so strong it stayed basically intact, just buried under twenty feet of concrete and rubble. I think grass and stuff has even grown up on top of the rubble, so the dinosaurs don't know it's down there. It's the largest and the only above-ground structure in any of the compounds. So it makes sense that it would become the center of government here at East."

"But if it's buried under twenty feet of rubble, is it

really considered aboveground?" Chaz asked.

Shawn groaned. "You're missing the point. Which is that it's huge, way bigger than anything underground, so it can house a lot of stuff. But the important thing is that it's big enough to hide a few thousand square feet without anyone being the wiser. That place had so many underground stores, restaurants, storage rooms, and mechanical areas that one or two of them could disappear from the current maps and no one would notice. That's why I think the Noah's headquarters have to be there, right underneath the floors of Grand Central Terminal." When no one said anything or looked properly impressed, Shawn sighed. "You'll understand when we get there. Which"—he pulled out his port and consulted it as we ran—"should be in just a few minutes. Turn right at this next tunnel." We did, and almost ran headfirst into two huge pentaceratops. We skidded to a stop. Chaz slipped, falling hard on her butt before scrambling to her feet and backing up hastily. She stretched her arms out, backing us up with her.

The dinosaurs' enormous bodies blocked almost the entire tunnel as they snuffled through what looked like an abandoned cart of turnips and potatoes. Their teeth crunched on the crisp roots as they devoured the hard work of the East Compound farmers. One of them looked up, inspecting us with big brown eyes.

"We need to find another route," Chaz whispered through gritted teeth. "Those guys could crush us or impale us in a minute if they wanted to."

"We can't," Shawn said with a quick glance down at the map he had pulled up on his port screen. "Every other route is going to take us miles out of our way. We need to go down *this* tunnel." The pentaceratops that had been eyeing us snorted and turned back to the cart. Lowering its head, it used one of the massive horns that arched over its eyebrows to spear a crate. With a quick flick it sent the crate crashing into the concrete wall, where it popped open, releasing a flood of small brown potatoes. The dinosaurs began eating, ignoring us completely.

"Who cares if it takes longer," Todd hissed. "We can make up the time."

"You might be right," Shawn said, consulting the map again. Suddenly we heard the sharp cadence of booted feet coming from the tunnel we'd just left, followed by someone shouting out orders. The marines.

"Well, there goes that idea," Shawn said, shoving his port back in his bag. "We have to go around."

"As long as they don't see us as a threat, we should be okay," Chaz said, biting her lip with a nervous glance behind us.

"I'll go first," Shawn said gallantly, already moving

to the right-hand side of the tunnel, farthest away from the two dinosaurs who were still gorging themselves on potatoes. The sound of approaching voices and footsteps coming from the tunnel behind us was getting louder by the second, and the knot of fear in my stomach tightened. Todd moved to follow Shawn, but Chaz grabbed him, shaking her head.

"One at a time," she whispered. "Less likely to spook them that way." We watched Shawn inch his way down the tunnel, his back pressed to the wall as he watched the dinosaurs warily. At one point, he was less than two feet away from the powerful hind legs of one of them, and if it had decided to back up at that moment, he would have been smashed. He finally made it past, and with a tiny wave he moved a good twenty yards down the tunnel to wait. Todd went next, followed by Chaz a minute later. The pentaceratops went right on eating. I was last.

I'd edged around the first dinosaur without any problem and was halfway around the second when a pack of six marines burst around the corner. They came to a fumbling stop, yelping in surprise as they caught sight of the living roadblock. The startled dinosaurs lifted their heads up with disgruntled snorts, blowing out hard through their noses as they inspected this newest intrusion. The dinosaur closest to me stamped its foot so hard the ground trembled.

"There they are!" One of the marines shouted, and before I could react, he'd shouldered a gun and fired. The bullet missed, blasting into the stone a foot above my head before ricocheting off to hit the flank of an already unhappy pentaceratops. It squealed, and I barely avoided being trampled as it dropped its head to charge the marines. Turning, I sprinted toward Shawn, Todd, and Chaz as bullets pinged off the ground and ceiling. A quick glance over my shoulder revealed that the two pentaceratops were standing their ground, heads bent as they defended their stash of potatoes. I could only hope they would buy us the time we needed to get to Grand Central Terminal.

But I'd forgotten about Sprout.

I tripped as my bad leg almost gave out, and she let out a frightened croak. The sounds from behind us changed immediately. The territorial snorts and grunts the dinosaurs had been making to keep the marines at bay turned into enraged bellows. The same bellows I'd heard when I was topside in the middle of their nesting ground, and I knew all too well what that meant. The pentaceratops whirled to face us and charged.

"We seriously cannot catch a break," Todd cried as we took off down the tunnel at a dead sprint. It sounded like we were being chased by thunder, and bits of concrete and dust fell from the ceiling as the tunnel shuddered and shook. We had a head start, and the pentaceratops weren't nearly as quick as the condor-raptors had been, but they would catch us eventually.

"Please tell me we're close to Grand Central," Chaz called to Shawn.

"It shouldn't be much farther," he said, gasping.

A quick glance over my shoulder showed that the pentaceratops weren't the only thing we had to worry about. Behind them ran the six marines. Even if we made it to the station, we were going to have them to deal with. One step at a time, I reminded myself. My injured leg was on fire, and I blinked away the black spots that clustered at the edge of my vision. The tunnel curved slightly to the right, and I saw a subway plat-form up ahead. The wall on our left transitioned from rough concrete to smooth white tile, and I could have cried in relief when I saw the words GRAND CEN-TRAL inlaid in small black tiles. Together we raced up to the platform and sprinted across it to the concrete staircase set in the far wall.

No sooner had my feet hit the first stair than the pentaceratops caught up with us. Unlike the condor-raptors, they didn't bother with the stairs. Instead they charged the platform. The corner they hit gave with an eardrum-shattering crack, sending concrete flying in all directions. One hundred and fifty years of rust and decay had made the underlying supports weak, and the decimated corner created a ripple effect, causing the rest of the platform to buckle and crack. I stumbled and would have fallen backward onto the collapsing platform if Shawn hadn't snaked out a hand and caught me, pulling me back at the last second. With a crash, the remaining concrete of the subway platform broke and crumbled inward. We raced up the stairs before the rampaging dinosaurs could maneuver their way over the rubble. I caught one last glimpse of the bigger of the two dinosaurs ripping chunks out of the narrow stairwell before we reached the top, and they disappeared from sight.

Shawn led us up another set of stairs, followed by an even longer hallway. Suddenly, Todd skidded to a stop, and I almost collided with his back.

We were standing in the doorway of the most massive room I'd ever seen. The tile floors gleamed, and a domed ceiling arched so far overhead I could barely make out the faint artwork etched on its surface. Bits and pieces of it had crumbled away, and cracks ran the length of the room, patched over with thick ribbons of concrete. Rectangular stone columns lined the sides of the space, and a sweeping double staircase graced the far end. In the center of the room was a circular concrete booth with an ornate clock attached to the top.

Hanging from the arched ceiling high above our heads was a humongous flag. The Noah's golden-ark crest was emblazoned across it. Behind the flag were windows, or what used to be windows. The glass was gone, presumably shattered when the building was buried over one hundred and fifty years ago. The holes where they'd once been were now filled with compacted rubble instead of sunlight.

"Wow," Todd breathed.

"This way," Shawn called impatiently, and I tore my attention away from the ceiling to see him standing ten yards into the room. He'd kept running, unaware that we'd all stopped to gawk like idiots. I elbowed Todd and Chaz in the ribs to get their attention, and took off again, our footsteps echoing eerily off the cavernous walls.

The first bullet was silent. We were almost to the circular concrete-and-glass structure that supported the impressive clock when a fine spray of concrete hit my back. I turned, not sure what was happening, and saw the second bullet hit the ground a foot behind Chaz.

"Watch out!" I screamed as another bullet pinged off the concrete to my right. A second later bullets were flying at us from every direction, and I glanced frantically around, trying to spot a shooter. The stairs were still too far away, and I knew there was no way we'd make it without at least one of us getting hit.

Shawn must have come to the same conclusion, because he dove for the much closer circular booth I'd noticed earlier. It had obviously been a ticket booth for the subway in its past life, but now it apparently functioned as some sort of office. I had just enough time to see the sign that said MARINES over the door before Shawn reached it, yanked his backpack off, and launched the entire thing through one of the opaque glass windows. He threw himself through the newly created hole, reappearing a moment later to haul Chaz inside. Todd didn't even slow down, diving through the ragged opening headfirst. I managed to somehow clamber inside, falling hard on my hands and knees. Stumbling to my feet, I turned around and froze. In the middle of the room stood two marines, grinning broadly as they pointed long black guns at my friends' chests.

CHAPTER 16

We had nowhere to run. The taller of the two marines grabbed a small black port screen out of his belt, tapped its surface, and waited a moment until it lit up.

"Report, soldier" came the voice of another marine from the port's speaker.

"We have apprehended all four children trying to infiltrate marine headquarters," he said. "Please communicate with the dinosaur prevention squad to hold their fire. All they're doing is wasting bullets and ruining our office."

"Affirmative" came the reply. "Detain the prisoners. Backup will arrive shortly."

"Yes, sir," the marine replied.

A moment later the sound of bullets ricocheting off concrete stopped, and in the sudden silence, I could hear Sprout's pitiful squeaking cry.

"What's that?" the other marine asked sharply. He was older than the first marine, with sharp blue eyes that shifted nervously from side to side.

"Who cares," said the younger blond marine. "We just caught the four kids the great General Kennedy couldn't. Do you know what this means, Rob? Promotions," he crowed.

Sprout let out a high-pitched shrieking cry again, and the older marine jumped. I really wished that someone so twitchy wasn't holding a gun on us.

"Relax," commanded the blond marine. He turned to us. "Take off those bows," he said. "Now."

Todd looked like he wanted to refuse, but he grudgingly took off his leather quiver with its handful of arrows and set it on the ground. He followed this with his bow, stepping back with a murderous look on his face.

"Now you," the twitchy marine said, jerking his chin at me. Not seeing many other options, I laid down my bow next to Todd's and stepped back.

"The quiver too," the marine barked. "Do it now."

"But—" I protested.

"Now!" he thundered. Swallowing hard, I removed my quiver and set it gingerly on the ground. Sprout was still curled up inside it, burrowed down in the bottom, and I prayed she wouldn't come out. The blond marine leaned down to Todd's quiver and pulled out the handful of arrows with a sneer.

"Do you see this?" he asked the other marine. "They just charged into our headquarters with nothing but a handful of sticks." Taking the whole bunch in his hands, he slammed them down over his knee, breaking them in half. Todd made a choking sound next to me.

"Kennedy couldn't catch you guys?" the marine went on with a sneer. "I think he might be losing his edge." Without taking his eyes off us, he reached into my quiver to grab my arrows, and let out a bloodcurdling scream.

He ripped his hand out of my quiver to reveal Sprout still attached to the meaty part of his palm. There was an audible crunch, and the marine screamed again, flailing his hand wildly.

"Get it off!" he shrieked. The twitchy marine raised his gun and fired at Sprout, barely missing Chaz and shattering the glass behind us. Todd dove for his bow, grabbing it and a handful of arrows from my quiver and jumping behind a metal desk. The older marine turned his gun from Sprout to Todd. Shawn and Chaz dove behind him while I lunged forward, snatching up my own bow and quiver before rolling behind another desk. Stringing an arrow to my bow, I stood up, ready to fire. But I was too late. The older marine was already down, two arrows sprouting from his shoulder. His gun clattered to the ground, and Chaz ran forward to scoop it up before training it on the blond marine, who still had Sprout hanging from his mangled and bleeding hand. He froze as he took in his fallen companion and the gun in Chaz's hands.

"Tie them up," Chaz said. "Hurry."

"With what?" I asked as I took in our surroundings for the first time. The room was sparse and small, with only a few desks and a black metal pole in the center.

"Improvise," she hissed, not taking her eyes off the two marines. Shawn stepped forward, already ripping strips of fabric off his compound uniform sleeves. He thrust a handful of the thick gray cloth at me before quickly tying up the older marine to a nearby desk. I approached the blond marine warily. His face was a mixture of fury and pain, and I risked a glance at Sprout, still attached firmly to his hand.

"I'm going to need some help," I called over my shoulder to Todd. A moment later he was at my side, pulling the marine's dinosaur-free arm roughly behind his back. Careful not to startle her, I gently grasped

Sprout by her round middle.

"It's okay," I murmured softly. "You did good. You can let go now." Nothing happened. "Please, girl," I coaxed. "That can't taste good." Just when I was beginning to worry that I was going to have to leave this brave little creature behind, she released her hold and huddled against my chest, trembling.

"We should have kept going for the stairs," I said as I carefully replaced Sprout in my quiver. "Now we're trapped, and these guys' backups are going to be here any minute."

"We aren't trapped," Chaz said. We all turned to see her standing by the thick metal pole. She was staring at the ground, and we hurried over to join her. At her feet was a narrow spiral staircase that disappeared into the floor, invisible unless you were right on top of it.

Without hesitating, Todd began jogging down them two at a time. We followed quickly and a few moments later we found ourselves in a dimly lit passageway. Unlike the subway tunnels or the hallways that had led up to Grand Central Terminal, this place was narrow, with a ceiling so low Todd's head missed scraping it by barely an inch.

It was obvious that this tunnel was not part of the original station. The walls were made by unskilled hands, and the stairs we'd just climbed down had a makeshift appearance to them. Mismatched lights borrowed from other sections of the compound hung at irregular intervals down the length of the slightly lopsided walls. "I hope you're right about this," I said. "I expected to find someplace a little more polished for the Noah's headquarters."

Shawn grimaced. "I was thinking the same thing."

"Well, there is only one way to find out," Todd said, pulling his bow up to the ready position. I did the same, and we led the way down the murky hallway.

Less than three minutes later, the makeshift passageway ended, and we entered part of the original station again. The room was small and made entirely of smooth concrete. Five large metal doors were set in the far wall. To our right was a hallway lit with bright fluorescent lights curving away out of sight.

"What was this place?" Chaz asked, glancing around. "It doesn't look like the Noah's headquarters."

Shawn motioned for us to follow him and turned toward the hallway. Todd shot his hand out, pulling him up short.

"It does look like a prison, though." He strode forward to yank at the closest door. Nothing happened. "It's locked." Todd grunted, giving it another frustrated tug.

"Well, it would be a really crummy prison if the

doors were unlocked," Chaz muttered under her breath, but she moved to help Todd with the door.

"Give me a second and I might be able to do something about that door," Shawn said, hurrying over to where a small holoscreen monitor was embedded in the concrete. "Maybe," he added. He stared at it for a second, brow furrowed, before pulling his port out. I jogged up to the next door and gave the handle an experimental jerk. It was locked as well. Todd shouldered me aside, giving the door his own yank before moving on to the next. His eyes were wide and frantic, and I knew he was picturing everyone he knew and loved trapped on the other side of those doors. From the tunnel behind us came the sound of running feet.

"We're out of time," I whispered. "That's the marine's backup."

Shawn was about to shove his port back in his bag when Todd pushed past him roughly to yank at the first door again. When it didn't budge, he pulled his bow off his back and notched an arrow.

"I'm not going," Todd said through gritted teeth. "My mom is in here. I know it. You guys run if you want. But I'm done running."

Shawn stood frozen for a second, looking torn, then he muttered something unintelligible and turned back to the holoscreen again. The sound of running foot-steps got louder, and I strung my own bow, ready to fire as soon as I saw movement.

"Got it!" Shawn whispered, and ran to the first door Todd had tried to open. He punched six numbers into the small keypad beside the door handle, consulted his port, and then typed in five more. With a click the door unlocked, and he held it open while Todd and Chaz rushed inside. The footsteps were getting louder by the second. I stood my ground, bow still drawn, until Shawn was through the door. Without taking my eyes off the tunnel, I quickly backed inside. Shawn shut the iron door softly. Immediately, I pressed my ear to the cold metal. The approaching footsteps got louder and louder, and I tightened my grip on my bow. But then the sound started to recede. They'd passed us, not bothering to check the doors they knew to be locked. I sagged in relief, and noticed Shawn out of the corner of my eye. His face was an alarming white, and his port hung forgotten at his side.

"Shawn?" I asked as I put a worried hand on his shoulder. "What is it? The marines kept going down the tunnel. It's okay." When he didn't respond, a surge of worry washed over me. Had he been hit with a stray bullet during our run across the station? Was he losing blood? Why else would he look like he was about to faint?

"Shawn, say something," I commanded. "You're scaring me."

"Sky?" said a low voice from behind me, and I froze, the blood draining from my own face in a dizzying rush that had my knees buckling. Shawn grabbed my elbow to steady me as I shut my eyes, not willing to believe that what I was hearing was true. It couldn't be.

"Sky?" the voice spoke again, and I turned slowly to meet the familiar blue eyes of my dad.

CHAPTER 17

I stared at my dad in shock. His face was thinner than I remembered it, the cheekbones standing out like sharp cliffs in his narrow face. Blue eyes the color of the sky at twilight looked at me in astonishment, earnest and wide set and achingly familiar. Two fat tears slid down his cheek to splash onto the floor, and he made a choking noise that was half my name and half a sob.

I don't remember doing it, but suddenly I was across the room and in his arms. Bending his head, he buried his face in my hair and cried. This can't be real, I thought even as I inhaled his familiar smell of lab chemicals and soap. Right when I'd given up, resigning myself to the fact that I'd never see him again, I'd found him.

"So . . . ," Todd said from behind me, "I'm guessing this is your dad?"

"Of course it is," Chaz said. "Don't you recognize him from the tape?"

"Shhhh," Shawn hissed. "Give them a second."

"We don't have a second," Todd groaned in exasperation. "Or did you forget the pack of marines on our tail?"

"I didn't," Shawn said. "Sky said they ran past us."

"But they'll be back," Todd pointed out. "And this place is obviously not a prison. Which means my mom and everyone else from the Oaks is still locked up somewhere." The disappointment in Todd's voice pulled me back to reality. He'd expected to find his family on the other side of the door, not mine.

My dad stepped back then, wiping at his still-streaming eyes. "It is a prison," he said to Todd, "mine." As though his words had triggered something, he grabbed my shoulders, his face suddenly etched with fear. "What are you doing here?" he asked. "How did you get past the armed marines outside?"

"There weren't any," I said.

My dad's forehead wrinkled in confusion. "Impossible," he said. "There is a twenty-four-hour guard posted at the marine's station entrance as well as outside that door," he said, gesturing to the door we'd just come through.

"Well, we met the ones at the entrance," Chaz said, grimacing. "But the ones outside your door were probably relocated because of the dinosaurs."

"Dinosaurs?" my dad asked. "What dinosaurs?"

"The ones Sky let into East Compound," Shawn said. "Oh, and there's the one she's toting around on her back." My dad blinked in surprise and glanced at my back, where Sprout was snoring softly, apparently sound asleep inside my quiver.

"I don't understand," he said slowly. "Has the Noah captured you?"

I shook my head. "Not yet. Although not for a lack of trying on his part."

"Why?" my dad asked. "Did you find my message? Were you able to deliver it to Ivan or Boznic?" Before I could reply, he'd paced away, shoving his hands into his hair in frustration so it stood up in familiar crazy tuffs. I'd forgotten that he used to do that. Except now his chestnut hair was shot through with streaks of gray at the temples. "Of course you found it," he said, more to himself than to us. "Otherwise, you wouldn't be here, and the Noah wouldn't be after you. But you couldn't have found Ivan or Boznic. They never would have let you come alone, or come at all for that matter. I never wanted you here in this kind of danger. Never."

"Dad?" I said nervously.

"I'm sorry," he said, striding back to us. "I've been talking to myself for too long. I'm out of practice. I just never thought I'd see you here. Or see you at all, for that matter. The boy said the marines are after you? Explain."

"We don't have time," Todd protested.

"He's right," I said, turning to my dad. "There isn't a lot of time before the marines figure out where we've gone. We need to get out of here."

"Didn't you hear me?" my dad asked. "This is a prison. You can't get in or out."

"I can," Shawn said. Holding up his port, he quickly walked to the small holoscreen beside my dad's door and got to work. I turned to my dad, the questions I'd been dying to get the answers to for the last five years burning in my chest with such a fury I couldn't hold them anymore.

"Dad," I said, drawing his attention away from Shawn. "What happened five years ago? How did you end up here?" I asked, unable to keep the hint of accusation out of my voice. Glancing around, I took in *here* for the first time. The room was bright and white, with a slight chemical smell to it, and lined with shelves filled with tiny plastic petri dishes and glass beakers. A long well-lit table ran down the middle of the room filled with microscopes and other scientific equipment. It was a lab, I realized. Very similar to the one my dad had worked in back at North Compound. The thought of North Compound had me turning back to him.

"I was found out," he said simply. "I stumbled upon that file detailing the Noah's plans, and the marines were tipped off almost immediately that someone had stolen confidential government information."

"How did you do that?" I asked. "Find the video of the Noah, I mean."

My dad shrugged. "I'd been keeping tabs on the Noah's correspondence ever since I was transferred to North Compound. The Colombe was gone, but I hadn't given up hope that things could change. That people *and* dinosaurs could one day inhabit the topside world, just like Ivan and your mother talked about. I'd spotted the file months before I actually managed to get it open, but when I did I knew that I had to do something. Unfortunately, with the marines on my tail, I had less than twenty-four hours to formulate some kind of plan."

"And that plan didn't include me," I said flatly. I had to know why I'd been left behind.

He shook his head sadly. "It was the best I could

do. I barely had enough time to get together what I would need to make the trip to find Ivan or Boznic, and on top of that, I knew I couldn't leave you without an explanation."

I swallowed hard. "But you did leave me without an explanation. I risked my neck checking the topside maildrop for years, hoping to get some clue about what had happened to you."

He flinched at my words. "You were so young, Sky." There was a definite note of pleading in his voice now. "How was I supposed to explain a secret organization and nuclear warfare to you? You were still afraid of the dark, for goodness' sake!"

When I didn't say anything, my dad sighed in resignation. "I did what I thought was best. There was no way I was going to take you topside so young. You weren't fast enough or strong enough. Besides, I fully intended to come back for you after I found Ivan or Boznic."

"But you still put that message for her in your compass," Shawn pointed out, glancing over his shoulder, from where he was busily working on the wall's holoscreen.

"I did." He nodded. "I knew there was a chance I wouldn't make it back. So I used a prototype mechanism I'd been developing inside my old compass and prayed you'd find the journal before the marines did."

"That prototype didn't work," I said, unable to keep the edge out of my voice.

"It didn't?" my dad asked, sagging in defeat.

"If it wasn't for Shawn, I'd never have found it," I said. "And, by the way, it wasn't even really a message. It was a note that made no sense and a map to the middle of Lake Michigan. Couldn't you have at least hinted about what was down there? And you never told me about Ivan! Why didn't I know I had a grandfather? And what about people living topside? Or Mom? She was murdered, Dad. Murdered." I was breathing hard; tears of frustration slid down my cheeks as years of pain and anger rolled through me.

"If the marines had gotten ahold of that note instead of you, it would have put Ivan and Boznic's entire operation in danger," my dad explained. "I needed to give you just enough to get there, but not enough to endanger them."

I knew he was right. Of course he couldn't endanger Ivan or the Lincoln Lab, even though I wished he'd been able to leave me more of a clue. A tear slid down my face, and I gave him another hard hug.

"How much longer?" Todd called to Shawn impatiently.

"Give me a minute," Shawn said. "This is harder

than I thought it would be. They programmed a different code for getting out than getting in." He shot my dad an admiring look. "They weren't taking any chances with you."

"But how did you end up in this place?" Chaz asked my dad, glancing around. "And what is this place?"

"It's a lab," my dad explained. "I was captured less than five hours after escaping North Compound. I'd been attacked by a pack of eotyrannus and had climbed a tree to get away. The marines were able to find me using an old tracking chip that was implanted without my knowledge on the day I was transferred to North Compound. Instead of killing me, or bringing me back to North, I was transported here." He gestured around himself. "I was the top biologist and DNA specialist in the compounds. And considering what the Noah was planning, they couldn't afford to kill me. So I've been here ever since. Kept under lock and key, not allowed to talk to anyone."

"DNA specialist?" Todd asked, shooting me a questioning look.

"I have been cataloging and saving the DNA of every topside plant, animal, fungus, and bacteria that I could get my hands on," my dad explained. "If the Noah does wipe out the topside world, it will be with my work that he is able to rebuild at least part of it."

"But Boz said the Noah's plan would do irreparable damage," Chaz cut in.

"Oh, it will," my dad said. "It will be thousands of years before evolution can bring back a sustainable ecosystem; unfortunately, by then, the human race might not be part of it anymore."

"I hate to interrupt," Shawn said, trotting back to us. "But I got the door open, and we might not be part of the human race much longer either if we don't get out of here before those marines come back."

"I don't know how you ended up here!" my dad protested. "You met Ivan?" He turned to Chaz. "And you mentioned Boznic. And how did you end up letting dinosaurs into the compound?"

"There isn't time," Shawn apologized, already pulling us toward the door. "Do you know where the control center is for the bombs?"

My dad nodded. "The same place the control center is for the entire compound. But why do you need to get there?"

"We can explain on the way," Chaz said anxiously. "Let's go."

"Wait," Todd said. "What about my mom?" He turned to my dad. "If this is a prison like you said, then maybe you know where other prisoners are kept?" He quickly explained about his village and my dad listened, his face focused and intense. I'd always loved that about him, the way he listened with every fiber of his being. It made me want to hug him again, but I knew we didn't have time.

"I might know where they are being kept." He nodded. "If I'm right, it's on the way to the command hub."

Shawn peered out at the empty tunnel. A second later he gave the signal that it was safe and disappeared. Careful to shut the door behind us, we headed down the far tunnel at a run. My dad took the lead, and after only a minute he turned right, and we wove our way through increasingly narrow corridors. While we moved, we did our best to catch my dad up on everything. It wasn't easy. So much had happened. It didn't help that he kept interrupting us with questions. When I got to the part about how I'd let a herd of pentaceratops into East Compound, he laughed out loud, shaking his head. A minute later we skidded to a stop outside a large metal door.

"This is the only place large enough to keep thirty-plus people," my dad told Todd. "It's the holding cell I was brought to when I was first captured, and it's had three armed marines standing guard outside it for a week."

"This has to be them, then," Todd said, jumping for the door handle. It was locked. The sound of shouts and running feet came floating down the tunnel behind us, and my heart lurched. The marines were heading this way.

"Can you get the door open?" Todd asked frantically, turning to Shawn.

"I think so," he said, already consulting his port.

I stared anxiously down the tunnel that would lead us to the command hub, feeling torn.

Todd saw my glance and nodded once, as though he'd read my thoughts. "You guys keep going," he said, putting an arrow to the string and turning to face the tunnel we'd just left. "Shawn and I will follow with the rest of my village if we can." Shawn jerked his head up, looking like he wanted to argue, but one glance at Todd's face had him turning back to his port.

"But—" I began to protest.

"Just go," Todd said as the noise of approaching marines got louder. "Saving my mom won't do us any good if you don't stop the Noah."

Knowing a lost battle when I saw one, I quickly pulled all but two of my remaining arrows out of my quiver, thankful that the marine who had broken Todd's arrows hadn't managed to do the same to mine. Sprout woke up with a startled squawk, but quickly resettled.

"Todd," I called, "catch." He deftly caught the arrows and jammed them in his own quiver. Whirling,

I signaled for my dad to lead the way. He did, Chaz and me at his heels. The last thing I saw before the curve of the tunnel hid them from sight was Todd letting loose an arrow as the first marine appeared around the corner.

CHAPTER 18

We followed my dad at a sprint as he led us toward East Compound's command hub. Shawn had been right; it was located in one of the old utility rooms.

"Do you think it matters which port screen we put this plug into?" I asked my dad.

My dad shook his head. "I don't know. Putting it in any of the ports in the command hub will do some damage. We can only hope it's enough. Do you have the plug ready?"

"It's inside your compass," I said, stopping all of us momentarily as I fumbled to unscrew the back. I gingerly removed the plug and handed it to my dad.

"Good." My dad nodded, but instead of turning to run again, he hesitated, looking back and forth at me and Chaz. "If I asked you to do something for me, would you?"

I blinked in surprise. "What?"

My dad exhaled hard, and I could tell that I wasn't going to like what he said next. "Will you stay back where it's safe? We passed a storage closet a minute ago where you two could hide. I'll go on ahead and do this? Then I'll come back for you."

"Not a chance," I snapped, and Chaz shook her head. "Give me back that plug."

"Sky," he pleaded.

"No," I hissed. "You may have been able to leave me behind five years ago, but you will not do it again. I'm not sure if you understand this, but I made it here on my own. I faced dinosaurs and sea monsters and marines, and I am going to see this through. Now give it here." I paused. "Please," I added.

I waited for my dad to argue. Instead he pressed the tiny port plug back into my hand, curling my fingers around it as he looked into my eyes as though reading something there.

"I guess you're not the little girl I left five years ago," he said.

"I'm not," I agreed.

"I can't decide if that makes me proud or sad." He sighed. From behind us came shouting and gunshots. Apparently Shawn and Todd were putting up a good fight. Pushing aside my worries for my friends, we took off running again. The tunnel was getting progressively better lit, and goose bumps broke out along my neck. We were close. I tightened my grip on my loaded bow, painfully aware of the quiver that carried only one more arrow and a very disgruntled baby dinosaur.

A moment later, the wall on our right transformed from smooth concrete to clear glass. On the other side of the glass was a circular room. Spread out in a wide arc were workstations, each with complicated-looking port screen setups. They all faced the far wall, where twenty huge monitors displayed rotating images of East Compound. Some simply flashed from empty subway tunnel to abandoned subway platform, but others showed pentaceratops methodically ramming into the side of a black helicopter or condorraptors on the prowl. The screen in the far right corner showed a large-scale fight, and I realized it was the marines battling the people of the Oaks. I recognized four of the villagers who had managed to pin a marine down. Ivan flashed onto the screen, slamming two marines' heads together.

"Do you see that?" Chaz said from behind me. "They found Ivan." But I was too busy taking in the rest of the space to answer. The room wasn't empty. Four people, three men and a woman, stood with their backs to us, facing the wall of screens as they worked busily at their ports. And standing in the center of the room was the Noah. As though he'd heard my thoughts, he turned and our eyes met.

Suddenly my muscles seized, bringing me to a wrenching stop, frozen in midrun. The feeling of electricity coursing through my veins made me want to scream, but my jaw clenched shut involuntarily, cutting it off. The arrow I'd notched to my bow clattered to the floor and rolled away. In my peripheral vision, I saw the same thing happening to Chaz and my dad as they too were caught by some mysterious electrical force field.

We had run right into a trap. Back at North Compound we'd used electrified gates designed to slam down if the dinosaurs ever found their way in. Whatever this was put those gates to shame. Unable to look away, I saw the Noah's face spread in a wide smile as he reached down to the desk he was standing behind to press a button; then he strolled over to the glass that separated us. The sound of running feet flooded the hall, and even though I couldn't turn my head to look, I knew what I would see. Marines.

As quickly as I'd become frozen, I became unfrozen again. My twitching muscles were unable to hold me, and I fell forward, barely getting my hands up in time to keep my face from smashing into the floor. The impact jarred Boz's port plug loose, but my hand shot out, closing around it seconds before I was grabbed roughly from behind and hauled to my feet.

"Hello, Sky," Kennedy sneered, yanking my arms behind my back with so much force my joints popped in protest.

"Don't tell him anything," my dad cried as his own marine manhandled him.

"Tell me what?" Kennedy sneered. "That you let dinosaurs loose? That you've cost us lives, time, and resources we couldn't afford to spare? That you're a traitor to the human race? Oh, don't worry. We know all that." I felt him rummage around on my back, and then my pack lightened. "So much for your little pet," he mocked as he tossed Sprout's limp body aside. She skidded across the floor, coming to rest in a tiny huddled mound of blue-green against the wall. "The electroshock was designed to incapacitate adult dinosaurs, but it kills about one third of its human victims," Kennedy went on as I stared in horror at Sprout. "It's a real shame you beat those odds. That much electricity should have finished off a little brat like you." With a jerk, he slammed me against the glass wall of the command center.

Kennedy glanced back over his shoulder at my dad. "Is this what you were hoping for when you stole the Noah's private correspondence?" My dad let out a strangled cry, and Kennedy chuckled. "Come now," he said. "Don't act so surprised. You had to know that this was how it would all end." Kennedy turned back to the glass wall of the command center where the Noah still stood observing all of this, his face hard and impassive. "May I kill her now, sir?" Kennedy asked. The Noah didn't say anything, just studied me with those dark eyes of his, searching my face.

After what felt like an eternity, the Noah shook his head, motioning for Kennedy to bring me to him. For the first time I noticed how bedraggled these marines looked. Their uniforms were ripped and bloody, and most of them sported visible bruises and wounds. The marine who held Chaz had a broken-off arrow shaft I recognized sticking out of his right thigh. Good for you, Todd, I thought viciously.

The six marines paused outside a wide glass door, and a moment later there was a faint click and it slid open. The Noah was waiting for us at the front of the room, his back to the impressive display of screens that still flashed images from East Compound. The room had emptied, leaving us with the Noah and his marines.

"So you are Sky Mundy. The little girl who has caused all of this," the Noah said. He flicked his eyes toward my dad. "Had I known the daughter you left behind was an even worse traitor than you were, I would have killed her five years ago. I was unaware that someone so young could cause such damage." He sounded mildly impressed.

My dad's eyes flashed defiantly as he stared at the Noah. "I know," he said. "I am incredibly proud of her."

His words sent a rush of warmth through me, and I squared my shoulders and looked the Noah in the eye. "Your plan to wipe the topside world clean will never work."

"Sky, don't," my dad started, apparently trying to stop me from saying something that would seal my fate. The marine holding him cracked him in the side of the head. I cried out, reaching for him instinctively, but Kennedy jerked me back to face the Noah.

"That's where you're wrong," the Noah said coolly. "Our world is resilient. In time, things will become as they once were, and future generations will be able to walk in the sun again. I do not expect a child to see or understand the need for sacrifice."

"It's not sacrifice," I spat, "it's murder."

"I'm sure the people who didn't get invited onto Noah's ark in biblical times thought the flood was murder too," he said. "The only difference between victory and murder is which side you're on. Remember, young Sky, history is always written by the winners." Suddenly the port in his hand buzzed, and he glanced down and tapped his screen.

"The tree-village prisoners have been recaptured" came the report. "There were few casualties. Two of the children have also been caught."

"What about the one-armed rebel?" the Noah asked, not taking his eyes off me.

"Critically injured, sir," said the voice from the port a moment later. I'd barely had a chance to process this before Chaz slammed her head backward into the marine holding her. There was a sickening crunch and he cried out, letting go of Chaz with one hand to grab his newly broken nose. She twisted sideways in an attempt to escape and bumped into Kennedy, who stumbled forward, knocking me into the Noah. Kennedy yanked me backward, but my brief bump had thrown the Noah off balance, and he lost his grip on his port screen. It clattered to the ground and skidded away across the floor. In that second, I saw my chance. I jerked out of Kennedy's hands and dove for the Noah's port.

"Shoot her," the Noah roared. There was a scuffling above me, and my dad bellowed. A second later a bullet ricocheted off the floor inches from my head. Someone grabbed for me, but my dad yanked free from his own marine and threw himself at my would-be attacker. With one last lunge, my hands closed around the port. I slid Boz's plug into the small slot on the side seconds before I was grabbed by the ankles and jerked backward, the port still clutched tightly in my sweaty hands. I twisted, trying unsuccessfully to free myself, and came face-to-face with a frazzled-looking marine, his gun mere inches from my face.

"Don't you dare!" my dad bellowed, and suddenly my head was being shoved down by the weight of his hand. I heard the smack of a fist connecting with someone's jaw seconds before a burst of gunfire almost deafened me. Bullets zinged around me like lethal rain, chipping chunks out of the surrounding concrete floor. A moment later a body fell heavily to the ground inches from where I sprawled on the floor. Before I'd even lifted my head, I knew it was my dad. He lay completely still, his eyes open and blank, having thrown himself in front of the bullets that were meant for me.

No, I thought desperately as I stared into his lifeless eyes, no no no. I tried to reach for him, but a booted foot landed hard on the center of my back, pinning me to the ground. He couldn't be gone. Not after everything I'd gone through to find him. This couldn't be it. I tried to reach for him again, sure that if I could just touch him I could wake him up, but the boot on my back pushed down harder and I remained trapped.

"I'm really going to enjoy shooting you," Kennedy said as a gun in his hand gave an ominous click. Three marines stood protectively in front of the Noah. To my left, another had Chaz in a headlock. Through the numb haze of grief I could see that the home screen of the Noah's port screen was still brightly lit, proving that it was still in full working order. I couldn't breathe, and I dropped my head to the cool concrete of the floor, letting out a strangled cry of defeat. I'd lost. The plug hadn't worked. All of this had been for nothing.

"Take my port away from her before you shoot her," the Noah commanded. "I don't want blood all over it."

"No problem," Kennedy said. Glancing up, I saw Kennedy raise his gun and take aim at my head while another marine bent to retrieve the port. There was a sharp crack, and then everything went black.

CHAPTER 19

For a second, I thought I was dead. The darkness was that complete and absolute. But then the screaming began. The pressure on my back lessened a fraction, and on instinct alone, I rolled sideways and out from under Kennedy's boot. Fumbling my way across the floor, I found the still body of my dad. Chaos erupted around me as I located his wrist in the dark, praying to feel a pulse, but no pulse came. Tears were already running down my cheeks as I found his other wrist, hoping that I was wrong. People were stumbling into me, and into one another, as Kennedy bellowed my name, but I ignored it all. Time seemed to stand still as I reached with shaking fingers for my dad's neck with one hand while I placed the other above his nose and mouth. There was no warm breath, no thud of a pulse in his veins, and I knew then that my dad really was dead.

My hands fell limply to my sides, my left brushing against the Noah's port, still lying at my side where I'd dropped it. I picked it up just as someone's fumbling hand attempted to grab the back of my shirt. Ripping myself away, I rolled in the dark until I collided with the cold metal of a desk. I crawled underneath it as the yelling got even more frantic. Something smelled sharp and metallic, and suddenly the Noah's port began heating up in my hands. Remembering how the port back at the lab had caught fire, I tossed it away from me. Its screen flashed white upon impact with the floor, and suddenly the room was lit with an eerie glow. In that moment of illumination I spotted Chaz, still being held by her confused and blinking marine. Kennedy's furious eyes met mine right before the port went black again. I dove out from under the desk seconds before he collided with it, sending the huge port resting on top crashing to the floor. Lunging toward Chaz, I crashed into her captor, who fell sideways, releasing her. Together we crawled away from the confusion of panicked marines.

Navigating in the pitch black was hard, and we

bumped into desks, knocking over chairs and upsetting port screens as we felt our way blindly across the unfamiliar room.

"Spread out!" Kennedy called. "They can't get out of this room. If you find them, shoot them."

"But, sir," another voice protested, "our guns aren't working."

"It's because the electricity is out" came the Noah's voice, sounding much less calm now. "They are useless without it. Not to worry. It should come back on any moment now."

"What did you do?" Chaz whispered in my ear.

"The plug," I said. "I think it disabled the entire room." The smell of something burning was becoming stronger and stronger, and I wondered just what Boz's plug had done to the Noah's port. Back at the Lincoln Lab, Shawn had removed the plug immediately, and his port had caught fire. I'd left the plug inside the port. Did that matter?

"Why are you delaying the inevitable, Sky Mundy?" Kennedy roared from somewhere to our left. "When I find you, I won't need a gun. I'll break that neck of yours with my own two hands." My stomach dropped. He was right. There was no way out of this room without the electricity to run the holoscreen that operated the door. Not that I had any idea where the door even was. It was only a matter of time before Kennedy or one of the other marines found us.

Chaz's elbow suddenly dug into my ribs. "Do you see that?" she whispered.

"I can't see anything," I whispered back, groping blindly in front of me to make sure I didn't crawl into another desk.

"Look," she breathed, grabbing my arm and turning me roughly around. A dim red glow was coming from somewhere to our left. It was getting steadily brighter, and I pulled Chaz with me under a desk as the command center was suddenly flooded with a warm red light. One of the marines shouted in alarm, but it was immediately drowned out by an ear-shattering crash as hundreds of glass fragments hit concrete. I poked my head out from under the desk to see what had happened, and was on my feet in an instant, dragging Chaz up with me.

A huge section of the glass wall separating the command center from the outer tunnel had been broken, leaving a jagged hole. And in the middle of that hole was a familiar wiry figure with one arm.

"Ivan!" I screamed, forgetting momentarily about everything else as the figure turned toward me, a makeshift torch held high above his head.

Ivan grinned. "Ready to leave?" he asked. "I think

your job here is done." Behind him I saw Todd and Shawn and the rest of the villagers of the Oaks, bedraggled and bloody, but mercifully alive. Chaz and I ran toward Ivan, but before I could get more than a few feet, something charged us from the left. I whirled to face the attack just as the sharp twang of an arrow being released sliced through the air. It found its mark, and First General Ron Kennedy fell to the ground and didn't move again.

I threw myself into Ivan's arms. He staggered slightly from the impact, but righted himself and chuckled as he patted me on the back with his good hand. "It's all right, child," he said kindly, and I realized that I was sobbing.

"This isn't over!" someone cried from behind me, and I turned to see the Noah, still protected by a human wall of marines, his face red and furious in the light from the torch.

"I'm afraid I'll have to disagree with you on that," Ivan said calmly. He gave the remaining marines a stiff nod and grabbed my arm to turn me away. Suddenly there was a loud popping sound and the Noah's port began sparking, the fiery flecks illuminating the command center.

"Uh-oh," Shawn said from behind us, "that doesn't look good."

Ivan didn't ask questions. He grabbed my arm and we ran, joining the already retreating members of the Oaks as they headed away from the command center at a run. The gleam of blue and green scales in the torchlight caught my eye, and I pulled out of Ivan's grip to bend down and scoop up the limp body of Sprout. Even as I cradled her still body against my chest, I was painfully aware that hers wasn't the body I really wanted to save from these horrible tunnels. Sensing my hesitation, Ivan again grabbed my arm and together we raced after my friends.

The explosion came a minute later, rocking the ground under my feet and causing a few of the villagers to stumble and fall. I whirled, looking back down the tunnel to see raw red flames and a thick cloud of black smoke pouring out of what had once been the command center for East Compound. I stood frozen for a second, taking in this horrific sight as the acrid smell of burnt metal filled my nose. Ivan grabbed my arm again to drag me after him. He was right. We needed to get out of there.

CHAPTER
20

We emerged blinking and stunned into the cool, crisp air of a bright fall afternoon. I'd lost all sense of time and would have sworn it was the middle of the night. It hadn't taken nearly as long to find our way out of East Compound as I'd thought, despite having to navigate the impenetrable darkness of the electrical blackout. We found ourselves standing on the edge of a massive green space, complete with ponds, graceful weeping willows, and the ruins of once-majestic bridges. Around this strangely picturesque landscape loomed the wrecks of skyscrapers and toppled buildings.

To our right a herd of speckled hadrosaurs stood

knee-deep in a pond, their heads lifted to inspect us as long tendrils of soggy algae dripped from their mouths. For a moment we all stood there, breathing in the fresh air and inhaling the vibrant smells of the topside world. The noon sun warmed my skin even as the cool breeze sent goose bumps rippling across my arms.

I looked down at myself. The bloody leg of my ratty compound uniform was ripped and hanging on by a mere thread. More of my hair had sprung loose from my ponytail than had stayed in, so that sweaty red curls twisted in tangled knots around my face and down my neck. My hands and feet were liberally crusted with blood and grime, and the fabric under my arms and down my back was drenched in old sweat. The rest of our group didn't look much better, and I suddenly remembered the radio report Kennedy had received, and turned to Ivan.

"I thought you were 'critically injured,'" I said. "What happened?"

"Well." Ivan shrugged. "It turns out a captured marine will say just about anything when he has young Todd over there pointing an arrow an inch away from his heart."

I nodded in understanding. "A false report. But what happened after we left Todd and Shawn?"

"Oh, that," Shawn said, coming to stand by us. "I got

308

the door open, and Todd's village and Ivan were able to help. After a week of awful treatment, let's just say they were motivated, and the Noah's marines weren't expecting to be outnumbered. We probably wouldn't have won, though, if half the marines hadn't gotten a call about you guys from the Noah and taken off. They hadn't been gone a minute when two condorraptors came up behind the remaining marines. They were attacked on all sides, and with Ivan's help we were able to get the dinosaurs killed and the marines captured."

Todd grinned. "It was awesome."

"Where are we exactly?" Shawn asked, turning to take in the flowers and weeds that sprawled out around us.

"This used to be Central Park," Ivan said. "It was a patch of green space for the residents of New York." It was beautiful, but at that moment all it reminded me of was how far we were from anything familiar. I'd thought that if we managed to stop the Noah, I'd feel this overwhelming sense of relief and accomplishment, but as I glanced up at the gigantic buildings around us, all I felt was a hollow hopelessness. Unarmed and without supplies, we didn't have a chance of survival.

Something moving in the sky caught my eye as the telltale whir of helicopter propellers met my ears. I stiffened, putting a hand on Ivan's arm, but as the helicopter came closer, I saw that it was an iridescent blue, not the black of the Noah's fleet. And it wasn't alone. Four more blue helicopters came behind it, flying in tight formation. As they got closer, I saw the red emblem of a long-necked dinosaur across the side.

"It's us!" Chaz cried, jumping up and down, waving her hands frantically in the air.

"Us?" Jett asked, moving forward to stand next to us. I'd only met the leader of the Oaks once. He'd accused us of being the Noah's spies, which, as it turned out in Shawn's case, wasn't that far off the mark. He was watching the approaching helicopters out of two badly swollen eyes, and I felt a pang of guilt for what he'd gone through.

The helicopters landed, and Chaz raced forward just as the door of the first one opened and Boz hopped out. Chaz froze, staring in wonder, and then continued running, laughing, and crying.

"Well, hello," Boz called as he walked toward our raggedy group, followed by twenty other men and women exiting the helicopters and approaching us.

"You survived the bombing!" Chaz exclaimed, her voice high and squeaky with excitement. "Did the lab not sustain too much damage, then? Was the entire conference wing lost? We didn't lose any dinosaurs, did we? What other parts of the lab got hit? What are you doing here? Wasn't the lab locked down?"

Boz chuckled, motioning for her to be quiet. "One question at a time. One question at a time. Obviously, I survived. The lab sustained some damage, and we lost a few lives, but not as many as we could have thanks to your early warning. And yes, the lab was locked down, although overriding the system wasn't nearly as difficult as getting our helicopters out without the Noah's men spotting us. Honestly, I was all for waiting a few days until things quieted down, but then we got a message from someone at East Compound urging us to hurry."

"My message made it through!" Shawn yelped, pumping his fist in delight. "I knew it would."

"That message came from you?" Boz asked, eyebrow raised. "Impressive work, young man." Shawn shrugged modestly, and Boz turned back to Chaz. "So after we got the message, we came here to stop the Noah. Although," he said, glancing at each of us, "it appears we may be a little late?"

"You are," Ivan barked, stepping forward. "But now that you're here, we could use your help."

Boz blinked at Ivan in surprise for a moment before holding out a hand for him to shake. "Ivan," he said with a smile. "The last time I saw you I was a young man studying biology right here at East Compound, and you were telling the Colombe about living life

311

aboveground. It's good to see you're still alive."

"The last time I saw you, you were a lot skinnier," Ivan said gruffly as he shook Boz's extended hand.

Boz snorted. "The same charming personality I remember." He glanced around at our bedraggled group again and raised an eyebrow. "Am I to understand the Noah's plan has been successfully stopped?"

"It has," Chaz cut in. "We used the plug we stole from you."

"You stole one of our plugs?" Boz asked in surprise.

"We did," I confessed. "We were planning on giving it back once we saw what it did. But then with the attack and everything, that obviously didn't happen."

"Those plugs were untested," he said. "We ended up having to redo over half the batch because of a destructive defect."

"What do you mean by destructive defect?" Shawn asked.

"They exploded," Boz said.

"Oh, that," Chaz said, waving her hand dismissively. "That happened. We blew up the entire command center with the Noah still in it."

"Really?" Boz said, sounding impressed.

"Yeah." Chaz shrugged. "About five minutes after Sky put it in the Noah's port, the whole thing went up in smoke."

"You put it in the Noah's port?" Boz exclaimed. "But his port would have had access to all of the controls and circuits in the entire East Compound! Putting it in there would disable the entire East Compound's electrical systems. Permanently. Did all the lights go out? What about the electronics? Did they shut down too?" he asked, glancing at us for confirmation.

I nodded. "Even the marines' guns stopped working."

"That's because they ran off the main electrical current of the compound," Boz explained. "My technicians told me that might happen, but I didn't dare hope."

"The lights going out and everything breaking is exactly why we need your help," Ivan cut in. "You see, my granddaughter let dinosaurs into the tunnels, and the citizens of East Compound are now sitting in the pitch-dark without any way of getting out unharmed." My jaw dropped in horror as he said this. I hadn't really thought about the over two hundred people left stranded underground. Ivan saw my look and put a reassuring hand on my shoulder. "Can you and your people get them out?" he asked Boz.

"We can try," Boz replied. "We brought a large supply of tranquilizer guns in case we saw any species of dinosaur we wanted to transport back to the lab, so we should be able to make the tunnels safe for people to evacuate."

"Good." Ivan nodded.

Shawn grabbed ahold of Ivan's arm, looking alarmed. "But the people of East Compound have never been topside before," he protested. "They don't know how to survive up here."

"I guess they'll have to learn," Ivan said sternly. "It's high time the human race got over this silliness of living underground. This world is big enough for everyone. Humans and dinosaurs."

"I believe you're right," Boz said as he turned to the group of men and women clad in the blue jumpsuits of the Lincoln Lab. "We have work to do," he said. "And if you run across those nuclear weapons, do be good enough to bring them up. I think we should drop them in the ocean for safekeeping."

"And while you're down there," Jett cut in, "could you see if there is a way to get the Noah's helicopters out? I think I speak for my entire village when I say that we'd really like to go home."

"Certainly." Boz smiled. "I'll have my pilots navigate them for you. Although would you mind waiting a bit? We can accommodate a few refugees in our lab, but if you could take some back with you and help them get their footing topside, I'm sure they would appreciate it."

Jett gave a curt nod. "We can do that," he said. "But don't give us any of those marines. I've seen enough of them for a lifetime."

"Fair enough," Boz agreed.

After that, everything started happening fast. The people of the Oaks began setting up a makeshift camp in the trees while Boz talked with Ivan and Jett, making complicated plans to evacuate the now-uninhabitable East Compound. No one asked for our help or opinions, which was absolutely fine with me. The adrenaline that had kept me going ever since I'd woken up to the marines trying to force their way into our hiding spot was long gone, and I was content to stand next to my friends and listen to other people make plans for once. We'd saved the world, after all; someone else could worry about what we'd all eat for dinner. The feeling of something squirming on my back pulled me out of my exhausted daze, and I yanked off my quiver to discover a disgruntled and very much alive Sprout peering up at me reproachfully. Pulling her out, I sat down on the warm, sweet-smelling grass as everyone bustled about me.

"Are you okay?" Shawn asked, sinking down next to me as he pushed his sweaty hair back from his face.

"Are you kidding?" Todd said from the other side of me, where he'd plopped down. "She just saved the entire topside world. She should be fabulous."

"Not the entire world," I said, blinking hard as tears pressing against the backs of my eyes.

"Oh." Todd frowned. "Chaz told us. I'm sorry, Sky. I can't believe you got your dad back just to lose him like that."

I nodded, staring down at Sprout, who was busily investigating a bumblebee.

Shawn shook his head. "It should have been me. I made such a mess of things."

"No," I said, my head snapping around to stare at my best friend. "You didn't. You risked everything to help me get here even though you thought it was a bad idea from the very beginning. Without you, we'd still be wandering the tunnels of East Compound with no clue where to look. Todd's entire village and Ivan would still be captured, and all of this," I said, gesturing to the beautiful remains of Central Park, "would be gone in a matter of weeks."

"Does this mean you forgive me for not telling you about the tracker?" he asked, his face painfully hopeful.

I nodded. "Of course."

"But," Shawn protested, "you lost your dad."

I nodded, still blinking back tears. I'd grieved for my dad five years ago when I'd thought I'd lost him, but this time was worse. A heavy finality had settled inside my chest, leaving a bone-deep sadness in its wake that I knew was not going to go away anytime soon. I needed time to think, time to come to terms with everything that had happened, time to grieve for my dad in private. My friends were eyeing me in concern, and I forced a watery smile as I ran a hand over Sprout's knobby head. Friends, I thought as I took a deep breath to steady myself. Friends I didn't have five years ago; friends who'd practically become family somewhere along the way. I would get through this, I told myself, and this time around I realized I wouldn't have to do it alone. "I'm not saying I'm okay," I sniffed. "Because I'm not." I brushed away tears as I watched Boz's people arm themselves with tranquilizer guns and headlamps before following Ivan toward the compound entrance. "But I think I will be."

Sky

Todd

The Oaks

North Compound

EPILOGUE

"You can't be serious," Shawn said, his face an unnatural shade of green. "Is this really where eggs come from?" He looked about ready to vomit as he wiped at the yolky mess covering his hands, and I did my best not to laugh. "You let me eat this stuff for months, and it came from them?" he accused, pointing to the nests of bug-eyed rhamphorhynchus, who rustled their webbed wings indignantly as they resettled themselves. I eyed the strange creatures with their long, lethal beaks and rows of razor-sharp teeth, remembering the first time Todd had taught me how to collect eggs.

"Yup." I grinned. "And you loved every minute of it."

"I could have lived without this particular lesson," Shawn complained.

"Not an option," I said, grabbing my basket of eggs. "If we are going to live here, we need to do our part."

Shawn paused from picking up his own basket to crouch down on the floor, his brow furrowed as he studied something. I was about to ask what he was doing when he stood up, something small, black, and oval-shaped in his hand. "Todd was right." He laughed. "That plug of Boz's you used really did look like rhamphorhynchus poop."

I snorted and leaned in gingerly to look at the small pellet in his hand. Resettling the basket on my arm, I turned toward the door. "Just make sure you wash your hands before you make breakfast, okay? I don't really want my eggs seasoned with poop."

Shawn tossed the pellet aside, wiping his hands on his pants as though he'd just realized what he'd been holding. I laughed again, and ducked out of the small door and back into the early light of dawn.

"Helping save all this wasn't enough?" Shawn whined, gesturing to the snow-covered tree branches that lofted over our heads. "I really have to learn how to cook too?"

I shrugged. "Only if you want to eat." An icy December wind whipped past, and I hunched my shoulders inside the thick sweater Todd's mom, Emily, had knit for me. The snow on the deck of the rhamphorhynchus's small wooden hut swirled up and disappeared over the edge, falling forty feet to the ground below.

Shawn stood next to me as I looked out over the snow-covered village nestled snugly in the bare tree branches. Comforting curls of smoke rose from the top of each tiny house, and a warm glow issued from their mismatched windows in the early light of a winter morning. I let out a contented sigh as the smell of frying dinosaur bacon met my nose and my stomach rumbled. Shawn picked up one of the large speckled eggs from his basket and held it up to inspect it. "You know," he said after a moment, "I actually kind of miss compound food."

"You can't mean that," I said, turning to start across the rope bridge.

"No." Shawn sighed. "But it had one thing going for it."

"What's that?" I asked.

"I didn't have to battle featherbrained dinosaurs for it."

Laughing, I glanced over my shoulder to see him marching across the bobbing bridge without even holding on to the railing. I bit back a smile. If Shawn wasn't careful, he was going to start being mistaken for a native topsider by one of the many East Compound refugees who had made their homes among the people of the Oaks. Another gust of icy wind had us hurrying back toward the tree houses we'd been calling home for the last two months.

Todd's village had reclaimed their homes among the trees, quickly fixing the damage the Noah's marines had caused and building new makeshift houses for the East Compound refugees before winter set in.

"Isn't it odd how quickly this all feels normal?" I asked Shawn as my new tree house came into view. It was easy to spot among the other houses of the village. Where the other houses were made of wood, mine was made primarily of brachiosaurus rib bones and a few strategically placed T. rex femurs.

"You mean living forty feet above the ground or in a house made out of bones?" Shawn asked.

"Both." I laughed.

Shawn wrinkled his nose. "I still can't believe you live in that thing."

"Ivan offered to build me a house." I shrugged. "Who was I to argue over what he used to build it?"

"I would have argued," Shawn said. "It gives me the creeps."

"I think it's perfect," I said, defensive of my little house.

"Are you still going to think it's perfect if Chaz moves back to the lab?"

"I think so." I shrugged. "I don't think she'll go back, though. She seems to be enjoying treetop living a bit too much."

"Treetop living," Shawn snorted. "I never would have believed it." I studied my friend's profile for a second, thinking how treetop living would lose some of its perfection if *he'd* decided to move back to North Compound. But I knew now that he never would. He'd loved living with his aunt, but she'd been part of the lie that had encased our entire life underground. A lie I knew he wouldn't be able to forgive her for any time soon. And besides, he'd never admit it, but he was really starting to enjoy fresh air and sunshine.

"Don't act like you don't love living with Emily and Todd," I accused. "She treats you like her own son."

"Her cooking is amazing," he admitted with a sheepish grin that quickly turned to a scowl. "So why am I being forced to learn about eggs again?" he asked.

"Did you get them?" Chaz called, interrupting our conversation, and I looked up to see her leaning in the open doorway of our little house.

"All by himself," I said proudly as Shawn grimaced. I gave Chaz a conspiratorial wink.

"Wonderful!" Chaz smiled, clapping her hands.

"Now you get to learn how to cook them!"

"Lucky me," Shawn grumbled.

Chaz leaned forward to grab his arm and drag him inside impatiently. "Will you hurry up and get in here already before my nose freezes and falls off?"

Shawn groaned, but she ignored him and pushed him the rest of the way inside, giving me an inquiring look. I shook my head, not quite ready to go inside yet despite the cold. She nodded and shut the door. Brushing a few stray wisps of snow off our small deck, I sat down, my feet dangling off into thin air. It was something that would have made me want to vomit a mere month ago. I heard Shawn yelp from inside, followed by a splattering noise.

"Well, that could have gone better," I heard Chaz mutter.

"Isn't it a little cold for sitting outside?" Todd called, and I looked up to see him crossing the rope bridge that connected our house to his. He wore a heavy coat made of stitched-together allosaurus hide with a fox fur lining. It had been a thank-you gift from Ivan for all the help he'd given us. I knew just how warm a coat like that was, having an almost identical one inside my small house. I shivered, wishing now that I'd thought to put it on this morning. Verde trotted behind Todd, chirping and scolding Sprout, who was close on her heels. My tiny dinosaur was not so tiny anymore, and I realized that I wasn't the only one who had adjusted to life in the trees. Coming up to just below my knees, she paid no more mind to the swinging bridge than Verde did. Upon seeing me, she let out a little croak of delight and almost knocked Todd over in her hurry to say hello.

Todd righted himself quickly, shaking his head at Sprout, who was busy snuffling my neck and receiving scratches behind her tiny horns. "She's going to kill me one of these days," he said.

"She didn't mean it." I smiled as Sprout let out a huff of contentment and flopped down on my left, her comforting warmth a soothing barrier against the cold. "And you're right," I agreed, "it is way too cold to be sitting outside, but I figure I have twelve years' worth of sunrises to catch up on. So a little thing like frostbite shouldn't stand in my way."

"If you say so," Todd said, sitting down on my unoccupied right side. We sat in companionable silence, enjoying the simple beauty of the sunrise until the calm of the morning was shattered by a crash behind us. Todd jumped in alarm, turning to look back at my house.

"Not that way!" Chaz cried from inside. Shawn

muttered something unintelligible, and Chaz's infectious laughter pealed out.

"What's going on?" Todd asked.

"Cooking lessons." I smirked, raising a skeptical eyebrow.

"Nice," he said. "Oh, by the way. Mom said you guys should come over for dinner again tonight. She likes to pretend she's the mother of four kids instead of just one."

The prospect of one of Emily's meals was a tantalizing one, especially since breakfast sounded like it was going to be a little rough this morning. But I felt a twinge of guilt as I thought about just how many times we'd eaten there over the last few weeks. Just two nights before, Emily had invited us over for a meal of roasted apples and vegetable soup in honor of Boz visiting with an update.

I smiled, remembering the way Boz had scrutinized the contents of his bowl so carefully that his nose had almost touched its steaming surface. Even though Emily was careful now to not serve dinosaur when Boz was present, he always double-checked before taking a bite.

That night, after determining the soup held only vegetables and broth, Boz had sat back, smiling. "So many exciting things are happening that I hardly know where to begin," he'd practically crowed. "Your grand-father sends his love, Sky, but he was too busy with East Settlement to come this trip." I nodded in under-standing, although I was disappointed. Ivan had been flying back and forth between the East Compound ref-ugee camp, now called East Settlement, and the Oaks for the last three months, much to his well-vocalized annoyance. The last time I'd seen him he'd called the East Settlement refugees a bunch of "coddled idiots who don't know a tree from their own blessed left leg."

"This is what your parents wanted," he'd told me two months ago outside the ruined East Compound when I'd burst into tears upon finding out that he wasn't planning to fly back to the Oaks with me. "Now, don't do that," he'd said, wiping at my face with the rough cuff of his sleeve. "I won't be gone forever, but I feel like I owe it to your mom and dad to give these people as much help as I can. It was their dream to have the human race living aboveground again. This is the first step. If these people can survive, we can send delegates to North, South, and West Compounds in the spring. They will be quite low on some key supplies by then, so they might just listen. If I can do anything to help that happen, then this is where I need to be." After a speech like that, how could I possibly have been selfish and demanded that he come back with me?

Ivan, as well as a group of volunteers from both the Oaks and the Lincoln Lab, had helped set up East Settlement just outside the borders of New York City. The East Compound citizens had been less than thrilled when Boz's team had extracted them from their dark and dinosaur-infested tunnels. Upon learning that the compound's electrical system was destroyed beyond repair and that so many dinosaurs had flooded the tunnels that getting them dinosaur-free again was impossible, they'd eventually come around to the plan that Boz, Jett, and Ivan had devised.

With Ivan's and Boz's help, they had quickly built temporary shelters in the trees to protect themselves from the dinosaurs that roamed the abandoned streets of the once-great New York City. Teams of volunteers had ventured back into the abandoned compound's tunnels armed with tranquilizer guns and headlamps to salvage what technology, materials, and food stores hadn't been destroyed by the compound's newest occupants. Those who chose not to stay at East Settlement had split up, some going to the Lincoln Lab and the rest to settle with the people of the Oaks. Under Ivan's gruff guidance, the people of East Settlement were learning how to navigate this beautiful and dangerous topside world. Someone, and I had a sneaking suspicion it was Ivan, had even created a small patch for the citizens of

East Settlement to sew onto their worn gray compound uniforms. When I asked him about why, he'd muttered something about the people needing something of their own to identify with, but I knew the simple silhouette of a rainbow was more than that. Just seeing that patch filled me with a sense of hope that maybe we would be able to convince the other compounds as well.

Even now plans were being made to send a group of volunteers to the three remaining compounds in hopes of convincing the inhabitants to move topside. Shawn and I had already put our names on the list for the team going to North Compound, and I wondered what it would feel like to walk those familiar tunnels again. I wasn't sure if we'd be able to convince everyone to give up the safety of life underground, but it was worth it to try. Life in the sun was too dazzling to miss. My parents had died pursuing the dream of humans and dinosaurs sharing the topside world again, and I was excited to be a part of making their dream a reality.

"I don't always approve of your grandfather's methods," Boz had said, and I'd jerked myself from my musings to focus in again on what he was saying.

"Methods?" I repeated.

"The hunting of dinosaurs." Boz sighed. "But I understand that the citizens of East Settlement do have to eat. He's been very good about only shooting the species that have become overpopulated in the area, so that's something, I suppose." Boz grimaced. He'd worn a very similar look the day that Ivan had flown in with supplies for the citizens of the new settlement. Rolled hides, bones, claws, and teeth of over fifty different kinds of dinosaurs, thirty bows made of carved dinosaur rib bones, and enough rib bones to make over one hundred more. Ivan had shown up at East Settlement like a short, grumpy, one-armed Santa Claus with his loot, and Boz's face had gone white. Over the next few weeks, the refugees of East Compound had used it all.

I'd thought Ivan had cleaned out everything he had, until the day a helicopter had landed at the Oaks, and he had appeared with four burly men. Out of the depths of the helicopter had come a small fortune's worth of T. rex femurs, allosaurus vertebrae, and brachiosaurus ribs. Up until that point, Shawn, Chaz, and I had all been staying in Todd and Emily's tiny house. Ivan had taken it upon himself to build me a proper home before winter hit. The result was the strangest and most wonderful house the Oaks had ever seen.

Constructed of the thick and surprisingly light rib bones of a brachiosaurus, its walls and roof arched gracefully, giving it a unique curved shape unlike any of its boxy neighbors. Ivan had insisted on weaving the stretched and dried hides of a T. rex through this structure for added insulation before finishing off the inside with wood. The main deck and floor were also made of wood, and two compact beds had been built to fold down neatly from the walls at night, making the small house almost roomy during the day. Inside, it had a fireplace and even a kitchen table, dragged up from the depths of East Compound. It was small, but it was mine, and it felt more like home than North Compound ever had. Of course, convincing Chaz to live in a house made primarily of dinosaur bones had been a bit of a challenge, but she'd eventually come around.

Thinking of my house brought me back to the present, and I ran my hand across the smooth boards of my deck and glanced over at Todd, who was leaning back on his elbows to enjoy the view, oblivious to the cold or the fact that snowflakes had begun to drift down to settle on his eyelashes.

"Tell your mom we'd love to come to dinner," I said as Shawn yelped again from inside. "We may be really hungry after Shawn drops our entire breakfast on the floor." Verde headed into the house to take advantage of Shawn's clumsiness, and Sprout lumbered to her feet and followed, clucking quietly to herself.

Todd grinned after them, shaking his head. "What are you going to do when Sprout gets too big to live up here? She's going to be gigantic, you know. I'm sure you haven't forgotten what a full-grown pentaceratops looks like."

"I haven't," I said, thinking of how I'd been almost smashed by one in the tunnels of East. I shrugged. "I'll worry about that when it happens."

"If you say so," Todd said, sticking his tongue out to catch a particularly fat snowflake on its tip. He missed and barked a laugh that echoed out through the sleepy woods. He doggedly tried for another one, and I grinned. He'd turned into a better friend than I'd ever imagined.

I pulled my old battered journal out of my pocket to add a bit of information about the rhamphorhynchus nesting habits and paused. Now that I had Chaz, Todd, and Ivan, walking dinosaur experts, it occurred to me that I didn't really need the journal anymore. I ran my thumb over its water-damaged cover. Just like me, it had beat the odds and survived the trip from North Compound all those lifetimes ago. Boz had brought it for me from the Lincoln Lab on his last visit. I'd greeted it like an old friend and spent hours filling page after page with pictures of pentaceratops, condorraptors, and Grand Central Terminal.

Flipping back to the beginning, I'd read a few of my early entries. The Sky Mundy of the compound was so scared and beaten and unhappy. My entire life had revolved around finding out what happened to my dad. For five years his abrupt disappearance had haunted me. It didn't anymore. I finally understood why he'd done what he'd done, and I knew he'd made the right decision leaving me behind all those years ago. Besides, I'd gotten to see him again, to hug him, to hear that he was proud of me. It was more than I'd ever hoped for. And in the end, that would have to be enough. Besides, I knew where he was now, buried on a hill in the beautifully overgrown remains of Central Park. It was where Ivan had buried my mom over twelve years ago, and after all this time they were finally together again.

Unbidden, my hand went into my pocket where a small piece of chipped concrete sat. I ran my fingers over the rough grooves of the dove symbol and felt an unfamiliar calm settle over me. It was all over. I'd succeeded in doing what my dad had asked me to do, and because of his bravery, and the courage of a group of people who dared to imagine a life aboveground, everything was going to be okay.

The day we'd buried him had been the same day Boz had finally located the Noah's nuclear armory. I'd stood by my parents' graves and watched the long metal tubes get dropped one by one out of the belly of a helicopter to sink to the bottom of the ocean.

I looked at my journal one more time. It was scarred

and broken, but I wasn't anymore. Before I could think too much more about it, I tossed it off the deck. It flew through the air, pages spread, and then fell, disappearing in the swirl of ever-increasing snowflakes.

"What did you do that for?" Todd asked in surprise.

I shrugged. "It was time," I said.

"If you mean time for breakfast, then you're right!" Chaz called cheerily from behind us. She was standing in the open doorway and a warm gust of air blew out behind her, carrying the scent of cooked eggs with a definite undertone of something burned.

"Did someone say breakfast?" came a rough voice from directly below our feet, and I yelped in delight as Ivan threw open the small trapdoor in the floor of the deck and emerged, shaking the snowflakes off himself and smiling broadly.

"What are you doing here?" I asked as I gave him a quick hug. He smelled of pine and earth, a combination I'd grown to love.

"I thought it was high time I visited my favorite granddaughter," he said. "Make sure she's getting along all right. Besides, I needed a break from those blasted refugees. Always sniveling about the cold or the wet. Bah," he said, making a face that clearly described his feelings on the matter.

"Well, I'm glad you're here." I grinned. "You must

be freezing. Let's go inside. Shawn just finished making breakfast."

"He did, did he?" Ivan said doubtfully.

"Be nice," I hissed. "He's trying."

"I'm always nice," Ivan retorted, looking offended.

Todd snorted from behind us, but Ivan pretended not to hear. He turned to me, my tattered journal held in his good hand. "I believe you dropped this. It about hit me on the head as I was climbing up here."

"Oh," I said, feeling silly as I took it from his hands. "I was going to get rid of it. I didn't think I needed it anymore."

"Keep it," Ivan advised. "Sometimes knowing who you were and what you came from is just as important as knowing where you're going."

"Will you guys get in here?" Shawn called, opening a window to glare at us. "I went to a lot of trouble, and it's getting cold."

"I hope you like your eggs crunchy," Chaz muttered under her breath as we headed toward the door.

"I heard that!" Shawn scowled.

"If I wasn't so hungry, I would pass," Todd said, already heading inside. "But I'm starved."

I was the last one on the deck, and I hesitated a moment, looking out over the horizon. The glow of dawn was just beginning to illuminate the tops of the frost-covered trees, and in the distance I could see green-and-brown speckled dinosaurs moving in a large herd over a snow-covered hill. I let out a contented sigh. The topside world had turned out to be more amazing and dangerous than I ever could have imagined, and I still had so much of it to see.

"My word, boy, these things have more shell in them than eggs!" I heard Ivan complain through the open door. Smiling, I headed inside, my journal a familiar lump in my back pocket. The next chapter of my life was going to be an exciting one, filled with friends and tree houses and, of course, dinosaurs.

Author's Note

Dear Reader,

I grew up on the border of Indiana and Illinois near Lake Michigan, so I spent a large part of my childhood playing on Lake Michigan's beaches, diving beneath its waves, and running up its dunes. But I was never able to look at that massive body of water without my imagination getting the best of me. Logically, I knew there probably wasn't anything monstrous living in those murky depths, but secretly, I wanted there to be. Scotland supposedly had a monster, why couldn't Lake Michigan have one too?

Many have theorized that Scotland's Loch Ness Monster, nicknamed Nessie, is really a plesiosaur left over from the age where creatures the size of yachts used to swim around snacking on dinosaurs. The mere idea of Nessie has haunted and terrified generations, so when I sat down to write *Code Name Flood*, I couldn't help but wonder . . . how much scarier would an entire lake full of these prehistoric sea monsters be? The answer? Terrifying.

Plesiosaurs, mosasaurs, pliosaurs . . . you name it, I had them swimming in Lake Michigan for book two. Then I dumped my main characters into the water and let the fun begin. However, as delightful as writing about sea monsters was, I kept stumbling over the fact that they *weren't* considered dinosaurs, just prehistoric marine reptiles. And it annoyed me in the same way that Pluto getting demoted to a dwarf planet did. My editors even asked me at one point to have Sky explain *why* the terrifying creatures swimming around in my book weren't considered dinosaurs. And I begged them not to make me. Why? Because the reasoning behind it is confusing and downright dull. It has to do with things like the position of the animal's hip bones and the exact placement of the eye sockets . . . snore. Besides the boredom factor, none of this information felt normal or natural for Chaz or Sky to explain. Thankfully, my editors agreed.

Elasmosaurus, the long-necked guy on the cover, is probably the most iconic of the plesiosaurs. Described as looking like a snake threaded through a turtle's body, it's the one most often credited as a Nessie look-alike. But that snake-like neck is the reason I had to rewrite the entire scene where Sky almost gets eaten. In my original draft, Sky was attacked from above as the elasmosaurus hoisted its neck and head out of the water. Turns out, the elasmosaurus couldn't do that. Paleontologists aren't really sure why it had that long neck, but they do know it couldn't carry it around like a swan like many of the most famous and fraudulent early photos of Nessie seem to show. Oh, and the bit about them being attracted to light? That is purely from my imagination. Without any research proving the contrary, creative license allowed me to make the Lincoln Lab a beacon for these toothy and terrifying creatures.

Pretty Boy, a kronosaurus, was probably my favorite sea monster to research, although Shawn in particular didn't appreciate its addition to the story. Kronosaurus, named after the unsavory Greek god Cronus, was one of the big hitters for prehistoric marine reptiles, and Sky's unlikely savior in this book. Which is one of the reasons it earned a spot front and center on the cover of this book. I wanted the image to have the same feeling as the original poster for the movie *Jaws*. You know, the one where that poor girl is swimming along peacefully, completely unaware that Jaws is coming up from below? Yeah. That one. The obvious difference would be that Sky knew exactly how much trouble she was in. But using Pretty Boy on the cover created a bit of a problem as its profile view looked a little too similar to the spinosaurus from *The Ark Plan*, who *is* the only swimming dinosaur to date. What can I say? I apparently have a thing for toothy crocodile-like dinosaurs! Our solution was to turn it so that readers could clearly see that this toothy beast had flippers.

Dinosaurs and now prehistoric marine reptiles (see what I mean about that feeling awkward?) have been a blast to research and write about, and I hope that I created novels that brought dinosaurs thundering off the pages of history books for you. If I did my job right, you'll never look at dusty dinosaur bones again without imagining how our world would be different if they ever made a comeback.

Until next time,
Laura Martin

ACKNOWLEDGMENTS

How do you begin to thank the people who helped make the most passionate dream of your heart a reality? Somehow, a paragraph in this book doesn't seem to cut it. But until I win the lottery and can fly everyone somewhere exotic and warm, this will have to do.

First, I have to thank my parents, Jim and Joyce Van Weelden, who gave me a magical childhood, supported me in my every endeavor, and prayed for me. For my dad, who taught me the importance of a strong work ethic and a good left-handed lay-up. For my mom, who read too many versions of my book to count and worked tirelessly to help make my dream a reality. Without her this book never would have happened. I am who I am, what I am, and where I am because of my amazing parents. Thank you both from the bottom of my heart.

For my brother, Aric, who reminds me constantly not to take myself or this life so seriously. When I wrote the character of Todd, it was with your mischievous and big-hearted personality in mind. For Allison and Jenna and too many friends and family members to mention, who have always been in my corner no matter how awkward or uncoordinated I was.

For the countless teachers in my life who pushed me to be better, specifically the teachers of Illiana Christian High School and Butler University. For Jeff DeVries, for challenging me even when I didn't want to be challenged, and Dan Barden for telling me to stop making excuses and just write a good book.

For the countless middle school students who walked through my classroom door every year at Clay Middle School. This series was inspired by and written for the quirky kids who made teaching the best job in the world.

For Alec Shane, who first pulled my book out of the slush pile and told me it would make a great middle grade novel. For Jodi Reamer, my rock-star agent, thank you for your excitement, feedback, and unwavering belief in this series.

For my team at HarperCollins: after years of dreaming of publishing a book, this experience has been better than I could have ever hoped. For Tara Weikum, Chris Hernandez, and Harriet Wilson, thank you for the brainstorming and insights that helped turn the Edge of Extinction into the series it is today. You are both brilliant. Thank you to my cover artist, Eric Deschamps, and the entire art department for making my characters and vision for these books come to life.

For the most important person in my life, my husband, Josh. I cannot begin to thank you for being my rock, my supporter, and my best friend through this entire journey. I couldn't ask for a better partner in this life. For my daughter, London, and son, Lincoln, you two are the inspiration that lights up my days and the push that makes me want to be better.

And last, to my creator, who makes all things possible, even the impossible dream of publishing a book. Ephesians 3:20-21: Now to him who is able to do immeasurably more than all we ask or imagine, according to his power that is at work within us, to him be the glory.